Apple

Apple

Colin Padgett

Matador
9 Priory Business Park,
Wistow Road, Kibworth Beauchamp,
Leicestershire. LE8 0RX
Tel: 0116 279 2299
Email: books@troubador.co.uk
Web: www.troubador.co.uk/matador
Twitter: @matadorbooks

ISBN 978 1789016 598

British Library Cataloguing in Publication Data.
A catalogue record for this book is available from the British Library.

Printed and bound in Great Britain by 4edge Limited
Typeset in 12pt Minion Pro by Troubador Publishing Ltd, Leicester, UK

Matador is an imprint of Troubador Publishing Ltd

For the family

1

THE END OF... JUNE

The hillside was a scene of neglect. There were a few fruit trees which someone must once have cultivated, but the grass between them was tall, wispy and pale brown, a sure sign that no-one had regularly walked or worked here for some time.

An occasional bird alighted and perched on an apple tree branch but each one flew away almost immediately. It was as if they sensed something was not quite right.

The whole scene was strangely quiet until, as if at a given signal, clouds of butterflies and moths fluttered up from where they had been settled in the gnarled bark of the trunks and branches. As they went, a breeze stirred. The air itself seemed to come alive as a wave of leaves followed the insects, up and down, between and around the trees. This undulating flow of brown, grey and green followed the wind, away down the hill and over the stone wall that bounded the orchard area at one end. And soon the orchard went back to looking more like it should in October than in June.

None of this was seen by the men who arrived just a few minutes later, and whose arrival may have been the cause of the brief, fluttering exodus. Maybe they were naturally unobservant; perhaps, cocooned in the air-conditioned cabs of their mechanical diggers, they would not have been able to notice anyway.

What did matter was that when they arrived a few rows of noble, if strangely leafless, apple trees stood on the hillside, and when they left later that day, there were none, each having been torn from its place. Decades of growth replaced by mounds of dark brown earth which stood out like over-sized molehills among the long grass.

In between their arrival and their departure, as the diggers tore their way through the orchard, the smoke from their exhausts combined with the dust from the old bark. The remaining leaves from the branches joined them to create a grey-green curtain in the air. The destruction of the site was therefore obscured until the act was over.

And as they left, at the end of the day, one last gathering of moth, leaf and dust swirled in the air at the very end of the site. It wavered, as if considering a return to the orchard field, in spite of the breeze that tried to blow it away. Then it seemed to give itself up to the wind, like the sail of a yacht caught in a contrary gust, flapping and then collapsing, over an adjoining wall and into a row of gardens, sloping sharply upwards on this coastal hillside.

Silence returned. No more men. No more machines. No more orchard.

2

A CURATE'S EGG

'Try turning timidly.'

'Not bad, Vic. Your turn Fish.'

'Unusual umbelliferae ululate.'

'Oh yes, very clever. Trust you to come up with one like that. Posh words aren't worth any more points, you know.'

'Shut up, *Victoria*! Wait until you have to do "Z"!'

'Oh really, *Fisher*. Well that just happens to be Dad's letter!'

'Alright, kids. We've had a good journey. No need to start on each other now.'

'Sorry, *Commander*. It's your turn now. You've got V!'

Victoria and Fisher's father grinned to himself at the use of the old family nickname. 'I'm sorry, but I'll need to concentrate from here on.' He said. 'In case you lot hadn't noticed we're nearly there. I'll have to drive carefully on these narrower roads. Lovely game, though, Vic. That book was a real find.'

As Dad eased the car off the roundabout and down the long hill into the bay, Victoria smiled secretly to herself, remembering what had happened a few days before their holiday.

Dad had been in the middle of cooking supper when it had occurred to him that he needed his cocktails recipes book for the trip. As his hands had been greasy he had asked Vic to fetch it from the cupboard under the stairs. This had taken her a little while. All of Dad's folders, tapes, old records and other bits and pieces were kept under the stairs. He had recently rearranged them so she had to scan the whole lot to find the cocktails book. In doing so, a large paperback book called "Word Games" had caught her eye. This, she had thought, sounded like the sort of book you took on journeys so, once she had delivered the cocktails book to her dad, she had also added "Word Games" to her holiday things, thinking, 'Well, I've done my bit.' She had been feeling guilty about not making a proper contribution to the holiday preparations and the guilt hadn't completely gone away because her split-second effort somehow didn't seem to compare with the whole afternoon of work Fish had put into planning the journey. But at least she had done something. And now her book was the hit of the holiday so far!

As if he had heard his name in her thoughts, Fish's voice came through from the back of the car: 'Do you want me to take you through the brochure directions to the house, Dad?'

'In a minute,' Dad replied. 'The folder's under the passenger seat. It's a green manila wallet.' He slowed the car down as they reached the bottom of the hill and followed the road sharply to the left. A small and rather scruffy bay was now visible on their right, partly hidden by a low sand dune. On their left was the usual selection of seaside shops and a petrol station.

While Fish fumbled around underneath the seat for the folder, Vic remembered the day when Dad had asked him to plan a route. She had noticed that Dad had spoken cautiously. She had found out a little later from a chance remark by Fish that when she had been very young it had always been her brother's job to plan a route to their family holiday destination. Although Fish's initial reaction to the request had been understandably lukewarm, a couple of days later he had made a start on the job. And not just a start. He had thrown himself into it as if he was seven or eight years old all over again.

He had taken over the kitchen table with the road map from the car, an Ordnance Survey map with Grandpa's initials on it which he had found in the loft and, most amazingly, not once had he turned on the computer and asked it to plan a route for him! The result of his efforts had been a set of cards – colour coded, no less! – tracing a route which managed to avoid motorways and other main roads from the edge of Suffolk all the way to South Wales. And what a route it had turned out to be!

Fish's preparation, he claimed, had involved putting a long ruler on the map and following the roads it went over. The number of times they turned sharply left or right, or even seemed to be going back the way they had just come, made Vic wonder whether he had been using one of those annoying bendy rulers the kids played with at school instead of doing their work. But strangely enough, even though he was the one who had to drive in all sorts of directions, Dad hadn't minded. Not that he was ever easily annoyed about these things – he could be maddeningly cheerful while plans were going wrong and delays were happening – but as the journey had seemed to get longer rather than shorter she had begun to worry that Dad would get tired. But he hadn't. Instead, he kept pointing out bits of road he remembered from years ago when he used to go "Up North", as he put it, with his parents. Apparently, in his early years, Grandpa Gordon had been a great journey improviser, as likely to stop for a snack and a look at the scenery than to press on to their destination.

Dad had proved to be just the same and even now he was driving at sightseeing pace, but for a reason they could all appreciate: they were approaching a mini-roundabout that seemed to have no proper signs to give them a direction. 'Have you found it, yet?' he said, his voice cutting across her thoughts.

'Have I found what?' she asked.

'No, not you. I was talking to Fish.'

'I have now,' Fish's muffled voice came through the back of her seat. 'Do you recognize this?' he said to Vic, more clearly now, handing a book through from the back.

Vic took it. 'It's one of my old annuals!' she exclaimed. It must have been under the seat for ages!'

'Two years, if the date on the front is anything to go by,' Fish observed. 'Or two-and-a-half if you count the months since Christmas.' Trust Fish to be pedantic. She tucked it down by her feet. She felt too old to be reading books like that now.

Leaving Fish and Dad to work out the last part of the journey, she turned her attention back to "Word Games" and the reason she had brought it. Dad had decided that she should be something he called "Ents", which turned out to mean Entertainments Officer. 'It's an army expression,' he had explained. 'You can give us all things to do between home and holiday home,' he had said, using the same tone of voice he had used on Fish to get him involved. However, try as she might, Vic had not been able to get enthusiastic in the way her brother could. She hadn't given the book so much as a glance between finding it and setting out for Wales. It was only when she had answered Dad's request for a game to play while they were stuck in heavy traffic that she had discovered how good it was. After that she had hardly taken her nose out of it!

On top of that, she had noticed that Fish's enthusiasm for the holiday had not stopped with the journey planning. He had been lively and chatty the whole way. When Dad had asked to look at the map he hadn't become grumpy about being checked up on, and even more amazing than that, not once had he retreated into music via his earphones! Instead, he had joined in listening to the car radio, and he had even asked Vic to find another game at one point. They had gone through a sizeable chunk of the book's contents, even carrying on one game in the restaurant of a motorway services area in South Wales, much to the amusement of the lady at the cash desk who kept winking at Vic as she struggled to keep up with the word gymnastics her much older brother and, of course, her even older father, were capable of.

Now the journey was nearly over. While Dad concentrated on the last part, Vic idly flicked through the pages of "Word Games" that she hadn't already looked at. When she came to the blank pages between the cover and the title page she discovered an inscription indicating that the book had been a present, a present from Grandma Alma and Grandpa Gordon… to Mum. In that instant Vic's mood slumped. The pleasure of the past seven or eight hours faded and a sort of remote, cold feeling grew in her as she saw the names and then, when she saw the dedication to her mother, real sadness filled her.

Since losing Mum, the old family holidays had been suspended and instead they had gone away with relations. Vic had always had cousins, uncles, aunts and Grandparents all around her to keep her mind off things, and in some ways it had worked. Now it was just her and Dad and her brother, and the book which suddenly made her feel sad. She stayed lost in a grey mist of empty memories until the sound of Fish fumbling about in the back again brought things back into focus.

'It's OK. I've found the sheet. It must have fallen out of the brochure when I opened the folder.'

'So what does it say?' Dad asked. 'I don't want to go round this mini roundabout more than once.'

'Oh, right. It says: "At the roundabout overlooking the bay take the first exit and follow the road down to the foot of the hill. With the white hotel building on your left, drive along with the bay on your right. Go straight across the next two mini-roundabouts by the entrance to the ferry terminal and turn sharp left when you see the fish and chip shop. Right?'

'Yes,' said dad. 'And when I've done all that? Which won't take long, he added. 'This place is not enormous.'

Fish went on. 'After about fifty metres, make an immediate turn sharp right and drive a quarter of a mile up the hill. Don't you love it the way we British happily mix Metric and Imperial measures?! '

'Yes, thank you for the observation, Fish. Let's just try the sharp right, shall we?'

Now they were going back uphill the view was more interesting but Vic's gaze out of the window was only vague. Her thoughts were still clouded and the only thing which brightened her at all was that Fish and Dad were too busy finding the holiday home to notice that she had dropped out of the chatter. Without caring very much, she took in a broad bay with a straight jetty extending a long way and, beyond that, an even longer one curving out from the headland and half way across the mouth of the whole bay. There were a lot of small boats in the bay and about twenty small sailing dinghies, out beyond the curving jetty, heading for a smaller bay in the headland opposite. The view suddenly vanished as the very steep road they were on, which couldn't have been less seaside-like if it had been trying, took them between trees and houses. They instantly forgot the bay altogether The road was quite gloomy, overhung with huge ancient laurel and the tops of pine trees which must have had their roots several feet below the road, so steep was the slope. Every so often there was a gap in the growth but each gap had a house in it and although their foundations were down at the same level as the pine tree roots, the roofs were right across their sight-line to the bay, so it remained out of view. Dad commented that the vista from these houses, high above the bay, ought to be wonderful. But all Vic could see was the tops of the hills on the far side. They could have been any hills. Her gloom deepened.

Dad spoke again: 'Are there any more directions, Fish?'

'I don't think so. No! Hang about! There's more on the other side. It says that the parking can be awkward.' Then he added, reading carfefully: "When you see the house, drive on up the hill and turn round." It says it's easier to pull in on the steep road if you're facing downhill,' he added, in his own voice once more.

'Unusual directions.'

'Yeah, and totally useless if you happen to miss the house, which I think we have as this seems to be the end of the road coming up – unless we're meant to drive vertically down into the sea.

Sure enough, they were reaching a dead-end with a parking area on the top of the cliff, and a pub next to it. 'Well that's no good,' said Dad, calmly. Vic did not know how he managed to do it. Driving all day the breadth of England and Wales and you would think he had done nothing more than forget to buy some milk on the way home! He pulled up and started a three-point turn. 'How can we have missed it?' he said. 'It's "The Pilot's Cottage". It's got to be a quaint building standing alone on a headland in picturesque grounds overlooking the bay. All I've seen have been thick plantations of overgrown laurel, with dull brown semi-detached houses in between.'

'Yeah,' said Fish. 'And don't forget the deserted garage forecourt half way up on the left. I noticed a couple of rusting petrol pumps and lots of weeds. Very quaint!'

'Actually,' said Dad, 'The houses on the left as we came up were quite pleasant. There was one with some wooden sculptures at the front.'

While the two male occupants of the car were chattering on, Vic was still looking out of her window which, now that Dad had turned round and let the car idle back down the hill, was facing the side of the road where their house was supposed to be. They went past a dull pair of semi-detached houses painted cream up to a line above the ground floor windows. Above the line they were a reddish, chocolaty-brown colour.

'Typical seaside colour scheme,' Dad observed. 'Anywhere else you would have the neighbours complaining to the council about...' his comments went unfinished as Vic shouted out.

'Here it is!' she said. Sure enough, next to the strangely coloured houses was an identical pair, the second of which was "The Pilot's Cottage", in name at least.

Dad put the brakes on *almost* sharply, in that way he had of not quite coming to a dead halt, implying that the passengers may not be absolutely right.

'Are you sure?' asked Fish, leaning forward and speaking quite close to Vic's ear. Dad had put the brakes on sharply enough to make him lurch forward in his seat. 'Where's the name plate?'

'There isn't one on the gate,' she replied. It just says "39". But there's something on the porch at the side of the house. It's got something growing down over it, but there's a bit of a word that must be "Cottage".

'That would narrow it down,' said Dad. She knew his sense of humour and took no notice. Instead, having been the one who had spotted the house, and with the prospect of something to do lifting her spirits a bit, she got out and went to see.

Vic was more observant than people realized. As she pushed the gate open she noticed all the well-known signs of rented property. The gate catch did not actually catch. The concrete path had spots of moss, grass and lichen which would not appear if feet regularly crossed it. There was a pile of flower pots with ants crawling all over them next to a black plastic rubbish bag, and next to that a discarded beach sandal. And the name plate did say "The Pilot's Cottage" There was also a miniature brass anchor hanging on the wall next to it.

'Dad'll have something to say about that,' she thought. 'This is it!' she shouted back at the others, who were now half out of the car.

She couldn't remember where the directions had said to find the key, so she had to wait. It would take Dad and Fish a couple of minutes to catch up with her, because Dad would insist on bringing a couple of things out of the boot. 'Waste no journeys!' was one of his more irritating catch-phrases.

She looked to see if she could get to the garden, which must have one of those views they had been teased with on the drive up the hill, but the owners had built a porch right out across the path up to the wall of the neighbours' driveway. It was obviously a place for holidaymakers – and maybe even the owners – to leave wet and dirty things after a day by the sea. Very practical, but she would have liked to see the view properly.

Fish arrived. 'What a slope!' he barked in her ear, making her jump. 'Do you feel like you're lurching forwards all the time? No, you wouldn't,' he replied for her. 'You don't even weave about like the rest of us after a day with Grandpa on the boat.'

Vic didn't respond. 'Where's Dad?' she asked, looking over Fish's shoulder.

'He's next door, fetching the key.'

Vic looked next door. 'He must have slipped in quietly. I didn't see him.'

'Not *that* "next door", the next one up. The other half of the semi and, therefore, technically, "next door". See?'

'Clever!' she sneered, and was glad to see Dad coming along the road and then down the path. He glanced at the name plate and the shiny ornament next to it. 'Here it comes,' thought Vic.

'Well, if we lived here it would be "Anchors away!" ' he said, with a grin. Vic smiled but the expression in her eyes really showed that she had no idea what he was talking about.

Fish stage-whispered: 'It's a nautical expression,' he said. ' "*Anchors aweigh!*" – a-w-e-i-g-h is what they used to say on ships when they were putting out to sea. He's trying to be funny.'

In spite of suffering the familiar mauling he always got for his jokes, Dad just grimaced and said, 'Well, what sort of joke would you expect from *The Commander?!*

Vic could see a family holiday catch-phrase in the making and was relieved when Dad finally got the key in the lock. Then he took it out again because it didn't work like the one at home, inserted it again, turned it and opened the door to the porch. At least, he opened the door that got you into the porch from the path. As the owners had built it right across the path, it actually had two doors.

Dad, of course, had to make a quip. 'That's an interesting arrangement,' he said. This must the shortest corridor in the world! We'll decide later whether we're going to leave the door to the garden side open all the time. Some people wouldn't...'

Victoria did not notice, but Fish told her later that this had been a significant moment as Mum had always insisted that such doors should be locked. Dad had obviously recalled this. Nevertheless, he had then briskly got on with installing them in the house.

Vic explored, while pretending to help unload the car. Dad unloaded the car and gave half an ear to her snippets of information.

Once again, Fish was surprisingly enthusiastic, though he did draw the line at the word "explore", which he clearly thought too childish. True to form, he also behaved as if all the moving in had been done and concentrated on what interested him. He discovered the owners' strange collection of old vinyl records in a cabinet underneath something Dad told him was called a "gramophone". He also discovered the house's dangerous spots: a beam for banging your head on; a cupboard door with a hidden panel just inside the frame, also for banging your head on; a door catch fitted too close to the frame, for grazing your knuckles and a window which, unexpectedly, swung both ways and knocked off anything you left on the ledge. He discovered all of these by accident and spent at least the first three days of the holiday moaning about them or clutching a bruised or grazed part of his body. However, he did like the bookshelves. He liked them partly because they did not look as if they ought to stay up, being made of impossibly thin wood which sagged dramatically in the middle. He confidently predicted that they would find they had collapsed by the morning, especially if anyone added anything to what they already supported. His other reason for liking them was that they held at least a dozen volumes which he would plough through before they left. Those he didn't finish would follow them home, to be returned by Dad, by post, at great expense and with an apologetic letter to the house's owner, some weeks later.

Vic made some discoveries of her own. The first was the pile of letters on the telephone table. There wasn't actually a telephone on the table, but there was a telephone directory and a rather neglected-looking vase of dried flowers where a phone might have been. Her discovery slowed everything down temporarily, for her at least, because one letter was addressed to her. "Miss Victoria Darwin" it said, "The Pilot's Cottage" and so-on. Amongst the junk-mail she also found two more for the others, each addressed with the same spidery handwriting that could only be Grandpa's.

'Mr James Darwin and Mr Fisher Darwin!' she shouted, taking them through to where Dad and Fish were making piles of stuff from the car. 'Letters from Grandma Alma and Grandpa Gordon.'

Dad smiled. 'So your Grandpa did write.' He threat... er... promised he would. No doubt there will be snippets of information about things to see and places to visit. Because...'

Fish completed his sentence, '... because Grandpa Gordon has been everywhere and remembers it all!'

'Correct. How about making us a cup of tea, Vic?'

Although they both took their letters, they both also put them down straight away, unread, and got on with the unpacking. Vic was disappointed that they did not seem to share her excitement, and her mood sagged as it had in the car. However, having slipped her own letter into her back pocket, she did put the kettle on for a cup of tea. Then she continued her own exploration of the house.

Her next discovery was the amazing stairs. They wound up two floors but they were at such tight angles to fit into a narrow space that they had four levels, sort of mini-landings. And there was a window at each level that gave a different kind of view. Because the house was built on such a steep slope, the window on the first level was scarcely any higher than the road and she could look straight at Fish and Dad as they lifted the suitcases out of the back of the car. The next level was the first floor and through its window she could see the roof of the porch and a selection of old and new aerials on the side of the neighbours' house. Up one more and it was a sort of large porthole – Dad was sure to make a joke of that before the end of the day – and it was in the corner so she could see quite a long way down the hill they had driven up. On the second floor, which was actually two low-ceilinged bedrooms and a bathroom in the old loft space, it was a skylight, but again, because of the slope, without craning her neck very much she could see the roofs and treetops which stretched back up the hill on the other side of the road.

Once she was there, she discovered her bedroom. It had to be hers because it had the sort of dark, old-fashioned, heavy furniture she would have loved in her own room at home. And it also had a dormer-style window cut partly into the slope of the roof, with a broad sill on all three sides for her to sit in.

'At last!' she thought. 'The view.' And she was not disappointed. She could now see all the way across the bay and even got a few tantalizing glimpses of what was on this side. Through the tops of the trees there were white and grey shapes which must be part of the approach to the ferry terminal. Further over, two or three chimneys and roof ridges marked the hotel which nestled in the headland in all the tourist brochures Dad had sent off for before booking the trip. And across the middle of the bay a long foot-jetty with what looked like an old turret on the end. Vic wondered how long it would take Dad to notice that and, more importantly, how long after that he would require them all to walk its length.

There was more to the view than that: the hills rolling away on the other side of the bay; the variety of boats moored this side of the jetty; the quayside of the village on the far side, which looked picture postcard-perfect even from here.

And at that moment everything she had been looking at faded in a few short moments.

In fact, a storm had arrived. It swept over the headland with surprising strength. The considerable height of the headlands on both sides meant that its arrival had been masked until the last minute, and even when it arrived the water remained quite calm and the boats tethered out in the harbour hardly bobbed about. Apart from the rain that was like a series of veils thrown across the view the only sign that something dramatic was about to happen was the sudden absence of any seagulls.

The Darwen's family home had recently been fitted with double glazing, and the sounds of traffic and weather had diminished behind the insulation. This house had its original single-glazed windows, in old-fashioned metal frames, yet Vic could hear no actual storm noise. What she could hear was the drumming of the sudden rain on every available surface, the sound of which drowned out everything else. For a few minutes, with the usually sharp lines of the harbour, the jetty, the headlands, the boats and even the clouds blotted out, it could have been the end of the world.

It ended just as quickly as it had begun. The harbour became visible again, the boats could be seen and the outline of the bay turned back into a clear dark mass, above and beyond which the heavy low clouds she had not seen coming continued to beat their way through the air, hiding the inland blue sky and seemingly forcing the returning birds to fly low for the time being.

Victoria went downstairs and out into the sun lounge, where she could still see the last of the sudden tempest sweeping inland. Her mood was still a bit wobbly over this being the first "family" holiday without Mum. Now she wondered whether the rest of their stay would be marked by such changeable weather. Normally it wouldn't trouble her. Why should it? She had no way of knowing what was normal for the local weather. Maybe it had been one of those swift storms that makes everyone run for cover but freshens things up so life can go back to normal almost immediately. She had been on holiday before in places where it seemed to rain every day, and one of their family sayings was "There's no such things as bad weather; only bad clothes". However, she couldn't help also remembering that there were usually about fifteen people on those holidays, giving endless combinations of company and distraction. This time it was just the three of them. Anyway, the noise of the rain drumming on the roof of the sun lounge, the rattle of a cascade dropping from a faulty strip of guttering on the next house and the impossibility of seeing a view seemed to hold her where she stood. Then she remembered that the "bad clothes" saying had actually been one of Mum's at which thought her spirits began to decline yet further.

"Vic!" Although her brother had not shouted, the suddenness of his voice only a couple of feet from her ear, made her momentarily dizzy with the shock. "You're supposed to be making the refreshing pot of tea while we install everything. Remember?" he said.

"Yeah, yeah. It's under control. The kettle's on."

"I think you will find that it works better if you also switch it on at the socket," Fish added sarcastically.

"Oh, thank you *Fisher*," she said, using the name he had been given at birth and had recently begun to hate.

He frowned at her for a moment, but then seemed to remember that he was in a good holiday mood and, with a smile, said. "Don't push your luck, *Victoria*," and went back to moving all their luggage to the various rooms and cupboards in this unfamiliar house.

A couple of hours later, after two showers, one bath, arguments over who had the best room and all the other little moments that mark a family holiday as a truly special experience, it was Fish's turn to stand and stare out of the sun lounge windows. In Vic's presently rather unhappy state, she would have said that it was typical of his luck that instead of the grey curtain which had held her attention and delayed the family's end-of-journey tea, his view was clear and appealing. He paused for a moment to take it in. The various jetties were also broad dark lines. But the boats were strikingly clear, their decks were shining white, almost unreal.

The reason was, once again, the high headlands that had sheltered the harbour from the storm and prevented them from seeing the weather approaching. This time, their height made sunset seem to come early, but the truth was that it really was still only late afternoon. The sky overhead was still clear and blue, and the upward-facing surfaces of the boats were reflecting that brightness. Although he was unaware of Vic's earlier thoughts, Fish's now ran down a parallel path as he, too, recalled other holidays where they had had to get used to the effects of the local geography, especially gloomy, pine-shrouded valleys in Scotland which made you think you'd best turn round and head for home, only to come to a clearing or a hill-top and find broad daylight. And he, too, recalled such holidays with Mum for company, which made him feel wistful and, more especially, made him wonder how it might be affecting Vic…

"Must keep making an effort," he thought.

3

STILL SATURDAY

Towards the real end of the afternoon, when they were more-or-less installed and a second pot of tea had been consumed, Dad asked, 'Anyone noticed that jetty across the harbour?' Vic choked on her tea and Fish snorted with amusement.

'I'll take that as a "yes" then, shall I?' Dad said, so convincingly that they couldn't tell whether he was annoyed or just resigned to their familiar mockery. 'So who fancies a walk along it?'

'We'll both come,' said Fish. Long experience had told him that Dad rarely sat down for long, not even on holiday at the end of a day's drive. Especially not then. However, experience also told him that the places he dragged them to sometimes turned out to be interesting, often in quite unexpected ways. Not that anyone in the family would ever let on that they thought this.

'Well let's go, then,' Dad said, springing up from his chair. 'Bring your kagoules in case another of those squalls happens along while we're three hundred yards out in the middle of the harbour.' He took two of the mugs out to the sink as he went.

'Waste no journeys!' Fish muttered to Vic when Dad was out of earshot.

Five minutes later they were ready to go. Dad had bought a postcard at the last service area on their journey and somehow – another of his familiar tricks – he had found time to write it and put a stamp on it too. 'It's for Granny and Grandpa,' he said. You can sign it as we walk down the hill!' Then, seeing the looks on their faces, he added, 'Alright, as it's been a long day we'll we take the car to the end of the jetty.'

'Which end?' asked Fish.

'Ha! Ha!' said Dad. 'Let's try the dry one, shall we?'

The jetty began from a small car park next to a building labelled "Museum of the Sea". It was one of those modern buildings which you can't be quite sure is open. There was no obvious "front" entrance and its walls were tall white curves which the architect had obviously decided matched the seaside location. However, it had no windows at ground level, so no clues to its contents were visible. They all agreed that they must take a look inside sometime. In fact, in two weeks' time it would be added to the list of "Places we never actually went to on our holidays".

'Let's go,' said Dad, taking a small rucksack from the boot of the car. 'Anyone remember a map?'

'But we're going to walk along a jetty, in a straight line, within sight of our house,' Vic moaned.

'I know that, you know that and Fish knows that, but there will be a test…'

'A test?'

'He means Grandpa,' said Fish. 'We'll get back home in a fortnight or, nearly as likely, Grandpa will turn up sometime during the next two weeks, and he will look at the places we've been on a map and then he'll start asking awkward questions and we'll need to have some answers to some of them or we'll incur his mockery.'

Vic looked at Dad. Dad gave her a resigned "It's true" look.

'So what do we do,' she asked. 'Go back to the house?'

'You can, if you like,' said Fish. 'I'm going for a walk along the jetty, with this map Grandpa gave me.' Waving the map, which he had just taken from an inside pocket of his kagoule, Fish strode off along the jetty. Dad and Vic shared a "typical Fish" look, then, on an impulse and much to her father's surprise, she looped her arm through his as they followed her brother.

From where they had parked the car the jetty looked decidedly lacking in promise. The car park itself was just a dry, light-brown sandy surface and, apart from a few stones which had been worn smooth by walkers, the jetty path was the same. But Vic couldn't stop looking at all the blocks. They were square, but not cheap and cheerful grey concrete; they were real stone. She tried to look at every single one, finding their square, individual beauty fascinating. And it was not only she who liked them. As she stared at each one she noticed that there were all sorts of creatures on them. The main one was a very bright green insect with wispy antenna which looked just like the thin strands of seaside grass which sprouted between the stones. There was one on nearly every block and each one crawled down the sides of the blocks very quickly if you cast a shadow over it but stayed in place if you did not come between it and the sunlight. There were also very small white butterflies soaking up the heat left in the stones by a long warm day. They were just like the ones Dad spent the Summer trying to chase off his cabbages, but so tiny that they were beautiful. However, pests or not, they, too, went away if you came near, only up into the air instead of down the cracks. But what she loved best were the lizards. Dad said that this was just the sort of spot to see lizards but she still couldn't believe how many there were; and they were so deep and dark black. And they didn't seem to care how close you got to them.

'If you're going to stop and look at each one,' Dad said, 'Then I will have to detach my arm from yours before you pull it out of its socket. Let's try to catch up with Fish, shall we?' They walked on more steadily, then he added. 'Can you see our house? I can't work out where it is.'

'You must be able to see it. We can see the jetty from up there so the house ought to be visible too.'

Vic glanced up to where she thought the house should be but, although she could see what must be the houses which had blocked their view on the way up the hill, the actual house was, indeed, hard to pinpoint. They resorted to trying to trace the route of the road.

'It must be even steeper than we think,' he said after three failed attempts to spot it. 'What's below it?'

Vic knew exactly what was below it: the hotel with the pointy roof, which she could see from where they stood. She felt a little guilty, however, when she remembered that, while she had been exploring the house and its surroundings Dad had done most of the unpacking work. 'The hotel,' she said, cautiously.

Dad's response was to hold out his hand and point at the hotel. Then he moved his hand upwards to fix what he was looking at, and tried to trace a line straight back up the hill to their house. 'Nope,' he said. Still no luck. Maybe we'll see it from the jetty's end. Come on, Fish is there already.'

They carried on down the jetty but it was a slow progress because they both kept glancing up at the hillside trying to get a glimpse of the house. When they eventually came up level with Fish he was chatting to two men down in the water in a dinghy. They were going along pulling up lobster pots. Most of them were empty but a few had something in them. Vic found the lizards and the view more interesting, especially as the structure on the end of the jetty was not the turret it looked like from a distance. It did have some shaped stone work along the top which made it look like a castle but close up it was just a square brick building with a plaque on it saying "Welsh Water".

'Anyone thirsty?' Asked Dad as he produced a flask out of his rucksack.

Vic never knew how Dad did this. Wherever they went, at a moment's notice, he always managed to pack a hot drink and some biscuits. Sure enough, when he had poured her some tea, with warm milk from a smaller flask, out came the Rich Tea biscuits – Fish's favourite.

While Dad and Fish exchanged jokey remarks with the men in the dinghy she sat on a wooden bench, mildly embarrassed by the public display of male chumminess and trying to look as if she was not with them. The bench was set in two of the square blocks that made up the jetty and, remembering the hot drink, she sipped it to keep the evening chill at bay. Why did the other two never seem to feel the chill? Dad had been known still to be wearing shorts in October, for Heaven's sake! Despairing of male behaviour, she peered at the hillside, trying once again to see their house. It was getting darker now and as lights began to go on in houses and the streets she thought that might give her a clue. But no matter how hard she peered and no matter how many other landmarks of the hillside she used as markers, she still had no luck.

All the while they had been occupied at the end of the jetty, lines of cars had gathered down at the entrance to the ferry terminal. Vic had noticed them occasionally at the bottom of her line of vision as she scanned the hillside but she hadn't really looked at them properly.

Dad and Fish eventually abandoned their shouted conversation with the fishermen and came over to where she was sitting. The map was spread out and they made a half-hearted effort at identifying points of interest. 'It's no use,' Dad sighed. 'Whatever we spot, Grandpa will top it and pour scorn on our feeble efforts.' He looked up and made them both jump when he exclaimed, 'Now there's a sight!' Vic jumped again when she looked. There was a huge boat the other side of the second jetty – the one that was built out from a point somewhere below where their house should be. It seemed to loom right over them, even though it had to be at least a hundred metres away. A moment later it wheeled away seeming, because of the jetty, to disappear out to sea far faster than ought to be possible.

'What is it?' she asked, genuinely surprised.

'Apart from an amazing optical effect, you mean?' said Fish with his usual annoying precision. 'It's the ferry, of course. It's a catamaran style,' he added, seeing from her look that she still didn't quite grasp what he was saying.

'Are catamarans that big?' she asked.

'Evidently,' her Dad commented. 'But I think it looked especially big because it was near the sea wall. Foreshortening, perspective, something like that. They only carry a few cars.'

This time Vic had something to contribute which might match Fish's annoying cleverness.

'But I must have seen a hundred cars go up the entrance road,' she said.

Dad said nothing and Fish ignored her snippet of information. 'Yeah,' he said, in an "I'd already noticed that" kind of voice. 'The rest of them must be on that.' He pointed to a boat which looked a bit more like the sort in which they had sometimes crossed the English Channel. 'There must be a choice of speeds for the journey. Anyway,' he added, glancing at Dad, 'That should be enough to impress Grandpa.'

'Ferry interesting!' laughed Dad, which was the signal to make their way back along the jetty to distract him from making more stupid puns. Vic had already put away the flasks and the remainder of the biscuits. When they were getting near the car park Dad said, 'I don't suppose you'll want any supper after the Rich Tea feast!' They knew he was joking but they treated him to a convincing mock-horror reaction so he could announce his obviously planned "treat". 'How about looking at that chip shop at the bottom of our hill?'

'But we won't have any warm plates back at the house,' said Fish, trying to wind up Dad, who always preferred to warm plates before a meal.

'Who's eating at home?' Dad replied. 'I was thinking of al fresco. That is...'

'If we don't mind your Italian friend joining us!' shouted Vic and Fish together. The Italian didn't exist but the joke *was* an old family friend.

Twenty minutes later they were all sitting on one of the strange seats dotted along the promenade. It was actually brand new, but made to look like an old piece of driftwood and an anchor. Fish was quite scornful, describing it as "a piece of tat" , but that didn't stop him joining Vic and Dad in devouring the fattest, chips and the meatiest fish cakes they had ever seen while a line of seagulls formed on the seawall.

'I think we're in a Hitchcock movie,' said Dad.

'He means "The Birds",' Fish whispered.

'I know!' she replied. 'I may be your kid sister but I do know a few things.'

'I apologise,' he said with an exaggerated roll of his eyes. 'Have you got any more tomato ketchup sachets?'

'We picked up extra on purpose,' said Dad. 'What are you doing with the things?'

'Eating them!!' Fish and Vic shouted together, completing yet another family catch-phrase. Then Fish stood up and said, 'Well, wherever they've gone, the chip shop is only just round the corner and I'm going to get some more.' With that, he was off, too quickly even for Dad to tell him to pick up some vinegar too as there wasn't any in the house.

Dad started to make a remark about Fish's sudden enthusiasm for tomato ketchup – something which Vic was more likely to consume in vast quantities – but their attention was taken by the arrival of two people in a beaten up old van which looked as though it had been built in Eastern Europe about fifty years ago. They opened the back of the van, threw a few things out onto the promenade, half-heartedly put one or two items back tidily and then shoved everything back in again.

While they did this they kept looking out into the harbour, which was gloomy now, and dotted with small motor boats and dinghies, until one put his fingers in his mouth and whistled, receiving an answering whistle from a small boat which was half way across the harbour. The fatter of the two men on the sea front scrambled down one of the small breakwaters and clambered into a rowing boat that was scarcely wider than him. He made a slow progress out to where the new arrival was being moored and then stowed a number of objects in the boat, with every move making Vic and her Dad wince as the dinghy threatened to capsize.

'What are you watching?' It was Fish, back from his chip shop return visit. 'Sorry!' he added, noticing their aggrieved expressions. 'Didn't mean to make you jump. I got some salt, by the way. So, what *are* we watching?'

Dad motioned in the direction of the boats. 'We were just wondering whether that man was going to try to get in the dinghy with the other chap and all the stuff they've just unloaded. It's a miracle it's still upright as it is.'

The answer was immediate. The rowing dinghy cast off and waddled slowly back to the breakwater. 'He's going to make two journeys,' said Vic. But she was wrong. The man on the other boat tied down one last tarpaulin, turned and with a graceful dive quite out of character with his size – and the fact that he was fully clothed – plunged into what must have been quite cold water and swam incredibly slowly to the shore. When he got there, he climbed carefully up the slippery blocks, which were the same as the ones used for the jetty, and stood there dripping, apparently unconcerned by the cooling of the evening. The others ignored him completely until they had everything stuffed into the back of the van. Then, when it seemed nothing more would fit, he squeezed into the back with it all and the van pulled away, almost as slowly as its wet occupant had just swum across the harbour.

'I think I'll need some extra pages for my diary today,' Vic said. She was pleased to discover that Dad and Fish couldn't think of a witty comment. She had the last word, for a change. Although the three people had seemed completely unaffected by the cold, Fish and Vic weren't. Dad decided they had done enough staring for one evening and, as it was getting dark and cold, he took them back to the house where he made them cocoa while Fish made a start on the first book from the sagging shelves and Vic filled in her diary. She had just finished the bit about the man diving fully-clothed into the harbour when she realized that she hadn't written about the book of word games. Remembering the dedication in the book doused her somewhat brightened spirits. She closed her diary, tossed it onto the coffee table and sat back in the sofa.

Fish looked up. 'You OK?' he asked.

'Yeah,' Vic replied. 'Why shouldn't I be?'

'I dunno. It's just that you sighed.'

Vic hadn't realized that she had made an audible sound. She put on a grin to try and get away from the subject, but Fish – unusually for him once he had started reading – closed his book, put it on the arm of his chair, and said, 'Do you like the house?'

Vic didn't know how to react. The question was normal enough, from anyone except her brother. He had never been the sort to make small talk of any kind.

'Yeah,' she said, still cautiously, in case this was just one of Fish's ironic wind-ups, delivered even more deadpan than usual. 'Why shouldn't I?'

'No reason. It's just that after years of big family holidays we've each got a room of our own...'

He seemed to run out of words – another unusual thing for Fish – so she filled in what she thought he might have been meaning.

'I'll be alright. I've got the best room. I won't miss...'

It was Vic's turn to run out of words. They were both finding that small-talk tended to lead back to the subject of Mum. Luckily, before the break in their conversation could become painful, Dad came in with home-made drinking chocolate.

'Here you are,' he said breezily. 'This will make you sleep soundly, as if you needed any help after a long day on the road. I'm just writing one or two ideas I had during the journey, otherwise...'

'"You'd forget 'em in a while,"' Fish finished his sentence for him. It was a line from one of Dad's favourite songs, which they had often heard him use. Dad smiled.

'Won't be long,' he said. 'Enjoying your book?'

'Yeah,' said Fish. 'It's really quite interesting...' but Dad was only being polite. He was already out of the door and half-way down the stairs. Fish glanced at Vic, who was grinning.

'You're lucky he didn't tell you not to destroy it!' she laughed. 'You know how fussy he is about books. Even a paperback looks brand new after he's finished it. I wonder why he's like that.'

'He told me once,' said Fish. 'You know he's got a huge collection of paperbacks back at home? Well, he's had them since he was a teenager; he used to hunt around the bookshops with an old school friend – they even went into London sometimes – and they spent their pocket money on them.'

'No wonder he behaves as if they're totally precious!'

Fish held up his hand. 'That's only half the story. Apparently, his friend's Dad belonged to some book club and bought all these hardback books, which he considered to be "real" books. He was dead snobby about it and actually threw away paperbacks when he'd read them. That's what made Dad really determined to look after all his books. I think he's right in a way, but I'm blowed if 'll put more effort into worrying about a book's cover than I use reading it. Anyway, a well-thumbed book looks like someone's had a good read out of it – several good reads, in fact. What better recommendation could there be for the next reader?'

Vic's thoughts were all over the place while Fish was speaking. She couldn't remember the last time they had had a conversation like this, and on top of that she was hearing family history for the first time. Fish was good at it, of course, as he had his Dad's easy ability with words. She wasn't so confident. 'So what's so amazing about the one you're reading?' she asked, wondering whether she sounded genuinely interested or not.

'What? Oh yeah. Well it's about a place near where we all went on holiday two years ago. You remember the Cornish expedition?'

'Do I remember it?' Vic moaned. 'We had to go and listen to Uncle Ben's choir every other night.'

'I thought they were pretty good,' said Fish. 'They've won competitions, you know. They were even on the radio once.'

'Yeah, yeah, they were good. But I could have done without hearing the same dozen songs every other night.'

'Cunning, though.'

'What? The songs?'

'No, Uncle Ben. Haven't you noticed that whenever the big annual holiday is arranged, Ben always manages to find something to do?'

'How is that cunning?'

'Don't you see? It's not really his thing, is it? I mean, who in their right mind wants to go away on annual communal holidays every year with a family you grew up with, or, worse still, married into?!'

'I still don't see how this is cunning.'

'Well, he always manages to make sure that where we go fits in with something involving his own circle of friends. It's the five-a-side football team tour, or the bell-ringing tour or the folk choir tour, so he gets time off from us!'

Vic was amazed that she had never thought of this before. She was even more amazed, though, to find herself having a conversation like this with her brother. She had been surprised enough at the pleasant journey from home but she had expected them to slip back into their usual sarcastic exchanges once they were settled in. She decided to test it further.

'OK, so it's cunning, but you haven't told me about your book. What's the Cornish holiday connection?'

'Well, I don't know whether there definitely is one. You see it's set a bit far back in the past for a start – early 1900s I reckon. And although it's an autobiography it's more about a property than a person. But the house – or at least the bay next to it, and the trees and gardens she describes, sound very like a place we saw when Grandpa hired that boat and we went up and down the coast exploring creeks and inlets.'

'Why don't you just check by looking it up on a map?'

'Well, I don't think I can. The writer spends half her time moaning about unwelcome visitors and tourists and she doesn't actually give the proper names of any part of the area. I can't find a village name or anything that I recognize. Not so far, anyway. It's odd. It gives the book a ghostly feel. As if the lives and everyday routines she mentions have all slipped away.'

The conversation ended here because Dad returned and came out with the words they always expected on these occasions: 'Did anyone else notice that poster at the bottom of the hill?'

'Uh-Oh!' said Fish, 'I think I hear the sound of a trip brewing. Hope we get the chance to use Grandpa's map, too. So where are we going?'

'Well,' said Dad, 'The sign said "Lighthouse Open Day".

I've looked on the aforementioned map and it's more or less at the end of our road. If it's a nice day to-morrow, how about taking a look?'

'At a lighthouse?'

'Well, why not? Anyway, Grandpa's map shows a lovely coastline. Let's take a picnic. If all else fails we can at least have lunch out.'

'Speaking of Grandpa, has anyone read their letter?' asked Fish.

'You mean the one that mysteriously arrived here even though it's not our home address?' said Vic, and she and her sister looked meaningfully at their father. He held up his hands.

'I had to give him some information,' he said. 'In case of emergencies and whatnot.'

'Yeah,' snorted Fish. 'It's the whatnot that worries me!'

Vic found the banter a bit disconcerting. 'What do yours say?' she asked.

'Mine doesn't actually say anything,' said Fish. It's just a verse of a poem.'

'Mine too,' said Dad

'I've got two,' said Vic, and as she put hers out on the coffee table the others put theirs down too. There was a pause. Dad and Fish looked at the verses. Vic looked at them, thinking that she had probably received two verses to make her feel special, but that then made her think again about Mum, and she felt gloomy once again.

'Funny how we were ready for this,' Dad commented wryly.

'Yeah,' said Fish, equally wryly. 'Well we all know Grandpa. So, what have we got Vic?'

'Not sure,' was Vic's non-committal reply.

Dad, meanwhile had moved the four stanzas around cautiously and then said, 'Well, I don't know the poem and, as Grandpa has left the title and the author off I guess that's that for now. It's an interesting one, though, and the poet mentions the gulls, which I had also noticed.'

'Me too,' said Fish.

In another mood, Vic might have added that she had seen them disappear when the storm arrived, but she didn't feel like chatting and, seeming to get the message, the others wandered off to bed, as did she.

Later, just before she went to sleep, Vic looked at the books on the shelf next to her bed with mixed feelings. The book of word games was there and she couldn't stop another pang of sadness about Mum running through her when she looked at it. On the other hand, there were books she had brought with her for the holiday, including a couple Dad had bought her just before they had set out. They were brand new and they reminded her of her surprising conversation with Fish, which was especially good because he often took the shine off things like holidays with his odd moods. And Dad was his usual self. He tired you out with his endless "things to do while you're on holiday" routine, but it was fun really.

The last thing she heard before she drifted off to sleep was a door banging shut somewhere downstairs. Probably Dad tidying up, or exploring, which he often liked to do on his own, at his own pace, she thought.

4

SUNDAY

Vic's sleep was interrupted several times in the night. At first it was simply the sound of more door banging downstairs. She only stirred and drifted off again, but it was enough to be annoying.

Then there was another, more irritating noise: the ferry terminal. One of Dad's reasons for choosing the house had been its position – on the sloping coastal strip overlooking a bay and a harbour. It *was* beautiful and ought to have been tranquil. Yes, he had said, there was a ferry terminal at the foot of the slope, but that hadn't looked like much of a problem on the map and anyway, he had said, how many times would big noisy ships pull in and out of a small place like Fishguard? But the reality of it proved to be that there were bright lights, which were on all the time, and hooters and sirens which sounded at intervals through the night. Vic knew that it always takes a night or two to get used to the unfamiliar noises and distractions of a holiday home or hotel room but this place was going to be a challenge and she wondered as she turned endlessly in her bed, whether she would ever get used to it.

And then there was the third reason – the real reason – why she wasn't managing to rest properly: she missed her Mum. Or rather, she missed the idea of her Mum. For Dad and Fish there were clear memories of times spent with her, but Vic's memories were from when she had been much younger. There were moments that she could summon up, but her chief memories were of the warm, cuddly times, those vague but lovely times when being put to bed or comforted when hurt. And since then there had been the big family holidays, packed full of relations. No-one had ever actually said that they were to make up for Mum not being around, but she could recognize the signs. So, if all the busy family holidays were left out, this one, was, for her, the *first family holiday without Mum.* And as she lay there, half sleeping, half thinking, she wasn't at all sure she had got over losing her.

She did not want to go and disturb anyone else: she was too old to sneak into her Dad's room and now was not the time to wake up Fish. So she turned on her light and tried reading, doodling in the margins of her diary and, eventually, just lying there with the light out, waiting for it to get light behind the curtains at dawn.

She eventually fell asleep only to wake up what felt like two seconds later. She looked at her clock: it *was* two seconds later! Well, more-or-less. It was half-past-five, which, when you are thirteen years old is a time which does not exist, especially during the holidays!

What had woken her up? Dad was always an early riser, even on holidays, but this was too early even for him. Anyway, he was always very quiet and she thought she could remember a loud rattling, banging noise, and the barking of a dog. Getting up, she went to the window and pulled the corner of the curtain up. Nothing rattling or banging, but there was a dog: one of those little terriers that people either found so endearing or so annoying. She usually liked them. "Wee stumpy dogs," she would call them, slipping into the style of her Scottish grandparents.

Fish disliked them. "Rat on a string," was his name for them whenever he saw one yapping along the road behind its owner. Vic could understand his view because as soon as she looked out, this annoying little dog, which was actually perched on the ridge of next door's garden shed, started barking at her. She stared at it, not wanting to make silly noises or to shout, in case she woke up the rest of the family. Then it stopped. She hadn't heard anyone telling it off. She hadn't stopped staring at it in that way that always infuriates a dog. It just looked down into her back garden, somewhere below where the sun lounge jutted out over the patio, flattened its ears and slunk back along the shed roof and out of sight into its own garden.

If Victoria hadn't been wide awake already, she was by now, with the bay clear in the sunlight and the seagulls gliding back and forth across the bottom of the garden. They looked as if they roosted in the pine trees which grew on the land beyond the gardens.

'Don't be stupid, Vic,' she said to herself. 'Seagulls don't roost in trees," But she made a mental note to be careful what she said if the subject came up with Fish. He always seemed to know whether things could happen which she was certain were impossible, and he loved to pour scorn on her for it.

She was definitely not going back to sleep in a hurry, and, for want of anything else to do at the crack of dawn, on holiday, with no-one else apparently awake, she decided to go and take a look in the garden to see what might be so interesting to a dog. She put a jumper and some jeans on and slipped into her trainers without fussing about socks. As she went downstairs through what was definitely a house in which no-one else was up, she still felt a little foolish. What would she say if someone heard her? "I just got up to go down for a drink." That should work. Actually, knowing either her father or her brother, they would probably be more interested in her words. Dad would probably make a holiday catch-phrase out of "Got up to go down". Well, she would have to live with that. At least going out this early might give her something to know that Fish didn't. "I might find something to impress him with later," she thought and, reassured by the thought of besting her brother, she finished her descent.

Not knowing where the door keys were kept, Victoria decided to try the back door in case no-one had locked it. The keys were in the lock. Dad must have left them there. He was always good like that. He took care of the little details, thought ahead and made things more likely to happen. When others were being lazy in front of the TV, or stumbling off to bed, he tended to pay attention to the little things which meant the next day would start just a little more smoothly than it might otherwise have done. It was always he who set the breakfast table each night, no matter how late or how tired he might be. Drinks and nibbles always got packed for any outing. Fish had once told her that Mum always joked that... Victoria felt a twinge at the thought of her Mum, but she had been teaching herself how to cope and she made the thought finish itself... Mum always joked that it was because he hated to spend money buying nice things to eat and drink when they were out. This was probably true; one of Dad's favourite sayings was "Look after the pennies and the pounds will take care of themselves".

Lost in these thoughts, Victoria hadn't realised that she had walked the length of the garden without noticing anything. This was no good. If Fish came along now she would have nothing to tell him about to impress him. She turned and looked around her.

The garden was really three different levels, each one a self-contained area. On the first terrace, just below the sun lounge, there was a narrow strip of concrete patio and a slightly less narrow strip of grass with a whirligig washing line in it. The next part was a miniature shrub garden, with a very low archway in a box hedge which made it almost impossible to enter.

The lowest part was just plain grass up against a stone wall which was completely blanketed with ivy.

The only interesting thing Victoria could see was an ornamental stone fountain in the shape of a large sea shell with the figure of one of those little boys you found in old paintings and Greek temples. She could try telling Fish about that, but he would just annoy her by knowing the real name for it. What was the use of pointing something out if you couldn't impress people with some technical detail!

Victoria sighed. How depressing! Here she was, thirteen years old, already one year into what Dad annoyingly referred to as "Big School" and she didn't know the proper words for things! With an almost audible sigh she turned and leaned on the ivy-covered wall. Over the other side there was just a neglected sort of field with nothing to see except tall brown patches of grass with mounds of soil here and there where someone must have been digging. A pretty rough job they'd made of it, she thought, and there was another sigh.

Victoria caught her breath. She was sure it wasn't she who had sighed. Maybe there was a breeze. There was ivy next to where she stood. Perhaps a breeze had shifted the leaves and the rustling must have sounded like her sigh. But there was no trace of a breeze. What she saw was nothing, except maybe a slight movement out of the corner of her eye, maybe just by the hedge on the corner by the fountain. Then the dog started barking, which distracted her.

She looked up to the shed roof where it seemed to like standing, expecting to see it barking at her, but instead it was looking towards her house, or at least the top of her garden. As she looked, it stopped barking and flattened its ears just like before. She heard a noise like a latch falling and expected any moment to see Dad or Fish at the back door. But there was no-one.

By this time, Victoria had walked up the path to the top patio. On the way down she had only noticed what you could see with the house behind you. Now she saw that there were two doors in the wall under the sun lounge.

One had a padlock on it, and a small window that she wouldn't be able to see much through even if it weren't just too tantalizingly high for her to reach. The other had no window, but a simple gatelatch which she lifted and let drop. Sure enough, it was the noise she had just heard.

She opened the slatted wooden door. Inside, there was just a pile of old wood, sloping from the bottom of the door to the top of the rear wall, about twelve feet back. And a smell, sort of musty but also sweet, almost fruity.

Victoria craned her neck forward and sniffed more deeply. It was the smell of apples.

'Anything interesting?' came a voice by her shoulder. She felt as though her heart was going to jump up her throat.

'Fish!!' she shouted. 'Don't *do* that!'

Her brother held up his arms to stop her threatening hand giving him a clout of annoyance.

'Sorry! Sorry! What are you doing up so early, anyway? I didn't know you had heard of six *a.m.*'

'Yes, very funny. I was just looking at the garden. I couldn't sleep because of the dog.' She indicated the shed roof where the dog had perched. It was no longer there.

'Dog?' said Fish.

Victoria's heart had only just started beating properly since her brother had startled her. Now exasperation took over. 'Don't tell me you can't hear it from your room?! It woke me up an hour ago with its barking.'

'So you decided to come out and look at the garden. Must be some dog to get you away from your clothes and CDs.'

'It wasn't just the dog,' Victoria started. 'I've been awake on and off all night, thinking... At this point even her annoying brother had enough sensitivity to recognize the signs. Her expression showed that sympathy was required. As her eyes began to moisten with tears, he took her gently by arm and said, 'I've got the kettle on. Come and have something warm to drink. Would you like some hot chocolate?'

He was now talking more like a parent than a brother. But she didn't mind. They went back inside and she stood and looked out of the kitchen window while he organized her drink.

'You can go and sit down, if you like,' Fish said, thinking that she was trying to appear useful. Vic didn't reply. She wanted to stand where she was because on this side of the building there were no big, overwhelming views, just a short patch of grass and a concrete ivy-covered wall up to the road, almost up to the limit of her sight. She was standing looking out of the window but she was only seeing her thoughts. She was also happier standing near her brother, but if he had asked why she probably wouldn't have said as much.

'I expect we'll have to go on the first of the many shopping expeditions soon,' said Fish, for lack of anything better to say. 'Dad will want his creature comforts but you can guarantee it will take him several attempts to track everything down that he needs.'

Once again, Vic responded to Fish's simple chattiness. 'He's like Uncle Ben.'

'Uncle… Oh, yeah. See what you mean. They do both like what Dad calls "quality of life" things around them, even on holiday. Do you remember the fuss about tea when we were all in Scotland the first time? Oh no you'd probably be too young.' He hesitated, and Vic knew that it was because the conversation was moving into the risky territory of Mum. She wasn't going to let it trouble her.

'Tea?' she asked, taking the cup of hot, sweet chocolate that Fish had now finished preparing. He took the signal and went on.

'Yeah. Tea. We all arrived pretty late on the first night. Only Grandpa had got there reasonably early because he did the journey up in two stages. When we had all got there we more or less had to go straight in for supper and then off to bed. Is your chocolate OK?'

Vic sipped it. It was still too hot. 'It's fine,' she said. 'What about the tea?'

'Yeah, the tea. Well, in the morning, Grandpa, having had a rest as soon as getting there as well as a proper night's sleep, was up just about before anyone. I came into the breakfast room just after Dad and I heard Grandpa offer him some tea he had just brewed. Well, you know Dad never drinks tea with breakfast...' He paused, as if waiting for a reply but it was obviously for another reason because he looked towards the bottom of the stairs, probably thinking he could hear Dad. He went on immediately, before Vic could say a word. 'Well, he said so but, being Dad, he couldn't help himself saying it in a way that, well, it wasn't rude, but it was clear that, having told him many times, he thought Grandpa really ought to know. Which he should have done, I guess, because it's the sort of thing Dad tends to go on about, you know, wanting to drink something with a bit of a kick in the morning and preferring coffee – real coffee – and all that. Anyway, to cut a long story a bit shorter, they were just starting to relax again after this slightly uncomfortable episode, when in came Uncle Ben, who *hates* tea. So, naturally, Grandpa offered him some of his specially freshly brewed beverage...' he hesitated, noticing Vic grinning. 'I know!' he exclaimed. 'It was just like a TV programme. And Uncle Ben is a *real* foodie. So whereas Dad had just been a bit ironic, your Uncle was scathing about the English habit of drinking an insipid leaf concoction at any time, let alone breakfast, and with so much milk that it was lukewarm. And of course, Grandpa said "What are you going on about now?" in that way he has of winding people up and they were still niggling each other about it when the rest of the family started to wake up.'

Before Vic could say anything he gave her a look and nodded towards the bottom of the stairs. Dad's footsteps could be heard, so they went and sat at the breakfast table and concentrated on being a normally happy son and daughter for their father.

The smell of apples was forgotten, for the time being.

***

Dad didn't come straight in. Something in the porch took his attention and they could hear him turning some pages. The only thing with pages that Vic had noticed was a telephone directory, so she guessed he was looking at that. It was another five minutes before he had finished whatever he was doing and came in to find Victoria and Fisher managing to seem quite normal. Fisher was doing a jigsaw he had found in one of the cupboards and Victoria had her holiday notebook pages spread out on the sun lounge coffee table. So far she had written what she called her "Holiday Habit". Whenever she was away from home she liked to break one of her routines and see how well she could stick to a different one. So, in her notebook it now said: "Noticed that I always put on my left sock first. Will start with the right one for the next two weeks." She hadn't written anything else as yet, but she thought she might produce a short poem about each day of their stay and she figured it would be more likely to happen if she had her materials at the ready. What she was actually doing was reading a very ancient Blue Peter Annual she had found on one of the living room shelves.

'Morning both,' said their Dad.

'Umm,' they replied, both absorbed in their respective activities. There were, after all, limits to how normal they were prepared to pretend to be.

'I suppose you've both had your breakfast,' he said, looking round the unfamiliar kitchen layout.

'Umm,' they said again, so he stopped trying to engage their enthusiasm for a moment and opened a couple of cupboards until he came across things he might like. There was a coffee maker and the owners of the house had left half a jar of real coffee, which, as Fish had just been saying to his sister, he preferred, so he put in a fresh filter paper and left the water to percolate through. Then he resumed his quest through the cupboards. Victoria gave half her attention to the page she was reading about how many guide dogs Blue Peter had bought in 1987. The other half she used to watch what her Dad would do. She guessed that her "holiday habit" ritual must have been an inherited trait from him because for some reason he always changed his breakfast routine when on holiday. He was a muesli and toast man at home, but he was perfectly capable of eating nothing but boiled eggs or porridge when away. Right now, nothing in the cupboard seemed to appeal and he seemed to lack his customary liveliness.

'What I'd really like is some fruit,' he announced, to anyone who might be interested.

'Well we ate all the fruit on the way down yesterday,' said Fish, who also watched these critical moments in his father's life as carefully, if even less obviously, than Victoria.

'This will do,' Dad replied.

'What is it?' Victoria abandoned the Blue Peter Annual and peered round the corner of the sun lounge arch to see. There was a peculiar arrangement which Dad would explain later in the holiday as straight out of the 1960s. It was made up of two tacky-looking veneered cupboards, each with a drawer at the top, half-screening the arch between the kitchen and the dining area. Each drawer and cupboard could be opened from either room, and supported a frame of wooden shelves. On one of the cupboards sat an old-fashioned shallow glass dish from which, as Victoria peered, her father picked up one perfect, crisp, green apple. Seeing her looking, he held it up.

'This,' he replied and took a firm bite out of it. 'Delicious! It's a russet!' he exclaimed. 'You'd think it had just been picked this minute.'

"Well it must have have been," thought Victoria, "Either that or Fish put it there. I certainly didn't." She looked in Fish's direction but he only seemed to study his jigsaw with even more interest.

Her father poured himself some of the coffee which had now successfully filtered through the ancient brown machine. He came through and sat at the table where at least something was as he wanted it because he had set it all the night before. Somehow she felt unsure of him this morning. And he had good reason to be a little edgy if he wanted to. This was an unusual time in their lives: a holiday as a threesome without Granny, Grandpa or the rest of the family. He had moods like anyone else, but she didn't know whether he was the type to brood.

'I've left my coffee in the kitchen,' he said. 'Must be getting old.'

'I'll get it,' Vic said, and she jumped up, giving Fish a look as she went past.

Fish wasn't stupid. He might have seemed to be immersed in his jigsaw but he got the message and spoke to his father. 'Are there any odd jigsaw pieces near you?' he asked.

'Can't see any,' said Dad. 'Are you missing one?'

'Think so. This gap here.' He pointed.

Dad leaned over and scanned the pieces. 'Might be this one,' he said, slotting the one he had picked up neatly into place. Later in the day, Vic commented to her brother that Dad always seemed to be able to do that sort of thing. Fish had replied that their Dad had a great many talents, if only people would shut up and pay him some attention occasionally. Vic had been surprised at the vehemence with which Fish had spoken, assuming it was a "boy thing".

'Thanks,' said Fish.

Vic came back with the coffee, poised to make her contribution to perking up Dad.

"Your Grandfather always used to say he did jigsaws upside-down, without seeing the picture," Dad observed.

' "What you should do is", muttered Fish, loud enough for Victoria to catch. She gave him a look intended to remind him that now was not the best of times to remind Dad of one of the more iritating of Mum's relations' sayings. He gave her a "Yeah, I know," kind of look in silent reply. She needn't have worried, however, because Dad didn't react to Fish's remark.

She put his coffee on the table and he picked it up and drank it in one gulp. 'Delicious!' he said, with feeling.

'So, what are we going to do today?' Victoria asked, as perkily as she could while continuing to grimace at her brother with a "Day One of First Summer Holiday Since You-Know-What!" expression on her face warning Fish to make an effort. She couldn't believe herself. She was meant to be the kid sister, still gloomy about a holiday without Mum, but here she was chivvying Dad along and reminding her brother of his responsibilities.

'I'm not sure I want to do anything very vigorous on our first day,' Dad replied. 'Not after my huge long driving job yesterday.'

Victoria and Fish were used to Dad's first-day-of-the-holidays speech. As usual, it was basically true. He was strongly of the opinion that a holiday began the moment you locked your own front door and set out for your destination. This meant that he always liked to take a scenic route to their holiday destinations, and appreciate wherever it was that they found themselves. So the journey was usually a long one and he always protested that he was exhausted at the end of it, and yet he always gave in and took part in an expedition or activity the very next day. Usually organised it too. However, although long experience should have taught Vic to expect the worst, she let herself believe that maybe, just maybe, Dad had forgotten what he had said last night.

'OK,' she said. 'You enjoy your apple and I'll...' Her offer to get him some more coffee was interrupted by a volley of barking outside. She also thought he heard a door banging but neither Fish nor Dad said anything about that.

'That must be the dog you told me about,' said Fish, without looking up from his jigsaw.

'Told you so,' Vic replied sharply.

'What dog?' asked Dad, and so Vic had to tell him about her disturbed sleep and even accompany him over to the conservatory to show the animal to him. She braced herself for his reaction because she knew what sort of things got him worked up. Dad was not like the rest of her family; most of them had the habit of being very prickly about tones of voice they thought they detected, especially from younger people. Pointless circular arguments often developed from the slightest chance remark. Some of them also seemed to like picking fights, just for the sake of it. But her Dad was the exception. He did not pick on the kids but, of course, he had his own mood changes and one of them was to get rather worked up about things which other people might consider to be a minor matter. The dog was a perfect chance for him to sound off about inconsiderate neighbours. She quite expected him to complain about letting a dog up on a roof like that in the first place. It would be even worse if he heard its owners' half-hearted voices pleading with it to stop and come down. He would then chunter on all day about "only themselves to blame", or some such opinion, because, again unlike the relations, if he got an annoyance in his head it tended to stick with him. Other members of the family might shout unexpectedly at you, almost for the sake of it, and then be all chummy within minutes. Dad could get *seriously* upset by some things, but you always felt he meant it. He wasn't grumpy for the sake of it but she was sure this would spark him.

On this occasion, she got a surprise. He just grinned, then he repeated Fish's "stumpy dog" saying and went back to his breakfast.

But that was where the surprises ended.

'So what about that lighthouse?' he asked as Vic gave him the coffee she had fetched anyway.

Fish couldn't resist it. Mock-dramatically slumping across his jigsaw, he moaned, 'Ah well! If it means we can tell Grandpa some more stuff from his map, it's gotta be worth it!'

'That's the spirit!' Dad laughed. Vic knew why. To anyone outside the family Fish would have sounded like a typical complaining teenager. Vic knew that Dad regularly needed getting off the hook of Grandpa's questions and Fish was actually helping him. 'Yes.' Dad went on. 'It could be interesting. Anyway, it's only just round the headland. We can always come back if it's not worth it. What's the time now?'

He leaned back in his chair to see the clock above the kitchen door. 'Half-past five,' he said. 'Must have stopped. Anyone got a watch on?'

'Yeah,' said Fish. 'It's eight-fifteen.'

'OK. Let's see if we can be away by nine. Fish, you make sure we've got all the waterproofs, cameras and everything. Vic, you can make a start on the picnic. Sort out some things kids like to eat...' They all grinned at this. It was another standing family joke that no-one in the family had ever particularly liked junk food. '... and I'll put some drinks and real food together when I've brushed my teeth.' He had cleared his breakfast things as he talked and was about to go upstairs when he looked at the fruit bowl. He hesitated a moment, an expression of momentary puzzlement on his face. Then the expedition plan reclaimed his thoughts. 'I didn't realize we had two of those excellent russets,' he said. 'Don't let me forget to put this one in with the picnic; they're delicious.'

Vic was surprised by the apples too, but she was determined to do her bit of the picnic preparation properly so she let it slip out of her mind, for the time being...

***

They *had* got away by nine, Victoria thought to herself as she lay in the bath at six o'clock that evening, trying to get rid of her various aches and pains and prevent others from developing by the morning.

The past seven hours – eight if you counted the time they had actually stopped to eat or be entertained – had proved that Dad was still basically his old self.

The drive up to the lighthouse had looked straightforward. Their holiday house was actually on the next road round from the one they needed, so they had driven over the hill they were already living on and found it quite quickly. When they did, it had taken quite a while to get out of the T-junction as half-a-dozen cars were already moving slowly up it, presumably also going to see the lighthouse. The trouble was, they were moving slowly because it was a beautiful but very narrow country road and you could not get past oncoming vehicles without stopping in little passing places. There weren't many cars coming the other way but as there was traffic in their direction even the occasional farm vehicle coming the other way had everyone stopping, backing up to a passing point or desperately hoping that the vehicle squeezing through six inches of space wasn't going to take the paint off their car. The drive across about three miles of seaside headland had taken the best part of an hour.

After all the tense manoeuvres, which only Dad didn't seem to mind, Vic's heart had risen as they reached their destination and even Fish had to admit the it was magnificent. They had come over a rounded hilltop approach and although the map showed the lighthouse standing on a small island right next to the mainland, it was actually so close that they could only see the building, which seemed to hover just yards away. With a grey sea cut by sunlight through banks of cloud, the white of the lighthouse looked even more impressive. Things had soon started to get a bit more complicated, however.

The car park hadn't seemed too busy, just an L-shaped field on the right of the road, but when they had turned into it a sign with the word "overflow" had given them all ominous feelings, admittedly not as uncomfortable as Vic's stomach muscles were now feeling after clambering over stiles and fences, but still that feeling that you get when a relaxing activity suddenly becomes harder when everyone else seems to have the same idea.

Vic gazed through the steam rising from her bath, added some more hot water and bath essence and relaxed again. The memory of the walk to the lighthouse returned and she smiled as she remembered how it had gradually put itself together from discomforting bits and pieces. The walk from the overflow car park had featured cow pats, nettles and brambles overflowing in fiendish combination across a narrow path. They could have got past them easily but for the fact that even at this early hour a surprising number of people were coming back up it as well as going down. At its end there was a stile which people seemed to be having a lot of trouble climbing over, mainly because many of them seemed to be accompanied by whiny kids who all behaved as if this was their first time away from their TVs or computer games. Several, who looked perfectly capable of simple physical activity, had even demanded to be lifted over the stile, something no self-respecting member of her family would have dreamed of doing!

Surprising herself with a positive thought about her relations, Vic returned to the present for a moment. She had noticed that the hot bath water had brought out the blotches on her legs which were her lasting reminder of the nettles and brambles, not to mention the independent mind set of the members of her family. She sighed at the memory and stretched her aching ankles under the warm water, letting memories of the day out gradually come back into her thoughts.

The three of them had finally negotiated the stile and made their way along a crushed stone path. She remembered that the stones of the dry stone wall to their left still glistened in places from an earlier shower.

And to their right the view across the sea had been so breathtaking that even a slightly unhappy teenager couldn't avoid noticing. The sea and the sky were both a deep shade of grey, but not quite the same shade. And down through them had streamed shafts of intense sunlight like spotlights which picked out, by some miracle arranged by a local tourist office, five or six sailing boats which swept round the headland and tacked past the outlying rocks about half a mile away. The only "fly in the ointment", as Dad had put it, had been the people. There was another, lower, dry stone wall between them and the cliff edge, and people were dotted along it looking worryingly like a queue. Fish, who was good at picking up these things, reported that he had heard one member of a family who were going back up the path saying that an hour's queuing was their limit!

They had found it unbelievable that, early as they were, others had already been queuing for an hour. However, they had pressed on because Dad always insisted on checking what they were queuing for. Vic and Fish had to admit that, embarrassing though it was, his willingness to investigate a line of people often revealed that they were waiting to do something quite different from what he had come for. But with a wry smile she remembered that this time his hopes had been in vain. Finally coming round the corner they had been met by a wonderful scene, made all the more beautiful by sailing boats which now to dipped in and out of the sunlight. The lighthouse, of which they had only had a glimpse so far, and then only of its curved top, was a brilliant white building, not very tall but above their sightline because of the island of rock which it sat on, surrounded by small outbuildings which encircled it like a ring. There was a brass band playing on the headland, which they had not heard because of the curve of the coastline, a display was being presented on the sheer rocks on this side of the island by the coastal rescue services and a burger bar set up beyond the gate the queue waited to pass through. Fish had commented that a burger bar was a bit out of character in such a traditional setting, not to mention rather soon after breakfast, but Dad had pointed out that it was a "wholefood" one and the people behind the trestle tables it was set up on were clearly volunteers, so it passed the "DFT" – the Darwen Family Test.

Vic's thoughts were interrupted by someone coming up the stairs. She hoped her planned bath – which was less than half way through by her standards – was not going to be interrupted. She was in luck: whoever it was only opened a door, then she could hear the barking of next door's dog, the door was closed again and whoever it was walked back downstairs. Vic wasn't going to call out to see who it was for fear of reminding them that it might be their turn. Instead she went back to her achy memories.

The pleasure of the visit to the lighthouse had stopped there. They knew from their walk down from the car park that they must have walked past about a hundred queuing people and at this end of the queue there was a narrow bridge. It was solid, but not much wider than one of those that Indiana Jones got trapped on in each film, and it could only be crossed in one direction at a time. Dad had spoken to someone who looked as if they were in charge at the gate and when he came back he had reported that not only was the queue moving very slowly but there was a safety limit on the island and in the lighthouse and they would definitely be queuing for at least an hour if they wanted to visit.

They hadn't been too disappointed: another of Dad's occasionally infuriating mottoes was "Enjoy what you get" and even if they didn't cross over and actually go into the lighthouse they had seen something worth the effort of the visit so far. So, for a moment, they had all agreed that, as it was "only a lighthouse", they could visit one another time, so why not use an hour more productively?

Vic smiled wryly again. In most families such an announcement would be a huge relief. The boring outing that a parent had insisted on dragging you out on was about to come to an early halt and it was time to pile back into the car trying hard to conceal your delight that you could go and slob around at home again. But not to Victoria and Fish. They knew Dad too well and so, instead of sighing with relief and turning straight back to the car, they had waited a moment. Vic grinned broadly this time as she remembered the look on Fish's face when Dad had pointed out that they had plenty of what he always called "provisions". This was the inevitable signal that another activity was about to be proposed, probably far more demanding than the one originally planned.

Sure enough, he had pulled out the map, shown them how the path they were on was actually part of the one that ran right round the coast, so why not walk a bit of it? Vic hadn't said anything at the time. It was actually such a beautiful morning that she didn't mind too much. If she had known quite how much she would itch and ache at the end of it she might have lent her voice to Fish's half-hearted protest.

Fish had played the "Aunty Margaret" card as his last-ditch tactic. Aunty Margaret was legendary in the family for organising walks which always went from "A to B" and back again so, on Mum's side of the family, an "Aunty Margaret walk" became shorthand for "there and back again". When no-one from that side of the family was within earshot, Fish was fond of pointing out that quite a lot of walks involve going somewhere and then coming back the same way, if only because of geography or pressure of time, so it was hardly fair to saddle Aunt Margaret with the label. However, logic did not come into it, and family expressions had a habit of sticking, so, whenever a repetitive activity took place it was always referred to as an "Auntie Margaret".

Dad had anticipated the tactic, however, pointing out a path which would take a circular route and bring them back to the car park. "Only four or five miles" he had said, and he sounded so keen that they had gone along with the suggestion.

The provisions had been left in the car to avoid carting them round the lighthouse, so Dad had gone to fetch them and left them sitting on the grass listening to the brass band and wondering how far he was going to drag them.

After he had been gone for a couple of minutes, which eventually turned into the best part of fifteen minutes, Fish had surprised Vic by making a direct remark about Dad.

'He's remarkably relaxed,' he'd observed.

'How do you mean?'

'Oh, I don't know. He's certainly been more easy-going while driving.'

'Hasn't he always been like that?'

'Well, Vic, that's because you seem to have inherited a family trait – the stating of things you think are obvious but which may not be.'

'I don't!'

'Don't get me wrong. It's no big deal. But Dad used to get very uptight when it happened. But not so far on this holiday.'

'I still don't see what you mean. Everyone points things out.'

'Absolutely! But look. I'll give you an example. Remember when we got held up in a jam about an hour into the journey, just when he was hoping we would make some progress?'

'Not really.'

'That's part of what I'm talking about. You've got that family characteristic of making a comment, but forgetting it soon after; or, at least, not seeing what effect it might have had on someone else.'

Vic bristled slightly. 'So, when am I supposed to have done this?'

Sensing her rising annoyance, Fish paused and then adopted a conciliatory tone. 'Well, on that stretch of dual carriageway just past where Granny and Grandpa live. We were in the middle lane behind a truck. The nearside and outside lanes were moving – in fact the nearside seemed to be empty. Dad got a bit annoyed '

'I thought you were saying that Dad hasn't let himself get annoyed.'

'That's not the kind of annoyance I was commenting on. What I noticed was that when he banged the steering wheel to show his annoyance you told him not to get uptight because obviously, as you put it, the outside lane was blocked and people were filtering into our lane, and the nearside lane was a filter lane, doing the same from the other side.'

'Yes? So?'

'Well, didn't you notice that a minute or so later the traffic started moving freely and the outside lane wasn't blocked and the nearside lane was actually an exit lane?'

'So the big deal was... ?'

'Dad's an experienced driver. He does all the driving. Always has done. He knows roads. He also knows that one we were on. He could have contradicted you there and then. I can remember a time when he would have turned on you, or whoever it was and made it clear, quietly but firmly, that you'd been talking rubbish and should give him some credit for understanding things. But he didn't. So far during this holiday he hasn't been defensive.'

The funny thing was, thought Vic, as she changed position slightly in the bath, that she hadn't minded Fish telling her this at all. Although she did not like having her personality analysed, it was a new and quite enjoyable experience to have a proper conversations with him instead of the usual brother-sister sparring. She was learning about the family and Fish was talking straight to her. It made her feel more grown-up, in a way. She supposed that *she* was getting more relaxed as well because she hadn't argued with Fish, who often irritated her by seeing huge significance in tiny little details. Instead, she had carried on chatting with him and by the time Dad had returned they were giggling like idiots.

'What's so amusing?' he had asked, to which neither of them was willing to give a direct answer. In fact, Fish had just been reducing Vic to helpless giggles with descriptions of Dad's funny habits, in this case the way he expressed his political views. He had been commenting on the fact that Dad always put his money in his wallet with the Queen's face to the back because he said he was a "republican". He might have been relaxing but they didn't want to push their luck. Instead, Fish had turned the question back at him.

'Where have you been? It's almost fifteen minutes since you "popped up to the car for the picnic", as you put it.'

The distraction had worked 'Oh, you wouldn't credit it,' he had replied. 'Queues both ways at the stile, of course, but you won't believe what happened *at* the stile.'

'What?'

'Well, I was a bit careless climbing over because I had been waiting for all these people to get over before me and I caught my T-shirt sleeve on a nail.' At this point he had shown Fish his left shoulder.

Vic, who was to his right, had said, 'But the tear's on this side.'

'I know,' Dad had replied, frustration in his voice. 'I walked all the way up to the car, cursing myself for tearing one of my favourite T-shirts, and when I came back down I went and did exactly the same thing on the other side!'

Fish and Vic had not been able to stop themselves laughing at this. When they had stopped giggling, Vic had realized that this was just the sort of thing Fish had been talking to her about, while they had been waiting. In the past, she could remember Dad getting quite "huffy" about being laughed at. Of course, no-one liked being laughed at. Several of her relations could make your life very miserable indeed if you just made a little joke at their expense. But Dad's way was to go quiet for quite a long time, which he didn't on this occasion. Realising that Fish was right was a new experience and, added to Dad's apparent changes, these thoughts had lightened the discomfort of the first part of the walk for her.

Victoria ruefully flexed her feet at this thought. She could still almost feel the cut of the limestone headland which they had had to negotiate before reaching the softer, grassier part of the walk. Although they had been walking across more-or-less flat rocky ground, there were deep scorings in the ancient surface, running from back under the fields out to where the cliff-edge marked the end of land. She had found it very distracting to clamber over, especially as Dad had kept stopping and looking back and going "Oooh!" and "Aaah!" at the view. When she had looked, she had to agree that the bay they were actually passing and the white top of the lighthouse and the changing blues and greys of the sea and the sky were all marvellous, but walking had been just *so* uncomfortable!

This memory brought her back to the present once more and she flexed her feet, which still felt as though they had been bashed against fossilised sandpaper all day. Then her back twinged, and she remembered why.

They had left the cliff-edge to walk around an outcrop of rock and as they had gone beyond it Dad had pointed out that from this point onwards they finally would not hear the silver band by the lighthouse. For some reason best known to himself he had said he would like to have some "nibbles", meaning picnic food, and how about going and sitting by the outcrop. This had changed Vic's mood because "nibbles" had been one of Mum's words and, to make it worse, they had to prop themselves against the same kind of rock which had tortured her feet, and it had dug into her back *and* that was why it ached now.

Sure enough, Dad was in Heaven because they could actually hear the band's music caught by the face of the outcrop they leaned against and he either didn't or wouldn't feel the discomfort. Meanwhile, the sea had changed from crystal blue to slate grey every few minutes and Fish had loved the feeling of being right out on the tip of a bay and it had brought out his boyishness and he had lobbed a stone out into the air to see if he could reach the water far below.

And Vic had brooded about Mum, although there had been a lively moment which had brought her out of her gloom a bit.

Fish's stone-throwing had disturbed some seagulls which they hadn't noticed from the top of the outcrop. Then, when he had thrown a bit of bread instead of a stone, one of the seagulls had actually caught it in mid-air and they had spent ten fruitless but hilarious minutes trying to make one of them repeat the trick.

Eventually, Dad had brought them back to reality by reminding them that they were actually at the start of their walk, part of which would have to be improvised across foot paths and bridleways to avoid doing an "Aunty Margaret". Vic had got to her feet wearily and then Dad had asked her for an apple out of the bag to munch as he walked.

"The green one," he had specified.

Vic had suggested that he had already eaten the last green one but he had simply said, "No, remember? There was one more left in the fruit bowl so I packed it."

Sure enough, it had been there, making Vic's thoughts drift back to her odd early morning experiences at "The Pilot's Cottage". So, having been lost in thoughts for a while she only had Fish's word for it that their Dad had crawled to the cliff edge on his stomach to get a look at the flumes of spray thrown up by waves in a narrow inlet far below them. She had no proper memory of exchanging pleasantries with thirty pensioners from Yorkshire who were negotiating a stile and filling the air with cheerful expressions which sounded harmless but were really the swear words of their generation, much to Dad's amusement, apparently. She even only vaguely remembered a Labrador dog which kept walking back for a look at them long after its owner had trudged round to the other side of the bay without even a look back of his own.

So, as she cheated by letting some of the cooling water out of her bath and topping it up again at a slow trickle so Fish wouldn't hear, her thoughts strayed back to doors banging and a little barking dog and green apples in a bowl that should have been empty and the sound of someone sighing.

The rest of the walk she *did* remember because they had taken a wrong path. It hadn't really been anyone's fault because it had been one of those complicated map details where the entrance to someone's property and a footpath seemed to be in the same place. They had gone down a metalled track past a bungalow with manicured lawns and hedges but flaking paintwork, past an old black dog which, unlike the Labrador, had shown no interest in them at all, even though it was attached to a barn door by a long chain, and on to a field full of cows – and cow-pats – which obviously wasn't the path. This they had not discovered until they had walked three-quarters of the way up the edge of the field, trying to persuade themselves that this might just be a very little-used path. When they were near enough to the end to see there was no way out they had no alternative but to turn round and walk all the way back again.

Having doubled back they discovered that the dog's sense of its own purpose was to challenge people who tried to *leave* and they had edged past, pretty sure that the chain would hold but not so convinced about the barn door! Still, Dad had made them laugh by pointing out that he had never seen a better example of a guard dog and he ought to get a job in a prison!

Back at the entrance they had decided to follow the road until they reached a stile or footpath sign and Dad had improvised the rest of the walk, using his famous "sense of direction". As it turned out, about four miles from where they had started, he had been going the right way in terms of points of the compass but having wrongly identified a small hill, he took them further inland than they wanted to be and about three miles had been added to the trek!

Vic sighed. "Only four or five miles!" she thought. "More like six or seven!" Dad usually underestimated things like that but at least it was more evidence that he was feeling more like his old self. She nearly jumped out of her skin when there was a sudden loud banging on the bathroom door. 'What are you doing in there?' Fish shouted, 'Reducing yourself to a pure solution? We would *all* like to use the facilities!'

Although it was a pain to have her thoughts interrupted, on the other hand, even though she never told her brother this, she did envy him for his ability to make clever remarks. In fact, she had been known to trot one out at school to impress her friends, and "reducing yourself to a pure solution" went into her memory banks for later use.

'There is a shower downstairs!' she shouted back.

'Dad's in that,' he replied. 'Anyway, I'm aching all over and I need a bath'.

'If it's so urgent, why didn't you let me know when you came up before?' she asked.

"I haven't been up. I was cleaning the picnic things in the kitchen.'

'Likely story! More like doing some more of that jigsaw. Suppose it must have been Dad. He wouldn't take a bath if you paid him... Yes he would,' she added, noticing herself using another of Dad's lines. 'OK, I'll be out in a minute!' she lied, settling back for another five.

Dad never took baths, he said, because he was dead keen on France, the French, everything connected with them, and he could always be counted on to remind them of the French horror at the fact that the English liked to wash in a bath and then lie in their own dirty water. Except for days like today, Fish agreed with him.

Victoria preferred a bath.

So had Mum.

Then she felt a bit sad again and climbed out of the bath to try and stop going all weepy again.

"That was quick," said Fish, familiar with Victoria's "minutes". Then he noticed her glistening eyes. :

"You alright, Vic?" he asked, making to follow her into her room, which was right at the top of the house, next to Dad's.

"Yeah, fine," said Victoria. She pushed her bedroom door half shut as a signal that she did not need him.

"OK. Give me a shout if you need me. I'll leap straight out of the bath. That should be shocking enough to make you forget anything!"

Victoria felt better as soon as Fish had made that joke.

***

When everyone had finished their various cleaning routines they strolled down the hill together and bought fish and chips. This was quite surprising because while Vic didn't mind eating the same things night after night – especially fish and chips, which was her joint-favourite with pizza – Fish usually complained violently if he had to eat the same thing *twice in a week*. Even when they were on holiday and they were just eating for convenience, or because they were too bruised and aching to cook!

Even more strange, two minutes after they had joined the queue Fish suddenly told them what he wanted and said he would meet them outside. When they came out they found him sitting on a bollard set into the end of a wall by the mini-roundabout.

'What's up?' Dad asked.

'Nothing. Just thought the queue was big enough without me adding to it,' was the reply.

Dad and Vic had exchanged looks and agreed, silently, not to press the issue.

They all strolled round to the quayside of what Fish had by now dubbed "Oilslick Bay", and this time they walked up to the first stone bench on the jetty to eat. Fish threw a chip in the air but no seagull would give them the time of day, let alone repeat the food-catching skills of the coastal walk birds. Vic wondered out loud whether the lizards or butterflies would perform, but her remark fell flat and they all ate in aching silence.

It was almost dark by the time they made their way back up the hill, Victoria with her arm looped through her Dad's and Fish, as always, walking a little way ahead of them.

Back at the house, Victoria was almost asleep on her feet after the day's exertions. Fish and Dad settled down to watch the second half of a film on the TV so she went upstairs and got ready for bed.

Her Dad's bedroom was on the same floor and it had the best view over the bay. In spite of being deliciously tired she felt that she would like one last look at the view As usual, when she went in she could see virtually no sign of its occupant. Whereas Vic's room had stuff strewn everywhere, Dad always treated holiday homes like real home. He would stow all his clothes and effects in drawers and on shelves as if he were moving in permanently. Seeking out the view, she turned the blinds and found that nothing much could be seen apart from the lights of the town on the other side of the bay.

A shadow passed swiftly across her window and looking up she could see that there was a bright moon and patches of cloud were crossing it rapidly. She opened the window and the noise immediately told her that there was quite a strong wind blowing. She listened as, down below from where her room was, the bushes and trees could be heard stirring and straining as it blew. She was about to close the window again when she heard another sound. Just distinguishable between gusts of wind, it seemed a like another sigh, but as she listened more carefully it became more like crying, and not at all like the sound she had heard before…

Now what had made her think about that? Even as she quizzed herself the sound went away, and the sounds were once again the familiar ones of leaves and branches responding to the weather.

Victoria closed the window, got into her bed and was soon fast asleep.

5

MONDAY

On Monday morning Victoria woke up before everyone else. A dream still lingered in her head, a dream of trees, some standing against the horizon, some fallen to the ground. As usual, her memory of the details faded quite quickly. She had heard somewhere that people analysed dreams for some reason, and she wondered who the people were who were lucky enough to be able to remember the details of their dreams hours or days later. Or "unlucky enough" if it was a nightmare!

Before Mum had gone, so Fish had told her, Dad had been the family early bird, but she seemed to have taken that role from him. Not that Dad had stopped waking up quite early, but that she woke up even earlier.

She went quietly downstairs and put on some milk to warm up so she could make herself some cocoa. She also put a slice of bread in the toaster and poured some fruit juice, which she took through to the breakfast table. The table was already set. Dad always did this before he went to bed, no matter how late. She idly picked up a sachet of vinegar which had come back with them, unused, from the chip shop. With nothing else to do, she started to read the small print. "Odd," she thought, as she scanned the ingredients. "Didn't know apple was used to make vinegar." As she read she heard a creaking from the stairs; either Fish or Dad making an early appearance.

She came back into the kitchen and was surprised to find no-one there. A quick look up the stairs and in the downstairs loo confirmed that she was still the only one around.

Back in the kitchen, she stood waiting for the milk to start to bubble and wondering whether to turn the radio on.

'Hi, early bird,' came Dad's voice behind her.

She almost jumped out of her skin and dropped the sachet.

'Sorry!' he exclaimed, before she had time even to complain. 'I thought I was the first one up. I crept down so as not to wake you and Fish. What was so interesting, anyway?' He bent down to pick up the sachet Victoria had dropped. 'Vinegar?' he added. 'Oh, yes. From the chip shop "Sharpening up" your reading, eh?'

Victoria was used to Dad's awful puns and treated this one with the usual family contempt. Having failed to find something to impress Fish with the day before, she now saw a chance with her Dad, which she now seized.

'Actually,' she began, 'I was looking at the ingredients. Did you know that there is apple in vinegar...' She got no further. Next door's dog set up such a terrific din of barking that she had to go and look out of the sun lounge to see what its trouble was. It was looking down at the patio, just like the day before. And as she looked at the dog, she thought she saw, out of the corner of her eye, a movement down along the rear wall of the house. Was that the storeroom door closing?

'Strange,' she said to herself.

'What's that?' her Dad said from the kitchen, but before she could answer or he could ask anything more, there was a sizzling noise from behind him. 'Milk boiling over in here!' he said urgently, and went to mop up the mess.

Vic snatched the opportunity while he was busy. 'I've, er, just got to put my boots out to air,' she said, knowing it must have sounded very feeble. Then she added, even more feebly, 'In case we go for another walk.'

She didn't actually know why she was being so devious, but she nipped out of the side porch door and was almost immediately beside the storeroom. Quietly, she opened it. As she did so, the dog stopped barking, but in the split second between the two things she could swear she saw a shadow in the corner, beside the pile of wood offcuts. But with the door fully open there was nothing, except that fruity smell again.

Victoria was not sure whether to feel intrigued or foolish. What was she looking for? Why was she looking? A dog barking; a creaking staircase; an unexplained apple; maybe some odd shadows. These were all just little things she could be dreaming up for herself. She was tired, after a long journey and all the strenuous things Dad immediately wanted to do.

No, she decided, it would take more than a few odd but easily explained events to get her started on some silly obsession.

She closed the door and went back indoors, only just remembering to pop her boots onto the back step as she did so.

'Boots OK?' asked Dad.

She nodded.

He was eating an apple. 'Good. These russets are amazingly tasty,' he added. 'Oh, and I've made your cocoa, the way you like it.'

Victoria ought to have said 'Where did you get that apple? We didn't get any more apples,' but for some reason she thought better of it. She sat down and sipped her cocoa, then remembered the toast. She knew it would be there and she knew it would not be burnt. It would be there because they weren't on a big family holiday. On those occasions it was like being at boarding school: every man for himself. Anyone could walk in and find some toast you were making or a cup of tea you had just poured and treat it like their own. But Dad wasn't like that and Fish, who might be, was still not up. She put it through twice: once to toast it the way she liked it and the second time, still on the lowest setting, to warm it so it wouldn't be burnt because she was fussy about her toast, liking it crisp on the surface, soft-ish inside and not too brown.

She pressed the handle down again and fetched the margarine and honey from the cupboard. The toast sprang almost entirely out of the toaster, which made her jump and stop thinking about mysteriously appearing apples and barking dogs.

Meanwhile, Dad had gone back upstairs with his bright green apple. When he came back down he started to put on his outdoor shoes and said, 'We're going to need to stock up for the old self-catering part of this holiday.' After a pause he added, 'I think I'll go round the bay to do some shopping. I might also reconnoitre that museum at the same time, if it's open on Mondays,' he added, munching his apple and blowing on a small cup of black coffee he had meanwhile made for himself. 'I think Fisher's waking up.'

Vic smiled at another of Dad's little quirks. He was doing his best to sound casual, but anyone would have been able to tell that he had made plans, mainly for himself. The mention of shopping was a clue that Fish might also be included. Fish had always gone shopping with Dad since he was a toddler. For some reason he loved it. Victoria was usually less keen, which on this occasion was handy. The museum detail meant he had looked up some tourist information and he was planning what Grandma Liz called a "mooch".

'Er, what kind of shopping?' Vic asked, trying not to sound too interested.

'Just provisions! Time to fill the cupboards of the Pilot's Cottage. Matey!' cackled her Dad, with mock glee. 'So we don't have to go the petrol station shop or the chippy every time we're peckish.'

Victoria pulled a face. 'I think I'll stay here and start my diary,' she said. He knew she had never been mad keen on shopping, just like her Mum, so he would understand. It was just a question of whether he would leave her alone in a strange house.

'Fine,' said Dad. 'No problem. We'll go out and look at beaches after lunch. Weather forecast looks better for the afternoon.'

'What's wrong with Oilslick Bay?' Vic said, keeping her face as straight as she could. However, only Fish had mastered the art of winding Dad up and he just winked and vanished off upstairs again, leaving Vic to complete her "perfect toast" routine and enjoy her holiday cocoa.

It was Fish, when he came downstairs a few minutes later, who said, 'Will you be alright here on your own?' Just like Mum would have said. Actually, thought Victoria, from what Fish had told her, Mum wouldn't have let her stay on her own. Or rather, Mum would have opted out of the shopping trip too and so the issue would never have arisen. Apparently, if there was one thing Mum had hated more than shopping, it was shopping with Dad!

Victoria just gave him a look. A scornful sister look. He got the point and turned his attention to fruit juice and cereal, which he ate in about three uncharacteristically quick gulps. He gathered up a couple of plastic bags from the cupboard under the stairs and went out to join Dad by the front door.

"We'll get you something nice!" called Dad, as he went out. Fish paused there. He looked back, seeming to have sensed something.

"You *will* be OK, won't you?" he said, but turned and left without actually giving her time to reply.

If Vic had felt like it, she could have told him that, on balance, she was more than likely to be "OK". The fact that he had been talking to her in such a chatty way made her feel that the next two weeks were something to look forward to. She might have been experiencing some mixed emotions about Mum. There might be some odd atmospheres, or whatever, to do with the view and the garden. But the prospect of her first two week holiday with just her father and her brother seemed a lot less daunting than it had when the suggestion had originally been made, especially if they were not going to drag her absolutely everywhere with them.

Victoria cleared the few dirty items from the breakfast table. Fish hadn't eaten much, as usual, and Dad's apple hadn't made anything dirty. The washing up didn't take her long so she decided to make herself useful by doing a spot of general tidying.

She went upstairs and tidied her Dad's bedroom and her own. Then she went down a flight and risked a look in her brother's room, hesitant even though he was well away from the house. She had to admit that Fish was good. Not just good by boys' standards which, as Mum had taught her, were about as low as you could get before crawling around on all fours, but good by anyone's standards. No-one ever had to nag him about keeping things tidy. He put books back on shelves and washed up without bidding – unless he was dashing out with Dad on a shopping trip! Her conscience tweaked, Vic went back up to her room and pushed her things into a semblance of neatness, at least enough to make her feel she wasn't completely letting the side down or waiting for someone to intervene, like Mum might have done. Like Mum…

Vic just stood and stared for a few moments, her spirits sagging once again, until her eye fell on her diary and she remembered that this had been part of her excuse for not going shopping, so she had better make an effort. If she wanted to be left alone from time to time, she needed to have her diary next to her when the other returned, otherwise they might realize she was moping, and drag her with them.

Picking up the book and a pen, she went down to the lounge. She resisted the temptation to turn on the TV, something they *never* did in the daytime at home, and went to look out of the window. The view was not directly out into the garden because, as Dad had pointed out as soon as they arrived, the house had either been built to someone's slightly odd specifications, or been modified for some reason, and the lounge was actually on the first floor. Dad had also said that just about every holiday home he had ever stayed in had seemed to have some quirky feature such as this, as if an owner or builder had decided that there needed to be something more to a house than just living accommodation downstairs and sleeping upstairs.

So, as she looked out of the window, her view slightly elevated, Vic wondered whether she would be able to see Dad and Fish, or rather their car, circling the bay on the way to the shops. However, her position was not elevated enough to see over the trees at the foot of the next door garden. She glanced down to see whether the other neighbours' dog was in its customary place, poised to annoy with a volley of barking. No, it was away somewhere.

Thinking about the dog drew her thoughts to the odd things which seemed to have been happening. The apples, the dog barking at nothing and the sighing noise at the bottom of the garden did seem to follow some sort of pattern. On the other hand, she wasn't stupid. She did also know that as she was also brooding, on-and-off, about her Mum, she could just be seeing things this way because of that. Anyway, things like this – things with no obviously sensible explanation – didn't happen, so why trouble herself over them. She was probably just adjusting to being on holiday with Fish and Dad and the daydreams would go away in time.

Even though she had wanted some time to herself to think this through, she had also meant it when she had told Dad she wanted to get on with her diary, so she made her way downstairs to do just that. As she reached the small landing half-way down to the ground floor, she paused, hearing a noise from the front door. Feeling slightly unnerved she hesitated a moment more, wondering whether her recent mysterious experiences were about to repeat themselves and how she could handle it knowing that no-one else was in the house. In the bend of the staircase where she was standing there was a window and, as no more noises reached her, she looked out. She could see most of the front path and on it a woman making her way back up to the road. As the woman closed the gate Vic could see that she was about Dad's age, though how she judged that she did not know as most people older than Fisher looked the same age to her! All Vic could see was that she had some sort of loose-fitting top over her shoulders and a knee-length skirt, both brown – Dad's favourite colour, she thought to herself, for no particular reason. The woman went down next door's path but took longer there, maybe talking to someone. After a while, when Vic thought her neck would stick at the awkward angle she had now held for a couple of minutes, the woman reappeared and, as she turned to close the neighbours' gate Vic noticed one more thing: she had an incredibly long plait of greying hair right down her back.

Rubbing her neck, Victoria finished her descent and went round to the front door. A card lay on the doormat. It had a name on it, and an address further down the hill from where they were staying. "Sculptures and wood carving" was its main message. Below that it said: "Commissions accepted. New objects soon in stock including our new range of applewood work."

'Applewood?' said Victoria out loud to herself. At that precise moment the dog started barking again. Without stopping to think, Victoria opened the other porch door and stepped down the six concrete steps to the patio.

The dog's barking became more furious and for some reason she didn't understand, Victoria braced herself as she stood by the storeroom door. What happened next still took her by surprise.

Round the corner came a small figure in very great haste. It was a boy, but no boy she had ever seen had looked like him. He was dressed, but not in what you would call clothes. Instead, he brought to mind another of Dad's favourite expressions: "Looks like he's been dragged through a hedge backwards". Except that, if he had, thought Vic, he seemed to have brought most of the hedge with him!

That was all she had time to register for the moment because the boy was looking back over his shoulder and so walked straight into her. He had scarcely touched her before immediately jumping back again. An expression of panic passed across his face as he looked past her at the door he seemed to have been making for. It was clear to

Vic that he wanted desperately to get to it and she would probably have got out of the way sharpish if he had made a move to get past. But he didn't. He stood stock still.

And then he burst into tears.

***

The boy cried and cried. He began with a plaintive, lonely, tearful whimper and soon built up to sobs which made his body heave so much that Victoria felt he was bound to make himself ill if he didn't stop.

'What's the matter?' she asked, too quietly shy to make any impact on the noise he was making. 'Who are you? What's the matter?' she said, rather louder. She was thinking to herself that she had better not shout at him for fear of attracting the attention of neighbours, or the dog, which was still strangely quiet. Then she realised that the noise the boy was making was easily loud enough to make someone nearby hear and stop what they were doing. So she reached out and took his arm, hoping that the contact would break his unremitting wails.

She was startled by the feel of his arm. Not only did his sleeve look like leaves, it actually *felt* like leaves; but what really surprised her was that she had to grip much tighter than she had expected to feel his arm within it. When she did tighten her fingers round what she thought would be the muscle above the elbow – the stray thought that Fish would know its proper name flitted across her mind – what she grasped felt like nothing so much as a bunch of twigs! As shocked as she was by the sensation, the boy seemed equally shocked. Her direct approach had the intended effect, like turning off a tap, firmly. The crying stopped almost instantly.

The boy stood, shoulders heaving silently, staring through misty eyes over her shoulder at the door. Victoria stood, almost as startled by her decisive action as he was, not knowing where to look. After a few seconds that seemed to last all day she decided to speak but before she could do so the dog decided to fill the silent gap left by the cut off sobbing. A renewed volley of barks threatened to bring not only a neighbour, but the whole neighbourhood out to see what was happening and Victoria felt forced to take a line of action which in a more sensible moment she would have dismissed as very foolish.

'Come indoors,' she said and, whether he had heard her properly or not, the strange boy allowed himself to be steered up the steps and in through the porch to the kitchen. Victoria was somehow only slightly surprised, as she led him to the dining table, to see a fresh green apple in the fruit bowl.

She didn't really feel comfortable with the idea of actually grasping him again and had managed somehow to get him there by putting her hands behind him and pushing. When she pulled out a chair from under the dinner table he stood for a moment seeming not to understand. Vic sat down on another and he then appeared to get the idea and copied her. He sat, very awkwardly, and so did she, mainly because all the chairs except the one the boy sat on were already occupied by Darwen family items. In her case, she was sharing hers with one of Fish's jumpers, a book belonging to Dad and a pen from her diary-writing equipment. Too distracted to think of moving them, she perched on the edge.

Unfortunately, the boy had turned sideways on in his chair and showed no sign of turning towards her, so she got up again and went round to one of the black plastic-covered armchairs. These made a rather embarrassing noise as the air rushed out of the cushions when someone's weight came down on them. She let herself down slowly onto it, hoping the boy would be too preoccupied with his distressed thoughts to pay any attention. She looked up as the last gasp of wind came gently out of the cushion. He was completely preoccupied, gazing towards the sun lounge and beyond. Vic realised that all her effort not to make a noise sitting down had been a waste of her energy. She also realised that she was going to have to go through it all over again because whoever he was she ought to offer him something, such as a drink, and if he accepted her offer she was going to have to get up to fetch it. And then she would have to sit down again and he would have a second opportunity to hear the embarrassing sitting-down noise.

Vic paused and considered the ridiculous pattern of her thoughts. What was she doing? These were the sort of mental games she played back in her "real" life, with her friends, all image-conscious and concerned not to be judged negatively by each other. She was on holiday, away from everyone she knew, with, what is more, a total stranger who didn't even seem especially *human*. What did it matter?

She jumped up, not because she knew the chair made less noise if you did but because she had had enough of dithering and wondering. Her "guest" looked round sharply at her sudden action and she almost felt unnerved again.

As he looked towards her she asked, 'Would you like something to drink?'

'I don't know,' he replied, in a tone which almost made it sound as if he would be able to decide if only he knew what a drink was, and his gaze moved back to the view outside. He appeared exhausted. She could not imagine him lifting himself from the chair. Well, he would have to before Fish and Dad came home. Fish and Dad! She began to be very busy.

A drink would have to be fetched and he could leave it if he wished. Going into the kitchen, she glanced at the clock over the doorway. It was ten o'clock. This was no real use to her because she was not quite sure what time her father and brother had left. Nor did she really know how long Dad planned to be. Even when he did not actually tell you he had spotted an interesting place he fancied visiting he tended to extend shopping trips with stop-offs in coffee shops and strolls to look at a view or interesting building. But he had left her on her own in a strange house, so he probably wouldn't be gone all that long, or at least Fish would not let him – with some reason, it now seemed!

She looked back to the dining area. Her strange guest had half lifted himself from his chair and was peering down through the sun lounge windows towards the bottom of the garden. She couldn't imagine what he was trying to look at. All you could see from there was the top of the garden wall and the tangle of branches leaning over it, with more piles of the same among the freshly-turned piles of soil that she had noticed on her first day there.

Having decided to force the drinks issue, Victoria brought him one anyway, figuring that if she got some refreshment into him she would have done her bit and she could then get rid of him before the others came home.

"I really think you should have a drink," she said, and stooped down to look in the fridge. "I've got some orange, milk, apple jui…"

Even as she said it she knew something was going to happen. The room was suddenly filled with a rustling sound like a million leaves stirring. Nothing actually moved, nothing changed at all, but a sighing sound, like a lament, swirled round the room, then the sound of the dog barking could briefly be heard and the sound of a door banging, and then it was silent again.

When Victoria straightened up, she was startled, but somehow not surprised to see that her guest was no longer there.

She checked whether the "boy" had really gone, of course. Her heart told her that there was no point, but with the return of her brother and father imminent her head advised her that a quick check would be a good idea. It took her about two minutes to go through the whole house. There was nobody there but her, not even in the storeroom which had been the scene of the appearance.

She fetched her diary and, as she turned to walk out of the kitchen and upstairs to the lounge she glanced at the fruit bowl and felt a peculiar sensation in her knees which made her wonder whether she was going to fall over. It now contained two bright green apples!

Upstairs, having successfully managed to stay upright before flopping down in an armchair, she began the most peculiar diary entry she had ever written. Her biggest challenge was to get round her vivid impressions of what had happened to her. The events of the past ten minutes or so were clear and sharp. If they had been hazy and dreamlike she could have indulged in a spot of poetic embroidering, or even pretended they had not happened. But she could remember every detail so, although she managed to write it all down, she wrote very slowly, trying to cope with the impossible qualities of the things that she was certain had just happened. She had met a strange "person" where there should not have been anyone; "he" had come into her house but she had learnt nothing from him; his appearance and disappearance had been virtually impossible and yet each had been accompanied by similar things: certain words, a dog barking and a door banging shut. And the apples. She had been trembling as she sat down, but writing the diary had calmed her somewhat. Now she had finished the trembling returned. She put her head back and promptly fell asleep in her chair, warmed by the mid-morning sun which drenched the room in between banks of driven cloud.

When Dad and Fish came home and woke her with their shouts she was annoyed with herself for falling asleep in the daytime. Her mother had been an expert at taking naps, shutting her eyes and switching off at will, but alert the moment her eyes opened again. The rest of the family lacked this skill, each dreading daytime sleeping because of the wooziness that stayed with them on awakening. Woken suddenly by the other two, Vic felt disorientated and unsure as to whether she had dreamed the episode with the strange boy.

***

Dad and Fish had, of course, done more than just a bit of shopping. They were full of news about various discoveries. They had found a museum containing a tapestry made by a group of local people who had set themselves the task of depicting a French invasion of Wales in Seventeen Hundred and Something, which Dad had never heard of before. He was especially full of it because he had found lots of connections with places in East Anglia where, apparently, a similar invasion force had also planned to land.

'But do you know what's really amazing?' he added. Giving Vic no more than a second to shake her head he went on. 'They had no idea how big it would be when they had finished, but when they did, the local council loaned the building it's in – a Victorian school hall – and since then they've got all sorts of grants and things and they're building a whole museum of their own to put it in!'

Vic was as interested as anyone can be who has just had a completely impossible experience and doesn't dare tell about it. She didn't need to worry because Fish was enthusing too. In his case, about the buildings.

'The school hall is just incredible!' he said. 'It's so small! Heaven alone knows how anyone ever does anything in it. There's a badminton court marked out on the floor and the white line runs along next to the skirting board beneath the stage!'

Dad grinned and said, 'Well, I've heard that people used to be a lot smaller.' The joke fell flat so he tried, hopelessly, to rescue it. 'You know, average heights and all that...' They still gazed at him until he realised that it was a wind-up. 'Funneee!' he said and got on with unpacking the stuff from the supermarket. Fish continued.

'The new building, though, it's just amazing. It's all futuristic – there are drawings and even a model in a case. It's all gleaming white with smooth curves. Like something out of an old Sci-Fi film.'

Fish never talked much about his future. In fact, he tended to clam up if anyone mentioned ambitions and careers. However, at moments like this Vic was always sure he would end up studying architecture or something similar. He rabbited on about it for another five minutes while their shopping was stowed in the fridge and various suitable cupboards. Vic showed polite interest while actually thinking about what had been happening while the others had been out. Little did Fish know how deeply grateful she was to him for chattering about architecture as, if she had had to talk about her morning she wouldn't have known where to start.

By the time Fish had finished she felt a bit more calm and said to her Dad, 'Did you get everything you wanted from the supermarket?' She caught Fish's eye as she said this and he grinned, sharing something they knew about Dad.

'It's not the supermarket mentioned in the Guest Book,' Dad said. 'We spotted it tucked behind a beer and wine place in the same road as the museum, so we shopped to take advantage of the free parking and then went to the museum. Cunning, eh?'

Normally, Vic would have responded with some light-hearted remark about Dad's habit of taking opportunities to save money. However, although she had started it, she didn't seem to feel like following up on this occasion. She smiled automatically but found herself thinking once more about what had just happened here in the house. Or rather, she mulled over what seemed to have happened and the more she thought about it the stranger it seemed and the less she felt like telling anyone about it. She decided that she really would have sounded very silly indeed and Dad would certainly not leave her in the house on her own again.

Fish interrupted all of this by asking, 'What are we going to do now?'

As fathers go, Dad was never selfish with his time, especially when they were on holiday, but he pointed out that they were on their third day and he did have a bit of work to do. In fact, both Vic and Fish were aware of what he was really saying. Since they had a lost their mother he had been trying to be two parents in one, so he needed a break when he could get one. Added to that, he was a teacher, and Vic and Fish had also learned that it wasn't just "a job with long holidays", and if one switched off totally at any time it was that much harder to switch back on.

Fish took the hint expertly. 'Vic and I will go rock-pooling in Oil Slick Bay,' he said. 'We'll take sandwiches and come back after lunch.'

Vic wasn't sure she fancied the bay very much but Fish gave her a look which meant she had better get on with the sandwiches while he got some drinks ready and she took the hint. Anyway, she thought to herself, if she wanted to do some serious thinking about the recent events it might be easier out of the house, and she might even speak to Fish about it…

Fifteen minutes later they were out of the gate and away.

'Do anything interesting while we were out?' Fish asked casually, switching the lunch bag to his preferred shoulder.

Vic only had time to say that she had been filling in her diary, which was not untrue, when he interrupted her to say, 'There's a sort of footpath down here. Let's see if it's a shortcut.' What he had spotted was almost completely obscured by overgrowing laurel and ivy: a gap in a wall with a strangely recessed kissing-gate just beyond it. But, once through this uninviting entrance they immediately found an informative board telling the history of the pathway which zig-zagged hugely across an almost vertical hillside. Unfortunately, being in the shade of some seriously dark and heavy trees, the sign had become rather mould-affected and one corner had completely rotted away, so most of the sentences lacked a word or two. Still, they managed to extract some details which told them that this very unpromising bit of hillside, which looked to them like a very steep and overgrown patch of waste land, had once contained some fine local trees and still had some excellent shrubs which flowered magnificently in the Spring or Autumn. Not right now, however, as Fish observed. At the moment it was just a rather gloomy green tangle with a steep, path which they followed, trying not to stumble over any of the roots which grew across it.

The end of the path was actually the steepest part and they had to be very careful because there was no pavement beyond it. Feeling the momentum of the hill behind them, they stepped out hoping no fast vehicles would be coming along. As it happened, it turned out that they were near the end of the other road which led off from the mini-roundabout and went up to the big hotel they had seen from the jetty. They could see its enclosed veranda and entrance porch as they crossed to the next part of their route to the bay, which was a very ugly concrete bridge which crossed the single railway line running up to the ferry terminal. It was totally enclosed in metal panelling and perspex windows and so stifling inside that they more than made up for the time they had lingered on the hillside by crossing it in a few seconds. Beyond it, the waters of the deeper end of the bay lapped against more man-made concrete, this time in the form of angular blocks like gigantic jacks, with rubbish and scum drifting on the surface. They pressed on until they were near where they had eaten their chips the first night. So dry and ugly had been the path that they found even Oilslick Bay a relief, though they could see that the sand dunes the other side of the jetty were filled with more rubbish – anything from bits of coconut matting to discarded broken beach toys.

'Let's go out across the sand,' suggested Fish, sensing that this was turning out to be even less of a pleasure than they had hoped while they left Dad to get on with his work. What he didn't know, of course, was that Vic was still thinking about her earlier experiences and hardly noticing details around her. Then he found something to distract him from the rubbish-filled beach and Vic's slightly distant mood. Out beyond the slippery stones and oily pools they found a stretch of cleaner sand edged with large flat stones and, already there, a little boy, about five years old, and what must have been his Grandfather, who seemed to be in his early sixties.

They were turning over rocks and the little boy was then delightedly picking something up and putting whatever it was in a bucket.

The man turned out to be just like their own Grandfather: the sort who would speak to anyone who came within range. When he spoke he reminded them of their *other* Grandfather because he told them, unbidden, that there were lots of crabs under these rocks, in a tone which suggested they must be here for that purpose and that purpose only.

'Thanks,' Fish replied. 'Actually, we're just out for an explore.'

He had used a favourite phrase of their mother's and, in her present mood, Vic instantly felt like bursting into tears. No-one seemed to notice as she stood back for a moment and, with a mighty effort, composed herself. Then, somehow, within a couple of minutes, they were all turning over stones to find crabs and her emotions calmed once again.

Fish paired off with the man and Vic found herself almost dragged away towards another bank of interesting rocks and pools by the lively little boy. An hour had passed, the tide had turned and the seagulls had all swooped over them noisily to find fresh hunting grounds before they looked up and realised how long they had been there and Vic realised she felt happier.

'Sandwich time,' Fish announced.

'We go to my Gran's for our lunch,' said the little boy and Vic smiled at him. 'Have you seen the mud-skippers?' he added.

'Mud-Skippers?' asked Fish. 'I've seen them on nature programmes on the TV. Do they have them here?'

'Indeed,' said the Grandfather. 'When the tide goes out. Why do you think the gulls hang around? It's not just the crab bits they like. You have to come back when the tide is going out, though.'

'We'll try and time our next visit for that,' Fish said. 'Where shall we eat our nosh?' he asked Vic as their two recent acquaintances made their way back to the promenade.

'Let's sit on those seats by the car park,' she said. 'Under the flags.'

'I thought you might choose that place,' Fish said, meaningfully.

'Why's that?' she asked.

'Well, mainly because it's the only place apart from the other end of the bay with any seats on it! Ever been had!!'

Vic tried to clout him but he was already scrambling up the concrete blocks onto the narrow promenade. She caught up with him and they sat down facing the bay. Neither said anything for a moment but they were both savouring the unexpected pleasures of the impromptu crab-hunt and thinking that Oilslick Bay wasn't all that bad.

'I don't think these flags are just seaside decoration,' Fish observed. 'They're from European countries and the one in the middle is the flag of the EU.'

'Oh, yeah,' Vic mumbled, her mouth full of tuna fish and bread. She swallowed and then added, 'There's a board over there, like the one by our hillside footpath, only newer.'

While she poured some tea out of their flask, Fish went to investigate. When he came back he said, 'I was right. The flags are from the European nations, but you'll never guess the rest...' He paused, partly to give Vic a chance to say "What?" and partly to fan his mouth because he had just sipped the tea without letting it cool down. Vic didn't say anything so, when he had got over his scorching he said, 'This ugly bay has been chosen for a grant from Europe. It's paid for the landscaped car park behind the flags and these benches, which we are now sitting on, courtesy of Brussels, or wherever it is these decisions are made.

Vic surveyed the row of seats, each one set neatly into the car park wall. 'That explains why they are so comfortable,' she said.

Fish nodded. 'Too right! Grandpa would approve. He's always going on about how much better the Europeans spend people's taxes. Coincidence, though, isn't it?'

Vic lost the thread of Fish's thoughts.

'Coincidence? The seats?' she asked.

'No,' he replied with a tone suggesting that Vic was not being alert. 'Don't you remember that wooden jetty on the Baltic, where Aunt Ronny's in-laws live? It's got the same flags all along it, and a board saying how it was paid for by the European nations.'

Vic had not liked Fish using his "keep up" tone and she took a rare opportunity to get ahead of him.

'Are you sure they were flags of Europe?' she said quizzically.

His expression suggested he was about to say "Of course" but he stopped before those words came out. 'You're right,' he said, mock-respectfully. 'They were the flags of the countries with Baltic coastlines. Who's a clever girl, then?'

This time Vic did clout him. Before things could descend into a real fight, however, there was a crunching noise from behind them. They looked round to see a monstrous foreign people carrier which had just backed into the wall of the landscaped car park.

'That proves it's a European construction!' laughed Fish. 'An English car park barrier would have crumpled and whatever had hit it would have gone straight on "To the promenade and beyond!"' he said, finishing on a Buzz Lightyear voice.'

'And through us!' laughed Vic. 'Grandpa would be impressed, wouldn't he?'

'The one who loves everything European?'

'Yeah. Of course!'

They returned to finishing their picnic. As they were packing up the remains, Fish asked,

'So what *did* you do while I was out with Dad?'

'I told you before: I wrote my diary. Why are you so interested?' she said. She was tempted for a moment to tell him more, but the pleasant hour on the beach had wiped away her odd thoughts and feelings and she didn't feel any need to confide just now.

Fish was also holding back a bit. He actually had his own reason for wanting a more personal conversation and was trying to get Vic to do likewise. But she wouldn't. She saved what she wanted to talk about and instead they chatted about crabs and nice old Grandpas instead. While they did, Vic noticed Fish reaching into the bag, which she thought was empty, and then he put whatever he had found in his kagoule pocket.

'What you got?' she asked.

'Nothing,' he replied, unconvincingly.

'Show!' she insisted, and reached across him.

'Gidorff!' he barked, too late to stop her discovering a Kit-Kat, a mint one, no less.

'What's this?' she asked.

'You know what it is. I was going to share it with you on the walk back.'

This was probably true. Fish was like Dad: not selfish, just occasionally secretive when he was preparing something to surprise you with later. She changed tack.

'What did you say just now?'

'I said I was going to share it…'

'No!' she butted in. 'Before that. When I tried to reach your pocket.'

'What? "Get off"?'

'Yeah. But that's not *how* you said it. You said…'

'"Gidorff!".'

'Yeah! That's it! Why did you say it like that?'

Vic didn't know it, but Fish took a deep breath before saying, 'It used to be a family saying. One of Mum's.'

'Oh,' said Vic.

Fish said nothing. He couldn't tell whether Vic would appreciate a little more information or silence in which to reflect. He glanced across at her and although she was looking fixedly out into the bay there was no sign of tears. He gazed at the bay as well and took a chance.

'Sometimes, if you tried to grab her arm or give her a hug, Mum used to say "Get off", just like anyone else would. Except she used not to pronounce it exactly the way anybody else would. She always said "Gidorff". And it became a saying that Dad and I used until…' He paused, gazed out across the bay and then said, 'Let's make our way back.'

He stuffed the flask into the bag and glanced at Vic as he did so. She showed no sign of emotion except that she remained quiet as they made their way back round the promenade. Fish didn't try to start any conversation until they reached the mini-roundabout by the fish and chip shop. Then he asked, 'Shall we try the path again?'

'OK,' Vic replied. 'But let's walk along the proper road and not that concrete monstrosity,' she added.

As they set off along the long, old road, in single file because of the narrow pavement and large number of parked cars, Fish became quiet again. Although he occasionally used expressions which he knew had started with Mum, he was by some way older than his sister and had clearer memories of her. A word could trigger his moods just as easily as it did for Vic, except he didn't tend to show it so obviously. "Monstrosity" now had that effect on him, probably as much because of the "Gidorff!" episode as anything else. Accompanied by the word "Bloody", it had been another of Mum's favourite words, in this case inherited from her own mother, and the memory now made him stay silent for a while. It was not until they had a special moment at the start of the hill path that they spoke again.

The special moment was all to do with something they had succeeded in deciphering from the board at the top of the path when they had been on their way down: an animal, in the form of a mole. They were so surprised to see a small brown animal wriggling up the hillside next to the path that they could hardly believe it. Like everybody who sees a mole for the first time they could not imagine how this tiny creature was capable of causing such upheaval underground. Added to which, it showed no inclination to burrow but just wriggled rapidly but very blindly up the hill, so they went through every other animal it could possibly be as they toiled up the path. Eventually they concluded that it had to be a mole and Dad was the fascinated recipient of the news when they got home.

Not only was Dad able to confirm that he had got some work done but he had also stowed away everything that he had bought with Fish on their morning's shopping trip. Inevitably, he had a joke ready about it. As Vic was going upstairs, he asked her to take the new soap he had bought up to the bathrooms.

'It's very thoughtfully labelled so you know what kind it is,' he said, with a giveaway twinkle in his eye. Sure enough, when Vic looked at it, expecting the name of an odour, like "Spring Magnolia" or "Scent of Autumn" she found just one word: "White".

'Helpful, isn't it?' he laughed. 'Wouldn't want to make any mistakes over the colour while you're washing, would you?'

Vic grimaced, as usual, so as not to encourage him, as Fish always put it, but a snatch of conversation she heard as she went up the first flight of stairs brought her back down with a bump.

'I thought we couldn't find any of those nice green russets in the supermarket,' Dad said to Fish.

'We didn't,' was the reply.

'Well, I found two in the bowl after I had finished unpacking the shopping.'

There was no more conversation on the subject that she could hear and she found herself grateful, for a change, that Dad tended to use what he would call "the right word" for things. When she got back downstairs an expedition had been planned. A more promising one this time, so she even forgot to look at the fruit bowl.

'There's a beach about eight miles round the coast that sounds really promising,' said Dad as she came into the dining area. He and Fish had Grandpa's map spread out on the table and they showed her a stretch of yellow labelled "Whitesands Bay".

'Don't be too sure,' Fish commented, with a wry grin. 'The guidebook to the area told us that Oilslick Bay was a charming port!'

'It has its charms,' replied Dad.

'Hidden ones,' said Vic. They looked at her with faint surprise. They still tended to think of her as the baby of the family and at times like this, when she joined in the general banter, their reactions usually reminded her of that fact.

'Well the guidebook says that Whitesands Bay is one of the finest swimming beaches along this section of coastline, so I don't think we'll find mudflats there,' Dad said. 'Anyway, I'd like to get out before the afternoon is too far advanced, so let's go.'

'Without flasks and chocolate biscuits?' asked Fish, with mock concern.

'Well we've got five minutes,' grinned Dad, and ten minutes later they were in the car.

'You've still got your odd socks on,' Vic observed. Dad always wore odd socks when he did a bit of writing. He would never explain why.

'Never mind. I promise not to get out of the car and embarrass you!' he said with a laugh.

***

Whitesands Bay, when they got to it, was exactly as promised. Headlands jutted out at each end, just like at Fishguard, but probably twice as far apart, creating an open aspect, dominated by the sky. The coastline sloped long and gentle down to the sea and a bright, genuinely white stretch of sand probably a mile from one end to the other. The sea was pure blue with slashes of gently curving white waves running across. The only problem was that they had come too late; the world and its relations obviously knew about it already and they had filled the car park and several hundred metres of country lane beyond. No matter how big the beach was, there was no chance they would get onto it without a parking place, so Dad risked annoying a few drivers by overtaking the line to get to a field entrance. Fish had the job of keeping his window open and shouting to any driver who looked like they would object to queue jumpers that they were only going to a place where they could turn. He was disappointed that no-one actually challenged them.

They drove slowly back past the long line of people who had decided that even at this time of day it was worth the wait, then out of the lane and, as was Dad's habit, a slow drive home down every back lane they came across, partly using the map and partly his sense of direction, which he thought was very good and which was partly true. Vic had been lively on the drive to the beach because it had got her out of the house where she was finding things a bit bewildering. She became quiet again on the way back because she had been hoping for a decent break. Dad noticed and, although he didn't know why she was quiet, he did realise she needed something to change the atmosphere.

'Will you cook supper, Vic?' he asked. 'Some of your special pasta?'

Now Vic did not cook what most people would think of as "special" pasta. If you wanted really tasty homemade pasta sauce then Fish was the man for the job. If you wanted an unusual preparation, more like a stir-fry with seafood or cherry tomatoes and an exotic oil then Dad was the master, though he acknowledged that he had picked up most of his ideas from Mum. However, Vic had always had the magic touch when it came to making very basic pasta-with-ketchup. Fish always called it her "Transport Café cooking", but he would still eat lots because it wasn't just over-boiled spaghetti doused in ketchup. All she did was boil some spaghetti, take out of the water just before it was completely soft, melt some butter in the pan with a quantity of pepper, stir the spaghetti back in when the butter and pepper were sizzling hot and then serve it up... with tomato ketchup and Cheddar, rather than Parmesan, cheese

You would think anyone could do it, and sometimes anyone could, but Vic could get it right every time so it satisfied the need for fast simple food which would still satisfy Dad and Fish's taste buds. And it made her feel great to be able to do so. And Dad knew this.

She guessed he was up to something but she didn't mind. 'OK,' she agreed. 'Aren't we too early, though?'

'Yeah,' said Fish. 'We've almost got time to squeeze in a walk or something.'

Vic glanced at him in surprise. The tone of his voice had sounded genuinely enthusiastic but surely he must be joking. She expected to see a grin on his face which would give away what he really felt. But no. He genuinely looked like someone who wanted to go for a walk!

It was not unusual for the Darwens to cram in extra activities when a day seemed to be playing itself out but there was something about the way he said it that made Vic and Dad look at each other in surprise.

'I suppose it *is* a bit early,' said Dad cautiously. 'But I was thinking of getting a bit of writing done before settling down for the evening.'

'And I want a shower,' said Vic.

'Well, I'll just go for a stroll by myself,' said Fish. 'OK?'

'Er, yes,' said Dad, wondering whether to ask any questions. He decided he would, but nothing too sensitive. 'Any chance of picking up a couple of postcards while you're out? I was going to get some at Crowded Car Park Bay, but not being able to stop spiked that idea.'

'Sure,' Fish agreed. 'See you in an hour or so.'

'Right,' said Dad as Fish rapidly exited the car. 'Vic and I should manage to unload the car.' But Vic's brother was already on his way down the hill, moving remarkably quickly for someone going for a "stroll".

Once they were inside, Vic and Dad did what was expected of them. Vic made a start on the spaghetti preparation. Dad switched on his laptop and poured himself some coffee from the unused flasks they had brought back from the beach. "Waste not, Want not" thought Vic, but, unusually for him, Dad didn't say it. He took a biscuit and disappeared off up to the first floor lounge.

Fish returned, as promised, an hour later with two strange postcards of the kind he thought Dad would like. One had a herd of cows looking straight at the viewer with such gormless expressions on their faces that Dad and Vic couldn't stop giggling for the rest of the evening. Both decided there was no way such a gem was ever going to get sent. It was natural scrapbook material. The other was a peculiar view of Oilslick Bay with a badly-drawn cartoon crab in one corner.

They discussed who to send it to over Vic's spaghetti. By the time they settled down to share their attention between a game of Monopoly and a film on the television they had still not decided, so the decision was left to Dad, who chose Aunt Marilyn. She had recently been to some exotic foreign location on an "all-expenses-paid" business trip and so he wrote a jokey message about their glamorous holidays, cleverly re-using some of the phrases from a card she had sent them. She had a good sense of humour and was bound to find it funny. He went to bed before the film had finished. Fish was in an odd mood, which seemed to have been with him since they had returned from Whitesands Bay and once Dad had gone to his room he abandoned interest in both the game and the film and read one of the books from the shelves downstairs.

Every now and again something would happen to draw Vic's thoughts back to the earlier strange events: wind tugged at the trees outside the window; the dog next door barked; some fireworks went off across the bay and drew her to the window. Each time Vic tried to frame a sentence which would give her the chance to share her thoughts with her brother, but nothing convincing would come to mind. When they both agreed to lock up for the night – a bit early for Fish; a bit late for Vic – any chance had gone.

She completed her diary, which she had partly but half-heartedly filled in after they had got back from Whitesands Bay, still turning over the morning's experience in her mind.

Sleep took her away from it all and she had unexpectedly pleasant dreams about endless empty beaches.

6

TUESDAY

Although Vic woke up quite early, as she went downstairs she passed two open bedroom doors, each of which revealed an empty bed.

Fish was in the kitchen, cleaning burnt crumbs from the bottom of the toaster.

'Where's Dad? she asked, pouring out some cereal into a bowl and dousing it with milk.

She anticipated a remark from Fish, who had always tried to persuade her that she ended up eating soggy cereal because she used so much milk, but all he said was, 'Oh, you know him. He was up before dawn even cracked. He's gone to post his card. I've been left to make a start on the packed lunch for the beach. He wants us to leave by nine at the absolute latest.'

'So what are we having?' she asked, fearing one of Fish's terrible multi-ingredient sandwiches and hoping she had time to influence what went into hers.

He surprised her.

'Nothing, yet,' he admitted. I had some coffee and then I got distracted by this toaster which doesn't seem to have been cleaned, *ever.*'

Vic was not surprised by his cleaning the toaster. Wherever they went, Fish would notice little bits of neglect and make it his job to do some cleaning or repairing. He would have hated being told this, but it was very much like his Grandfather.

She was surprised that he hadn't started on the picnic lunch but this proved not entirely true. Typically, he had got something on the go. Three eggs were boiling in a pan on the cooker and three packets of crisps were also waiting to be stowed away in the picnic cool box. However, it was still less than he would normally have done by now and Vic wondered what might be slowing him down. With Dad out, she again wondered whether she could take the chance to confide in him, but his slow, preoccupied manner put her off. Then Dad returned from his postcard posting mission, which meant that she would have to seek out another opportunity. Maybe at the beach…

'Have you done the sandwiches?' asked Dad. Then, when the reply was negative, 'Good! I've just bought three delicious-smelling pies from a van down the road. The driver said he was really on the way to his round – he does the campsites – but he had stopped to post a letter and I took the chance to get three. They'll be cold by lunchtime but the man said they are just as nice eaten that way. I've got a game pie for you Fish, cheese and leek for Vic and ham and onion for me.'

Dad and Vic were actually both vegetarians, but Dad made a small exception when on holiday so he could try what he called the "local delicacies". His explanation was that local food was part of the tourist experience. If you didn't try them, he said, there wasn't much reason going away for a holiday. Vic was not convinced, but she had given up arguing. Anyway, he didn't do it too much as he was also mad keen on fish, which was part of their regular diet, and would choose that as often as meat on holiday. And he never cooked meat for himself, even away from home, so she forgave him.

The pies were duly packed with various chocolate bars and biscuits. The customary flasks of tea and coffee were added last to ensure they would be as hot as possible when needed and they set off, the sky already a promising blue.

When they reached the bay there was a short queue but it was moving steadily and the car park was only one-quarter full. Dad parked next to a VW Microbus, partly because Fish was fixated on them and it was fun to watch him drooling and partly because he figured it would shade the car a bit when, later in the day, the sun moved round.

They did not have much in the way of beach gear with them but, even before the small amount had been unloaded from the car Dad announced that he needed to go the loo and that they should go ahead and leave him to bring the cold box. Vic wondered whether Dad might also perform one of his little detours and leave her with enough time to start a serious chat with Fish. She was startled to discover that Fish must have been thinking more-or-less the same because as soon as they began the trudge beach-wards he spoke seriously to her.

'How do you think Dad's managing?' he said
'Managing what?'
'Our first proper holiday together. I mean, the first proper one without the rest of the family since… well, you know.'
'Yeah, I do know. You mean since Mum died.'
She had said it. Someone had to be the first and the men hadn't looked like getting round to it. Trust the woman to have to do the work!
'He's doing well,' she added.
Fish left it at that. Vic thought, "He's thinking that I'm taking it well. I wonder whether he's right?"
They walked across the last section of the car park thoughtfully but the scene that morning was so stunningly beautiful that their spirits rose at the view. It was like a postcard. The white sand was even more clean and dazzling than the day before. The sky was dark blue, the few streaky white clouds making it seem even more blue. In between, the sea was like lace, the white crests of the small waves making curving patterns between the twin green headlands which seemed to reach out like arms to welcome it.
'Wow!' said Fish. 'I hope Dad likes it. He always hates too much heat and dazzle.'
'Well you're going to find out,' replied Vic. 'Here he comes.'
'It's bright?' isn't it, said Dad, squinting, but he settled down under a parasol, hat clamped down firmly over his eyes, and with sunglasses on as well. Although he had never been one for lazy beach life, they didn't hear a word of complaint out of him all day. Vic decided that if Dad

was in a good enough mood not to let the brightness and the heat trouble him then she wouldn't repeat what she had instinctively tried out with Fish. As it turned out, she was going to get plenty of chances to talk to him about her feelings, his feelings, anything in fact, and quite soon. In the meantime, she spread some sun tan lotion on her shoulders and legs and stretched out on an old mat which was really on its last legs but which Dad had insisted on bringing along. Then she got back up because although Dad hid his head in the shade on beaches and he never took his T-shirt off, he was terrible at remembering to protect his arms and legs, so she did the honours for him with the lotion.

Then she lay down again and Dad pulled one of his little stunts by producing a magazine that he must have bought for her up in the beach shop on the way down from the car. Feeling warm and protected by this typically thoughtful act, she lay and grinned to herself for some minutes before getting round to actually reading it.

Fish, of course, had gone for one of what Dad called his "wanders". When they peered out towards the sea they spotted him picking his way along the line where the waves broke, all the way to the rocks at one end of the bay. He seemed to Vic to spend quite a long time gazing into the pools and she wondered whether she had upset him by mentioning Mum. But the next time she looked up she was surprised to see that he was jogging up the beach towards them and when he came up the soft sand to where they sat he revealed that he was not all unhappy. Quite the opposite, in fact, because he gave them the surprise of their lives by announcing that he was going to buy himself a body board.

He delved into a bag to dig out some money and while he made his way up the beach to the shop Vic and Dad exchanged looks of frank astonishment.

'I thought Fish hated the idea of going in the sea,' Dad commented. 'They must have heated this bit specially.'

Vic laughed and they both lay there preparing comments to fire at her brother. However, she had no time. It turned out that he had his swimming trunks on underneath his shorts and when he returned he quickly took sandals, shorts and T-shirt off, picked up the newly-acquired body board and jogged down to the water where, without breaking stride, he went straight in.

When Vic looked at her Dad with fresh astonishment, he just grinned and said, 'Now that *is* typical of Fish. He might take ages to decide to do something but once he's made up his mind there is no further hesitation. You'd think he was a Water Baby, wouldn't you?'

Vic didn't understand the reference and Dad spent the next few minutes explaining about characters from Victorian children's stories while Vic pretended to listen but was actually watching her brother behaving as if he had never done anything else on holiday except cavort in the sea.

He finally came back up the beach, dripping and bursting with enthusiasm for them to join him.

'We might,' said Dad. 'But have something to drink for now.' As well as the pies for lunch, it turned out that he had bought elevenses in the form of three jam doughnuts to have with their coffee. Although the sky was clear and the sun bright there was still something of the early morning in the air and coffee was a good idea.

'These hit the spot,' said Fish before grabbing Vic's magazine.

'Hey, Magazine Thief! I haven't finished that,' she protested. 'Why aren't you going back in the water?'

Fish rolled his eyes and patted his doughnut-filled stomach. 'Not wise straight after eating,' he laughed.

Before Vic could protest any further Dad intervened. 'Don't worry,' he put in. 'Let's you and me go for a walk. Time to find what Fish found so interesting up that end of the bay.' He pointed, and waited for Fish to say something, but "The Magazine Thief", which was what Vic now resolved to call him for the rest of the day, was already absorbed, as always when there was *anything* to read.

The walk didn't last as long as expected. Dad obviously thought she would stop every time a shell or interesting stone presented itself but she had grown out of that really. Anyway, Dad discovered that the sea was actually rather warm and he started muttering about joining Fish next time he wanted to go in.

Struck by the oddness of not just Fish but also Dad being enthusiastic about sea bathing turned Vic's thoughts back to the odd things which seemed to be happening to her at the holiday home and she didn't hear Dad clearly when he said something to her. She looked at him with a "come again" expression.

'How about going back?' he repeated.

'Oh, yeah. Why not?' she replied.

There was nothing in his voice but a look in his eyes suggested that he too might have had something he wanted to say. But he didn't. Instinctively, Vic looped her arm through his and they stood for a moment surveying the bay. Then they walked back to Fish, who was keen to get back in the water.

'Will you be OK looking after the stuff?' asked Dad.

She gave him a "Seriously?" look.

'Sorry to fuss,' he said, and for a moment it felt as if she was the adult and he was the child.

'Have your walk. I'll be fine,' she said

He looked her in the eye to reassure himself, then he and Fish turned and Fish must have said something cheeky because Dad grabbed the body board and dashed ahead. Vic watched them playing like a couple of kids in the water for a few minutes then went back to her magazine, which she read from cover to cover, as you do on holidays when nothing else is demanding your attention. Although she preferred crosswords, she was just becoming absorbed by a wordsearch when she became aware of a ragged shadow across the sand just next to her. For a moment she thought of her mysterious visitor but when she looked up it was only a large, rather hairy dog which was standing on its hind legs to try and get some attention from a boy. 'A normal boy and not even a stumpy dog!' she said to herself and rolled over to spread the tan she hoped would be building up by now. She was quite dark in complexion, like her mother had been, so being brown after a holiday was usually rather easy for her. Her friends were jealous, apart from the ones who were cultivating being "fashionably pale", which she thought was a line from a song in her Dad's record collection.

'No, that's "fashionably late", she said to herself.

'First sign of madness,' chuckled Dad, arriving suddenly and picking up a towel.

'What is?'

'Talking to yourself,' he explained.

'Know what the second sign is?' said Fish.

'OK, Magazine Thief, tell me. I know you want to.'

'When you start hearing replies!' he said, ignoring her jibe.

Vic laughed but she couldn't help thinking that their jokes were connecting with her recent experiences at the holiday home. For the second time that morning she went quiet but she did enjoy her pie and when Dad broke with his tradition and went and bought them cans of drink instead of producing home-made over-diluted orange juice with fizzy water she perked up again. They even had ice creams an hour or so later after she and Fish had been in the sea, and they decided to head for home at about half-past two.

It was just gone three when they got back. 'Tell you what' said Dad as they started to unload the car, 'It's about time for tea. Why don't we have a quick shower and go and pamper ourselves in the hotel down at the bottom of the hill?'

Fish, always eager to pamper his stomach, agreed instantly. Vic needed a little more persuasion but Dad, who tended to dwell on things that he or other people commented on, reminded her that they still hadn't solved the mystery of why their house couldn't be seen above the hotel from the jetty. He also remembered to express an interest in seeing the hill path where she and Fish had seen the mole, so she had to agree.

Although they saw nothing that Vic would think of as special on the walk down, least of all a mole, Dad's spirits were raised by everything else he saw. He loved the exposed roots of the trees which interlaced across the path; he also loved the way the light slanted down through the branches; he even loved the ivy and other deep dark green foliage clinging to the trunks; and he especially loved the smell of the warm, damp ground where the sun had not been able to get to it.

When they reached the road he was bursting with it all and talked of little else until they had sat down in the deep old leather chairs in the hotel lounge, waiting to be served with tea and biscuits. Then he only stopped talking about the path because he was loving the old-fashioned atmosphere in the hotel, and especially the charming man who had come to see what they wanted after they had made themselves comfortable. He was much older than all the other staff they could see; even the manager must have been about thirty years younger than this silvery-haired man with a long moustache, twinkling eyes and an accent which suggested he was genuinely local.

He set down a huge tray containing pots with two different types of tea to satisfy Dad and Fish's fussy tastes, a mountain of irregularly shaped biscuits which definitely were, as advertised outside the hotel, "Home Made" and some bone china cups and saucers which felt like silk to the touch.

Dad commented on the texture. 'Bone china,' replied the waiter. 'Delicate to the eye but just about as tough as you can get. It's because of the actual ground bone which they put in the clay before moulding and firing it. Excuse me,' he added. 'I've got a brother who used to work in the Potteries. He would never stop talking about it.'

'Don't apologise,' said Dad. It's very interesting.' He turned to Vic. 'Granny and Grandpa used to live up that way, in Nottinghamshire. Mummy and I took Fish there when he was little. Must take you back there sometime.'

At the mention of "Mummy" Vic was quiet again. The waiter, with all the experience of his job, sensed an awkward moment. 'Call me if you want the pots topped up,' he said, and quietly went out.

They sipped tea and munched biscuits and, although Dad made remarks about the excellent biscuits and Fish insisted on sampling both pots of tea, the atmosphere was flat.

After about twenty minutes, Dad went to get some hotel details to send to Granny and Grandpa, who were always on the lookout for comfortable hotels for short breaks. Fish went off to the loo and Vic, left to her own devices for a while, wandered round the oak-panelled room looking at the pictures on the walls. There were drawings and paintings of the hotel and the bay and one or two photographs of the building. While she was looking the waiter came back in.

'Been deserted?' he said.

Vic nodded. His choice of words was unfortunate in view of the reason she had just been feeling a little low. However, he was not to know and he was a charming man so she couldn't help smiling. He asked her whether she was on holiday.

'Yes,' she replied.

'Silly question, I suppose,' he said with a grin. 'Why else would you be here?' Then, after a pause: 'Where are you all staying?'

'The Pilot's Cottage,' Vic said. 'But it's not really a cottage.'

'Of course,' he said. 'I know it well. It doesn't look like a pilot's cottage, but that's because it isn't one!'

'Why not?' asked Vic with some surprise.

'Well, I'm not saying that there never was one. But the house you're in is part of a development from about fifty years ago. It's just built on the plot where the original one was. I can just about remember the old one being pulled down. They were going to just extend it and they found out that it had no proper foundations. Miracle it had lasted at all, especially up on that slope. I'm afraid to say that I don't think the replacement is very attractive.'

Vic agreed and told him that they had had trouble locating it from the jetty.

'Ah, that's probably because there's actually a ridge on the hillside, where the old orchard was. You don't notice it when you're looking down but it just about obscures the house from some angles.'

Vic heard most of what he said but her real attention had stopped at the word "orchard".

'What kind was it?' she asked.

'What kind of what?' he replied.

'Orchard.'

'Oh, I see. Yes. Well.. Apple trees, naturally. Beautiful local Russets. Magnificent it was. There are photographs of the hillside up on the first floor landing. Would you like me to show you them?'

Vic, trained from a young age to be careful, even with charming adults in reassuring situations, hesitated. The waiter sensed her caution but just then Dad came back in and readily agreed to let her go with the man and look at the pictures he wanted to show her. In fact, still thinking about the reference to her Mum that he had made earlier, he welcomed something which would distract her.

She followed the man out into the lobby and then walked next to him up the curve of the heavily carpeted staircase to the first floor. Being next to him as he moved she noticed that he breathed slightly heavily at the effort the stairs required, reminding her of Grandpa. Another one, she thought. Two in two days! At the top of the stairs he showed with a sweep of his arm a gallery of black-and-white photographs, all dated, taken since the hotel had been built. They mainly showed the building, and the drop of tree-clad hillside behind it, but some were taken from a low angle and in them you could see much further up the hill to where, in the early ones, a single-storey cottage sat among neat rows of fruit trees, and, in the later ones, the house she was now staying in looming over a more overgrown plot of tangled branches, cut back by a few rows to leave room for the extended garden but still covering a sizeable chunk of hillside.

'So that's what was on that churned up patch of ground behind our garden,' she observed. 'When did they do it?'

'When did they do what?'

'Cut them down.'

'Not long ago, actually. Only this year,' he said. 'But they weren't cut down to my way of thinking. More like an uprooting, it was. Huge digging machines. Call me old-fashioned, but I think even when you take a whole plant out you should do it with some care. It's all gardening. And trees deserve special respect.'

Vic said nothing but her thoughts were churning away while she looked quietly and closely at the rest of the photographs.

Dad came up the stairs to join them. 'I've settled the bill,' he said.

Vic told him about the orchard and then wandered along the curved landing as Dad, inevitably, fell into conversation with the waiter. When she had done the full circle back to where they were still standing, they were talking about one of those strange subjects that Dad always got round to. She stood and listened patiently.

'Good Lord!' exclaimed the waiter, when Dad had finished. Then, seeing Vic he asked, 'Well, young lady, do you like the pictures?'

'Yes, they're interesting,' she said.

'You should be proud of your daughter,' he said to Dad. 'She gives a boring old man the time of day with good grace! Well, I'd better get on. There are more customers down in the lounge. Cheerio!' And he bounced off down the stairs with the vigour of a man half his age. Still like Grandpa, thought Vic. Dad just stood there beaming proudly.

Fish was waiting outside in the porch and as they walked along the drive, which was really only an extension of the road up from the town, Dad said he didn't want to go home quite yet. He coughed and said, 'That hotel was a bit too dusty for my liking.' So Vic and Fish gave him a guided tour of the horrible perspex bridge over the ferry railway, which almost put him off enough to go back up to the house. However, this time they turned left when they were over it and were able to walk up to a viewing jetty where you could see the ferries loading and unloading. One was just in the last stages and got underway as they watched. Dad made his usual "Oooh! And Aaah!" noises as it edged past the jetty and then tacked indecisively back and forth round various sea lane markers that they couldn't see from where they stood. Eventually, satisfied with its position, it blared its horn and moved steadily off. 'Presumably towards Ireland,' Dad observed.

While they watched, Vic kept looking back up past the hotel to try and see their house, or at least the plot where the orchard had been, but without success. This wasn't especially surprising but Fish's behaviour was. He had gone quiet soon after they had left the hotel and he seemed hardly to hear what Dad wanted to talk about as they watched the ferry.

Eventually, they turned back and crossed the bridge where, just as they were going to climb back up the zig-zag path, Fish said, out of the blue:

'Tell you what: you two go up and get the plates and things ready and I'll get fish and chips for us all.'

Vic was on the point of saying "Chips again?" when she caught a look in Dad's eye which she took to mean "Not now". Then he said to Fish, 'OK. Alright with you, Vic?' Fish had caught Vic's eye by now and his expression made her agree automatically. But she would make him pay later, no question!

'That's OK then,' Dad said, again. 'Do you need any money?'

'No, I've got some,' said Fish. 'What do you want?'

'Haddock for me, please. No, make that Hake!' and they grinned at yet another catch-phrase they were used to hearing him use. 'How about you, Victoria?' Dad never called her by her full name unless he was anxious or distracted. Vic assumed this occasion to be the result of Fish's sudden offer to get some fast food.

'Just a fishcake,' she said, 'If a Magazine Thief can manage that.'

'Fine, I think I can afford that,' Fish laughed, sounding slightly forced, and he set off along the road. See you up at the house.'

'Sure you don't need help?' she added, but Dad tugged her arm.

'Come on, girl,' he said, using favourite term from when she had been very little. 'Let's go and get some plates warm and a drink ready,' and they trudged back up through the trees.

**

By mid-evening Vic was becoming exasperated with her brother. He had been slouching on the sofa since they had eaten their fish and chips, doing nothing but make silly remarks about the programmes Vic wanted to watch. Her patience had finally been exhausted when he had said, 'Why is it called a sofa?' Back at home, Vic would have made an immediate bee-line for Dad's dictionary – the etymological one he had been given by *his* Dad – and bored her brother to death with a word-hunt. But tonight she was intrigued.

'Oh, come on Fish. Do we have to play this game all night?'

'Probably not.'

'So? What's on your mind?'

There was a pause, so long that Vic nearly repeated the question. But he did eventually reply.

'Well… You know I went to the chip shop tonight?'

Vic was about to be sarcastic about this piece of non-news. Instead she opted for non-committal. 'Uh-huh.'

'Well, I was served by this girl…'

Fish didn't get any further. Vic's hoot of laughter was probably loud enough to reach the ferry which was making its way round the terminal jetty.

'A holiday romance!' She nearly called him "The Magazine Thief" again but instead she just said, 'You?' almost crying with laughter, which was something she had thought only happened in stories. Unusually for him, Fish did not get up and stalk out. He just waited until the hysteria died down. When it finally did die down and Vic had wiped her eyes he was about to say 'Seriously, though,' when another thought flashed across Vic's mind and she hooted again. '*Fish* 'n' chips!'

Fish didn't get it. 'Yes. I saw her when I went to get the fish and chips.'

Normally Vic would have made some remark about how he always pronounced all his words instead of shortening them like normal people. To-day she just had to make her joke work.

'No,' she gasped. 'Fish. *You.*' She pointed at him just in case he still hadn't got it. 'And chips.' He was still staring at her. 'Oh, come on! This is simple compared with the ones you and Dad come up with. If you went out with the girl from the chip shop you would be "Fish 'n' Chips." Still no smile. This must be serious, she thought.

'Well, thank you,' he said, with no trace of gratitude in his voice. 'That's the last time I confide in you about relationships. Can't think what I could learn from my kid sister, anyway. Stupid to ask.' His words were scathing but Vic knew his voice well enough to know that he wasn't really stopping the conversation. Sure enough, after a moment's pause he went on. 'I'm just not sure it's appropriate...'

He sounded as if he was struggling to finish the sentence, also unusual for Fish, so she cut across what he was saying. 'What do you mean "appropriate"? Do you think she might not be good enough for you?'

'Don't be stupid!' he said, looking quite fierce for a moment. Normally, when things reached this stage with Fish he would close the conversation. This time, he went on. 'I'm just wondering whether it would be fair.'

'Fair on who?' Vic asked, still perplexed, but then it struck her. 'Oh!' she said. 'You mean...' and this time it was her voice that tailed off mid-sentence.

They both knew what he meant now but neither actually wanted to say the words. They were on holiday. With each other. With Dad. Without the extended family tribe. Without Mum.

And on top of that, Vic thought to herself, there's all the stuff I'm going through that no-one else knows about.

Abruptly, and with no idea why she made the decision, she killed all those thoughts stone dead.

'Go for it,' she said, realising as she said it that it was one of those expressions all her friends used and which Fish hated. Mentally she gave herself a kick, but Fish didn't comment, yet another sign that he was serious about all this. She added, 'Ask her out.'

'What? As simple as that? "Saveloy and chips twice, and would you like to go out with me?"'

'I don't know,' she replied, quite sharply, and for at least the second time since they had arrived at The Pilot's Cottage she felt more like an adult than a child. 'Why do boys always think there's a ritual; some perfect line that will work with all girls? We're all different, you know. But this isn't like swimming in the sea. We have only got two weeks' holiday, and we've been here a couple of days already, so do you think you've got time to wait for her to notice you across the greasy counter?'

'I suppose not. And it's oil.'

'What?'

'It's not a greasy counter. There's a sign up in the chippy: "We only use the finest vegetable oil for our cooking".'

'Oh, very sharp. How do you do it? One minute I'm the only person who can advise you about getting off with girls and the next you're making smart remarks again!'

'I know. Sorry, but I didn't think you'd react that way.'

Vic sensed that he was about to go all serious on her. Although she had managed to keep her own feelings hidden it didn't mean they had gone away. She wasn't sure how she would react if he started dredging stuff up about the holiday.

'Well, there you are,' she said.

'So, I just go down there and ask her?'

'For Heaven's sake, YES!' Vic was exasperated. She paused, took a silent but deep breath, then added, 'And lose the beret.'

'Do what?'

'Your beret; don't wear it.'

Vic knew she was taking a big risk with this last piece of advice. Even if you got on with your brother as if he were, well, a brother, there were aspects of his life which you did not say were stupid. Fish's beret was one such aspect. Clothes-wise he was not what you would call *fashion conscious* but, by and large he would "pass muster", to use one of Grandpa's expressions. Unfashionable but inoffensive, that was Fish, but he would insist on wearing a beret and not at a jaunty angle, like someone with what the fashion magazines called "Gallic style", but square on the top of his head, with a little cord-like bit dangling down the nape of his neck. The truth was, it looked reasonably OK on him, but it was still a naff piece of clothing. Vic knew this because all her friends took great delight in reminding her whenever the opportunity presented itself.

Fish grinned and said, 'I will take your suggestion under advisement', which was one of Dad's stock of phrases borrowed from the world's of business and politics. He also liked "with all due respect" and "I hear what you're saying". Whichever one he chose, it could be taken to mean; "You're wrong".

"Oh my God!" thought Vic. "It must be love if he's even joking about not agreeing!" Any other time Fish would have sulked for days after a remark about his precious beret.

'I'll go and ask her now,' he added.

'Now?'

'Why not? You're the one who told me to "go for it". Vic smirked to hear how odd the expression sounded when he said it.

'Well,' she replied, 'You've just had fish and chips. Are you going to just queue all over again and ask her out instead of asking for fast food?'

'Yeah, I'll try the saveloy and chips line.'

'Oh, for Heaven's sake!'

'Alright! Alright! I'm going. I'll think of something good on the way down the hill.' And just like that, he went and, although such a bold move was a bit unusual for Fish, it did occur to Vic that whenever her brother decided to do something it was usually as good as done.

***

It was only when she had heard the front door bang shut that Vic wondered whether she should have been so obliging. Her good advice had got rid of the very person she had wanted to talk to. And if by some strange chance he was lucky tonight she might not get his interest in her problems at all. She idly flicked through a couple of magazines, looked at the strange collection of records the real owners of the house had left in a cupboard and even stared out of the window hoping to be able to make the dog bark, but there was no sign of it, so she settled for what Dad called "Brain Porridge TV", which translated as anything you watched just to fill up time.

After three-quarters of an hour of utter boredom she heard the front door again so she turned off the TV. Fish's scorn for it was even more fierce than Dad's, especially if he was in a mood. And he could easily be in a mood by now.

She had just managed to pick up a magazine when he came in. Most annoyingly, he picked up the remote and immediately flicked the TV to the first available channel. Incredible! Fish *never* turned on the television without checking the listings in the paper first. She had no idea what to say but she could not bear to stay silent. But what? As she had never seen Fish voluntarily watching "Brain Porridge TV" she couldn't tell what mood he was in, so how should she start?

She *had* to know, so she had to ask.

'How did it go, then?' she said, bracing herself to be snapped at.

Fish turned the sound off and grinned broadly, as if he had just been waiting for her question.

'She said "Yes"!'

'Really!'

'*Really!*' he repeated. Mimicking her astonishment. 'Actually, that wasn't the first thing she said.'

'What was, then?'

'She said: "Where's the beret?"'

'You're kidding!'

'I am not. Your so-called good advice nearly lost me a date.'

'*Sorry!* So, spill the scoob, then.'

'You what?'

'Oh, for Heaven's sake, Fish. Are you that old? Scoob. Scooby Doo. What's new? Geddit?'

'Yeah, yeah. I've been in the presence of you and your friends long enough to grasp something of the language you all claim to speak.'

'Oooh! Get him. You must be happy to even stoop to insulting us. NOW, TELL ME WHAT HAPPENED!'

'OK. I walked down the hill, taking off my beret and putting it back on. In the end I saw someone else in a stupid hat, so I decided to keep mine in my pocket. I joined the queue in the chippy. There were about six people waiting but by the time I got to the counter there was still no-one else behind me. So it was my turn to be served.'

'What did you ask for?'

'I didn't. I never got the chance. She was serving. She recognised me and asked about the beret. I told her my kid sister had instructed me not to wear it if I wanted to ask a girl out.'

'Kid sister!'

'Yeah, that's you.'

'I guessed. I didn't like it.'

'Well you are...'

'Never mind,' Vic interrupted. 'And she said... ? And don't tell me she said "You should if you want to ask this girl out" because I'll puke!'

'She said, "Could be bad advice" and she asked me who I was thinking of asking. And I just blurted out "Well, you, actually". And she smiled and said she would be off at 10.30 if I wanted to meet her. And she guessed I wouldn't be wanting any chips.'

'Fish! You've actually got a date!'

'Try not to sound too surprised. I have been out with the odd girl, you know.'

'Odd's the word,' Vic said, getting her own back for the "Kid sister" bit. Then she jumped on him and tried to tickle him until he managed to tickle her more and she jumped off again. 'You still smell of the sea, or chip shops, or something,' she observed. 'Are you going to have a shower?'

'I'm not sure I trust your advice after the beret business.'

'Believe me on this one,' she insisted. 'I've just been close enough to tell. And I'm telling you a shower wouldn't be a bad idea.'

'OK,' he grumbled, and he climbed over the back of the sofa and went off to his room.

Vic sat for a while, still enjoying the feeling of happiness that Fish had brought back with him. Then the dog began to bark.

'Damn!' she thought. 'And I still haven't got anyone to talk to.'

Vic went downstairs. She had two good reasons. She wanted to see what the dog was barking at, of course, but even more importantly she needed to get to Dad before he could make any silly remarks to Fish. As it happened, she accomplished both at once. Dad was coming in the back porch door as she got down to the hallway.

'Hello, Vic,' he said. 'Have you heard that yappy little stumpy dog?' he asked, also using Fish's expression.

Yeah,' she replied, trying not to sound too interested.

'Is your brother around?

'Yes. He's in the shower. Don't say anything.'

'What do you mean: "Don't say anything"?'

'He's going out.'

'Going out? It's nearly ten. Where's he going? No, don't tell me. I may be old and slow but I'm not stupid. Wouldn't happen to have anything to do with his new-found enthusiasm for fish n' chips, would it?'

'Could be. But you *won't* say anything, will you?'

'I will try to resist the temptation.' Dad was slightly put

out. He liked to be part of things but Vic knew he was likely to make an unsuitable jokey remark.

Dad struck a dramatic pose in the kitchen doorway. 'My little boy!' He wailed.

'*Dad!*'

'OK, OK. So we're going to be on our own and you're staying up late because we're on holiday. Fancy a game of cards to take my mind off whatever your brother's up to?'

Vic joined her Dad in the breakfast room and when Fish put his head round the doorway to say 'See you,' Dad behaved perfectly, absorbed, or pretending to be absorbed, in a game of Rummy.

Ten minutes later he said, 'I fancy something to nibble.' Vic froze, hoping he didn't mean fruit, but soon an assortment of biscuits and cheese found its way onto the table with them and, not long after that, some drinks. As usual on these occasions, they were cocktails: an alcoholic one for him and non-alcoholic for her. Dad loved making them, especially on holiday. The non-alcoholic ones were from a book he had got from a second-hand bookshop; the alcoholic ones were from a book Mum had once given him. The only restriction was that he could only bring a few bottles but, as he stuck to a strict limit of two cocktails at any one time – and none if beer or wine had been taken that day – a few was enough. Anyway, there was often driving to do when on holiday so his intake was modest to say the least.

While they played cards, Dad regaled Vic with a story from school about a rather coarse girl who had asked him if he drank.

'When I said "Yes", she turned to the class and said she was trying to imagine me drunk, so I said I never got

drunk. Well, you know the saying "teaching is learning"?'
Vic just nodded, concentrating on her cards because with
Dad telling stories she sensed that she stood a chance of
winning.

'Well,' he continued. 'I told her I didn't get drunk and
she replied, "But you just said you drink". When I observed
that is possible to enjoy alcohol without getting legless she
said, "Not in my family!" Luckily she added something
about not seeing the fun of just one drink so I was able
to steer the conversation in a general direction rather
than ending up saying something that might sound like
a criticism of her family. If you're not careful these things
have a habit of coming back to bite you. Nevertheless, to
judge from the reaction of the rest of the class, they shared
her experience, so I learned something about one of life's
realities.' He paused then said, 'Oh, by the way: Rummy!'
and set his cards down with a flourish.

'Oh no! How do you do it?' Vic exclaimed.

'Natural talent,' he said, with a laugh. 'Would you like
another cocktail? Non-alcoholic of course. Don't want you
legless with all those stairs to climb!'

They played on and Vic did actually win a few hands.
It was gone eleven-thirty when they heard the front door
bang. There was the sound of shoes being discarded in
the hallway, footsteps up the stairs, a couple of steps onto
the flight leading to their bedrooms and then a pause.
Fish's face, with a big grin on it, then appeared round the
doorway. 'I've locked the front door,' he said. 'See you in
the morning.' And he disappeared again, about four steps
at a time.

Dad and Vic exchanged meaningful looks.

'I have a feeling we're going to be keeping each other company quite a lot in the evenings,' he said, with a smile and started clearing the table while Vic began to get out the breakfast things.

With the table set and the lights all out, they made their way to their respective rooms.

"Oh, well," thought Vic gloomily as she climbed into bed and turned her bedside light out. "Maybe this is turning into the holiday I expected after all."

7

WEDNESDAY

In the morning, Vic woke later than usual and heard, immediately, the annoying bark of the neighbours' dog.

The noise was particularly annoying because up to that moment her waking dreams had been of the more normal kind, including fish and chips, her brother's grinning face, cocktail glasses and, of all things, a bowl of cereal. She rolled over and looked long and hard at the clock, which said 9.30. She had one last snuggle with the bear she always brought with her on holiday and started to haul herself out of bed. When she looked down to the foot of the bed she realised that at least one of her dreams probably hadn't been one at all. There was a small table there with a tray on it. On the tray was a bowl of cereal, a jug of milk, a glass of apple juice and a little flower in a narrow necked miniature vase.

Tucked in between the jug and the vase was a slip of paper. She reached for it and sat on the edge of the bed to read its message: "Didn't want to disturb you. Gone to the shops. F & D." For some reason, and not just because she would have to wait to find out how Fish's date had gone, Vic felt like crying. To avoid this, she blew her nose, pulled the table round to the bedside, tucked her bear in beside of her and made a start on her breakfast.

When she got to the glass, a thought slipped into her mind. "Apple juice." Her favourite. She immediately wondered whether one of them had mentioned it by name. After all, the dog had been barking. In fact, the dog was still barking... With a sinking feeling she slipped out of bed and scooted downstairs, pausing only to notice another suspiciously shiny green apple perched on top of the fruit bowl.

Heart sinking further, she went out of the back porch door, almost certain of what she would see...

But there was nothing.

Yet when she looked up at the dog it was still barking, as it had been on and off since she had woken up. Maybe it was just in a barking mood, she thought. The only pets they had at home were fish in a garden pond so she had nothing against which to judge the dog's behaviour. Maybe it was barking at her? No, it was definitely looking towards the door of the wood-store. Perhaps she could risk a little look, as there was no-else in. She cautiously opened the door and inside she saw... wood and stuff. Feeling slightly foolish she closed the door once more and turned to go back inside the house. Then another thought struck her. Opening the door again, she squeezed in for a closer look. At first, all she could see were planks and other odd bits of wood. Further back, however, she noticed some older pieces. Not cut and ready for use, but bits which she guessed were old window and door frames, or skirting board. She remembered what the old waiter in the hotel had said and found herself wondering whether these had been salvaged from the original Pilot's Cottage. But even if they had, she couldn't really put the pieces of her thoughts together in a meaningful way.

She closed the store door again and walked thoughtfully back into the house.

Now she had got up, she decided she had better complete the process by dressing for the day and tidying all the things Fish and Dad had left around. She glanced through to the kitchen and, yes, there definitely was a distinctly green-looking apple among Fish's favourite shiny red foreign ones.

Vic found this very confusing, especially as it had actually all happened in the minute or so since she had tumbled out of bed and her thoughts were still half back there with her bear and the bowl of cereal. And she didn't really want strange happenings, even if she had half expected them. Who in their right mind, she asked herself, would believe that apples could appear out of thin air or that strange people dressed as if they had just uprooted themselves from a field, could exist?

Anyway, there could be a perfectly sensible explanation for the appearance of an apple in a fruit bowl and there had been no-one in the garden or the wood store. So where was her mystery? She started to go back upstairs.

But the dog was still barking.

She paused. Yes, why hadn't it stopped? She had to have just one more look, so she walked through the breakfast room and into the sun-lounge. She could see the dog clearly and it was still barking but it wasn't looking towards the wood-store now. It was looking down the garden. Not down its own garden but down theirs.

Vic's gaze followed the direction it was looking, down the length of the three terraces she had explored on her first day here. She could see the outlines of the group of statuettes which stood by the wall at the bottom. How many were there? How many had there been when she had gone down there on that day? Two? Three? She couldn't really remember, but she had a feeling, just a feeling, that the number had changed and, as she gazed down she also had the peculiar feeling that one of them had just moved.

This was not nice. She was not enjoying her experiences. There was no-one else around to help and the only living creature that also seemed able to see what she could see was a dog which barked so much that no-one took any notice any more. On the other hand, the explanation could be simple. Maybe it was Fish or Dad at the bottom of the garden. Either or both of them could have come back since they had left her breakfast note.

She stepped back from the sun-lounge window and tip-toed half-way across the room. Only half-way because it then occurred to her that this was a stupid thing to do if you were out of sight of the garden, in a house! So she strode the rest of the way to the porch, and even half-way down the garden until she reached the step down to the third terrace, at which point she became more cautious once again and slowed down.

And then she stopped.

She could clearly see a figure through the wispy shrubs that fringed the path, and it looked very much like the one she had seen before. But she wasn't certain. Maybe the figure was a little bit smaller; perhaps it had less green about it; did it not also seem slightly thinner? How she could tell all this at a glance she could not be sure, but she wanted to find out.

What she decided to do was so simple she felt quite embarrassed even to think of it. She would pretend she was there by chance and just step around the corner into view. So she did, and to her surprise the figure didn't react at all. "He" was gazing over the wall at the disturbed soil and orchard debris.

Vic's next action was another stupidly obvious one: she cleared her throat. The figure shifted his stance a little but did not look at her. While she was trying to think of what she could do next, he surprised her by speaking.

'You're up early,' he said. His words were matter-of-fact but the tone of his voice was different. Strained and somehow distant.

'No, I'm not...' she began. Then she realised that he was joking. Why had she not expected him to be doing so? What did she think he was that ruled out that possibility?

'You're right. I had a lie-in. Fish was out late and I waited up for him with the Commander.'

'The Commander? Fish?' he asked, the words coming out like a rattling sigh.

'Fish is my brother. It's short for Fisher. "The Commander" is just one of our silly names for my father. He went on a computer game at a Navy museum during our last holiday. Fish tried to show off because he thinks he's really good at computer things, but he only reached Petty Officer level. Then Dad astonished us all by getting right through the programme, even though he never really takes an interest in computer games. He got to Commander level and spent the rest of the holiday saying "Who's the Commander?" at every opportunity.

'I still don't understand,' said the strange figure dully. 'But thank you for trying.'

Vic was speechless again. There was actually only one thing she could think of to say; the obvious question.

'What's your name?' she asked. Then, when he glanced at her quizzically – the first time he had looked at her – she added: 'What are you called?'

His reply was a cluster of brittle sounds. It did not mean anything that she recognised but it left her with a selection of impressions which, if asked, she would have compared to the things you heard "experts" say about food, or wine, or gardens. She could hear a sound which made her think of a breeze blowing through branches; there was almost a smell, of Autumn decay; there was also a crackling rustle like dried leaves crushed between your fingers.

'Thank you,' she said, really meaning it. 'But I don't think there is any way I could pronounce that. Would you mind if I called you something easier for me?'

He made the effort to speak once again. 'What would be easier?'

'Er... I don't know. Vic scanned back over her thoughts when he had repeated his name. 'I can't call him any of those things,' she said to herself. 'It could sound almost rude. Especially as most of what I thought sounds like a mess, which is how he looks!'

Then inspiration struck.

'Would "Apple" be alright?'

He nodded, vaguely, as if he understood, but then he asked: 'And what does that mean?'

'Well,' she began. Then she paused because she was going to start explaining all the things she thought had been happening to her, and this person might just be some gardener, or tramp or intruder who she shouldn't be speaking to anyway and who would probably laugh even if he didn't turn out to be dangerous. But something compelled her to confide.

Taking a deep breath, she began: 'Well, it's all to do with what seems to happen whenever you app... er... turn up.' She had modified her words because she knew this was weird but she didn't want to sound totally out of her senses.

He stirred his arms and took a deep breath before saying, 'What does seem to happen?'

'Well, someone in the house says the word "apple", one appears in the fruit bowl, the dog barks and you turn up somewhere nearby.'

'I see,' was the extent of his comment on this explanation. Then he resumed gazing over the wall.

Vic gazed as well. She had spoken to him and got an answer she didn't understand – literally. She had told him her secret and he had registered none of the reactions she might have expected. And still he stared at that rough patch of land on the other side of the wall. Who was he and why was he here?

She was just going to start asking those very questions when another voice cut across her thoughts.

'Vic! Vic! Where are you?'

It was Dad, standing in the side porch and sounding anxious.

She turned back to explain this to her mysterious new acquaintance, but he was gone. There might have been a scrabbling sound on the other side of the wall, and then again, maybe not. There could also have been a sound like a door closing up in the direction of the house, but she couldn't be sure. Anyway, the dog had stopped barking at last.

'Over the wall and away,' she said to herself and, with one last glance over the wall in case she could see anything, she turned and made her way back up the path, somehow not at all surprised that there had been no sign of him.

'I'm here, Dad!' she shouted as she went up the concrete steps and into the entrance porch.

***

Fish, of course, did not talk about his date, but the fact that only the laws of physics were preventing him from actually walking about a foot off the ground made it clear that he was happy.

'Did you like your breakfast?' said Dad.

'Yes, thanks,' began Vic, then, 'Oh!' as she disappeared rapidly upstairs to fetch the tray which she had forgotten about since the dog had barked again.

'Why did you go shopping?' she asked, once she had come back down again and successfully placed the tray's contents by the kitchen sink without anyone asking any awkward questions. 'Didn't you get plenty on Monday?'

'Yeah,' said Dad, 'We only picked up a couple of things.

What I really wanted to do was check something at the tapestry museum. Do you fancy going to visit a few sites with us? There are a whole lot of interesting little places associated with the French invasion on the tapestry.'

'Well, OK,' Vic agreed cautiously, looking in Fish's direction. She was wondering whether he was going to be "otherwise engaged" but didn't dare actually ask.

'I'm coming, too,' he smiled. 'Sarah does have a half-day off but she has to go on a family visit with her parents. She's doing her evening shift so I'll meet her after that. You've got my delightful company for the day.'

This news saved Vic from herself. She had maintained her calm demeanour during the latest encounter with "Apple", which had been interrupted by Dad's return, but it had unsettled her more than she liked to admit and it had made her very anxious about the rest of the day. She didn't want a bits-and-pieces, holiday-type day. She wanted a stable, everyone-together type of day. No, better still: an everyone-*out*-together type of day.

Of course, Fish and Dad had no idea of all this. All they knew was that she seemed happy, strangely so, in fact. And they went on noticing it for the rest of the day because every so often she would grab their arms and walk affectionately between them. They noticed it even more when she showed an unusual amount of interest in local geography and history.

Within half an hour they were equipped with a suitable quantity of picnic and snack provisions and Dad's "Invasion Trail" list, copied out from various leaflets and books. Then they set off for what turned out to be more than just a textbook family outing. Although she did not realise it at the time, they visited some places not unconnected with what was happening to her in the "secret" part of her holiday.

The places they went to were not typical tourist locations, which made it all the more amazing to Dad and Fish that Vic seemed keen to be there with them. Half the places were just vaguely identifiable spots on an Ordnance Survey map. More often than not they found themselves looking at roads, railways or industrial estates while Dad read to them about how some small group of French soldiers had taken over a farm building or held out in a clump of trees against a few locals and one or two English militiamen who, it seemed, hardly took the whole thing seriously.

Of course, Dad sweetened the day. They had morning coffee and biscuits in the lounge of a tiny hotel on a hillside, up a lane, which he had followed on impulse, even though it really wasn't wide enough for the car. The owners had been delighted to see them but had virtually no knowledge of the historical events the Darwens were tracing.

'Well, at least they knew about the tapestry,' Dad said afterwards, as he got them out of the lane by using his famous fifteen-point turn.

'Yeah,' said Fish, unimpressed. 'But they saw it on the regional news! How sad is that?!'

'Be fair,' replied Dad. 'I remember when we moved to our present house, visitors would quite often ask us if we could go and visit some place they had heard about but which we hadn't. When you live in a place you often think of it as just the place you live, you know, shopping, eating out, working. To a visitor, it's somewhere to explore.'

'But these people are locals, Dad!'

'True, but that's human behaviour. Anyway, this is all giving me an idea for a writing activity for my students, so just give me a moment to jot it down, and then we'll get on.'

When Fish was expressing righteous indignation you couldn't really stop him, unless you changed the subject. When he had finished his note-making, Dad did change the subject, because he thought he noticed a change in Vic.

'Alright, Girl?' he said.

'Uh-huh,' she replied with a bit of a smile. It was enough to reassure him but it concealed a change in her mood that he had been right to notice. When he had said "we moved" she knew that "we" meant Mum and him and, although it didn't last too long, her spirits sank for a while.

She perked up later, in time to be good company when Dad unexpectedly ditched the picnic plan and stopped at a pub for lunch. She played a game of pool with Fish, and then one with Dad while Fish read everything in the room, as usual.

'What about our sandwiches?' she said, as Dad lined up a shot.

'We didn't order sandwiches,' he said, looking up in puzzlement.

'No, the ones we packed,' she explained.

'Ah!' he said, settling down once again to his shot. 'They will just have to be our picnic supper, I suppose! Ah-hah! Did you see that cannon? Told you I used to be the pool champion in my youth!'

'Well I've only seen you beat a girl, Grandpa and our cousin when he was ten,' commented Fish, sitting down from his poster-reading tour of the room. Then it was Dad's turn to sulk.

Three Ploughman's Lunches arrived, so they finished the game quickly and when Fish asked one of his semi-serious questions about whether it was a plural and oughtn't it to be "Ploughmen's Lunches", his remark about Dad's pool playing prowess was forgotten. This was just as well because although Dad was very easygoing you occasionally got the feeling that he took such remarks a bit too seriously.

The afternoon was not quite so successful as the morning. They did find a spot on a hillside where you could see all the way to the sea across a series of hillsides, like a valley of ridges. And the tourist information almost succeeded in getting them to imagine thin lines of French soldiers straggling up in their direction so many years ago. However, they couldn't find anywhere for afternoon tea, which disappointed Dad most of all because he loved the feeling of being pampered and drinking tea you didn't have to brew for yourself.

And the final attraction, which they had saved up for last, was closed when they got there. It was a walled garden, which they could not believe was not open. There was a tangle of plants for sale on a trestle in the layby next to the door, with a pot for money. And the door itself was just a rickety old wooden thing which, even though it was clearly padlocked, looked so frail that it would surely have fallen over if they had leaned on it.

However, no matter how hard they studied the guide leaflets and the faded sign by the door, all they got from their visit was a tantalising glimpse of the tops of some lichen-covered trees. And they could only see them if they stood on the other side of the road, on tip-toe. Then Dad said, 'Your Mum loved walled gardens.' And it wasn't just Vic who went quiet as they drove back home.

8

THURSDAY

Having gone along on Dad's history trail for a day, Vic felt she had earned another day at the beach. Not that she hadn't enjoyed the day of visits, if only because the activity had taken her to some places which took her mind off the stranger aspects of her holiday so far. However, it had also given her what she thought of as "one last chance" to do something with Fish. Using what Dad called the "worst case scenario" she was assuming that his holiday romance would turn out to be "serious", and that he would therefore spend the rest of their stay trying to juggle girlfriend and family. And Vic had a good idea which was likely to win. Or rather, who would lose. So, starting with today, she decided to start thinking in terms of her and Dad only.

When she came downstairs she found Dad already preparing the snacks for the day. He must have been up for hours because he had made the picnic basket into a maze of individually labelled containers, with their names and suggested eating times on little labels. Dad really was on form.

'Isn't Fish up yet?' she said. As she did so, she poured herself some cranberry juice, carefully diluting it according to some advice she had read in the magazine Dad had bought her during the last beach visit.

'Is he ever!' barked Dad. 'Not only is your brother up but he is also out, and has been for nearly an hour.'

Vic sipped the juice and pulled a face as she discovered that diluting it had removed all the flavour. 'Where's he gone?' she asked, slightly concerned at what the answer could be.

'To see the new love of his life,' Dad grinned.

Vic's heart sank. She had expected something like this but she was still disappointed. Surely her brother could at least have popped into her room and said goodbye for the day. Her face must have been an absolute picture of instant despair that even Dad didn't think it was caused by the flavour of the juice. He looked at her sympathetically and immediately put on the most comforting voice he could.

'Don't worry, it's not permanent,' he reassured her. 'He's still coming to the beach with us. Sarah's working at lunch and this evening, so, with the sort of energy only found in worker ants and young men in love he has arranged to see her for an hour before we go. She has to be at work at ten anyway, so they will have to tear themselves apart. I wonder if they can be seen from here...' he added.

'What do you mean?' asked Vic, suddenly feeling more enthusiastic.

'He said they would go for a walk on the jetty,' said Dad. Romantic, eh?' By now he had wandered out to the sun lounge. 'No,' he said, after peering down into the bay. 'That's a shame. If I could have seen them that would have given me something better to make embarrassing jokes about all day!'

'You'd better be careful,' said Vic.

Dad noticed something in her tone and asked, slightly anxiously, 'Careful of what?'

She grinned triumphantly at having caught him out. 'Careful or you'll turn into Grandpa!' she laughed.

He stuck his tongue out at her. 'Oh, ha! ha!' he laughed. 'If you're so smart you'd better have your breakfast or you'll be the reason we're delayed when Romeo gets back,' and he went on making the day's mini-feasts.

Vic couldn't resist taking a look at the jetty but she couldn't see her brother either. As she sat down there was a bleep from one of the dining chairs.

'Did that chair just make an electronic noise or do I detect a technological intrusion into our lives?' asked Dad. When Vic looked faintly perplexed at his words, he translated: 'I think it's the mobile phone.'

Dad did not approve of mobile phones. For years he had used a favourite put-down to stop classes being too chatty. He would accuse them all of being in training to be radio disc-jockeys. Then, when they looked at him blankly he would explain: "People who have nothing to say and spend all day saying it." Since just about everyone now carried a mobile phone he had adapted his joke. He would say that now anyone could spend all day saying nothing without any formal career training at all. If he had his way they wouldn't have a mobile phone at all but Grandpa had given them one as a present "For emergencies" and although

Dad had resisted, saying that surely Granny and Grandpa could wait a few minutes to hear about any family tragedy which might occur, he had eventually given in, reasoning that he could just leave the damn thing turned off most of the time. In fact, he left it off *all* the time. It was usually Fish who remembered to switch it on, which was probably why they could hear it now. But the beep was a voicemail signal, thought Vic.

Dad noticed her expression. 'No,' he said. 'I haven't suddenly changed my mind about the things. 'But I have a feeling that some member of the family is going to want to get in touch before much longer, so I switched it on after Fish went out. I've only just brought it downstairs so someone must have tried to call while it was upstairs.' He took it out of the pocket of his bag, placed it on the table and looked at it, then he looked up to see her still staring at him.

'There's no need to give me one of Grandpa's "Surely you don't know how to use that" looks,' he said. 'I do actually know how to turn it on, you know!' he added. 'Remind me one of these days to explain to you the meaning of the expression "Know thine enemy".'

Vic changed her expression and made a mental note to herself not to remind him. She knew how easy it could be to end up back in the classroom when you were with Dad. 'So, are you going to access the voicemail?' Vic asked.

He grinned. 'I only said I know how to turn it on,' he said, making as if to hand her the phone but as she reached out for it he turned away. 'Hah! Only joking! But you can access it anyway as I am trying to get the food finished.' He handed it to her properly and started filling the flasks

'It's from Grandpa!' she said.

'Don't tell me,' said Dad, mock-wearily. 'They're coming to see us and they're going to stay at the hotel down the hill.'

'You got the first bit right. They're coming. Tomorrow, it says, but there's nothing about where they'll stay. It also says to phone back.'

'OK,' said Dad, 'No sense putting it off. After all, it's probably my fault for sending the details in the first place. I just shouldn't have used a First Class stamp. It's a bit early to phone, but I guess the message proves they're up. Can you dial their number for me while I get the lids on these flasks?'

Vic obliged. She got a ringing tone and then Granny's voice.

'Hi Granny!' she shouted, because her Grandmother was slightly hard of hearing. 'We got your message. Yes, Dad would like to speak to Grandpa.'

She handed the phone to her Dad, saying, 'Granny says it's another of Grandpa's hairbrained schemes. See if you can talk him out of it.'

'She must be joking!' snorted Dad. 'He'll have the route planned and half-a-dozen important facts about the place at his fingertips already… Oh, hello Doug! So, we can't escape from you, then! Uh-huh. Uh-huh.'

Vic finished off her toast while Dad listened to Grandpa. Fish came in while she was clearing the table. He paused a moment to listen to Dad.'

'So, Granny and Grandpa are coming down,' he said.

'How do you know?' she asked.

'Pretty obvious. Haven't you noticed that whenever anyone in the family goes off on holiday, Granny and

Grandpa tend to arrive for a few days at some stage. Now we've gone off on our own for the first time without… well, you know, on our own, then if they didn't muscle in at some stage it would be worth a place in The Guinness Book of Records.'

Vic tries to put her "listening with interest" face on, but she was actually feeling sad inside at what Fish had found so hard to say. "Without Mum" is what he had meant and she was relieved that by the time he had finished, Dad's telephone conversation had also come to an end.

Fish himself went ahead with the sentence he had been intending to deliver, because he thought it sounded funny and he would never let such an opportunity pass.

'Actually, it was all the Uh-Huhs.'

Both Dad and Vic looked at him blankly.

'You asked me how I knew Grandpa was on the phone. I knew because Grandpa always does most of the talking!' he explained. 'Dad always says "Uh-Huh" automatically when he's listening to Grandpa.' Vic and Dad continued to stare at him blankly and he was just about to embark on a fresh version of his explanation when he realised that it was his turn to be the victim of a wind-up. 'Oh, very funny I do not think!' he said, while the other two celebrated their moment of comic timing, laughing and making "Duhh!" noises just like they did at school.

'OK. Enjoy yourselves laughing at me but we'll be too late to park at the beach if we hang about much longer,' he said.

That shut Dad up straight away. He was always anxious about getting to places on time. Not early, or in time, but at *exactly* the time he planned. Not that he ever mentioned this as one of his aims, but you could just tell by his movements and tone of his voice. And the fact that they usually did arrive exactly at the due time anywhere. He quickly put the finishing touches to the picnic and started to transport the various bags and boxes to the car. Because he had prepared something special he didn't want any help This was another of Dad's characteristics which could sometimes be annoying. He was secretive about treats; so secretive that he left others guessing what he was doing and uncertain whether there was a problem or not. But today it didn't matter because it averted what Vic was sure would have been a disaster. It also helped that Fish needed to pick up a few things from his room, so he was upstairs at the moment that Dad looked back from the porch and said to Vic, 'I've forgotten to pack any fruit. Do me a favour and stick some in the backpack over there.'

Vic's heart had skipped a beat at the possibility that he might mention a specific type of fruit, but he went out and she breathed again.

Then disaster struck. He stepped back in through the porch door and said, 'Make sure there's at least one green apple for me.'

He could only have been a couple of paces back out of the door and Vic had time only to stiffen slightly in anticipation when, simultaneously, the dog barked and a brisk wind blew through the porch and slammed shut the door Dad had just used. Instinctively, Vic made for the porch. She was distracted by Fish shouting, 'That bloody dog's yapping again!' but she still noticed with sinking heart that there was a green apple in the bowl where there had been none before. A moment's relief that Dad obviously hadn't noticed that there wasn't one when he asked was quickly dashed when, reaching the porch, she found the familiar figure of "Apple" standing in the open doorway from the back garden.

Trying to indicate with her arms and expression that this was not a good time, Vic glanced up the path towards the front gate to see how much time she had. A minute or two might do but Dad was already coming back down! The only thing preventing him from seeing what was happening was the fact that the path was so steep that you didn't actually have your head level with the porch doorway until the very last step. As he came down, she turned and hissed 'Stand against the wall,' and, as there wasn't time to check whether he understood, she put her arm across him and pushed him as gently as possible. Then she turned to face Dad as he arrived, just hoping that her body would conceal the figure which must surely be half-visible behind the porch door frame. She was sure it wouldn't work. This was real life, not a television drama. He would have to be stupid not to notice. She held her breath and waited for things to suddenly become very complicated But he didn't notice. He just said, 'Are you getting the beach things? Don't worry about the fruit. I'll get it now.' And then he walked past.

'She watched his back for a moment, in case he decided to say anything else, but he didn't. She turned and immediately got some idea of why Dad hadn't noticed anything. Against the wall, "Apple" looked like not a lot more than a couple of twig brooms with a cloth covering them. Unless you knew what he was or you were looking for him, you wouldn't necessarily notice him.

Still, she wasn't going to take any further risks. Beckoning, she went down the path to the corner of the house. As soon as they got there the dog barked furiously. She stopped and held up an arm to prevent "Apple" going any further. She still couldn't quite get over how frail he felt to the touch. The way her luck seemed to be going just now she would not have been surprised to find Fish peering out of a back window, pulling faces at the dog to wind it up. Or maybe its owners would make their first appearance just when she least wanted to see them. Luckily they showed no more interest than they usually did. She thought she could hear a faint "Shut up!" from somewhere back behind the dog, but there was no-one to be seen, not even Fish, who was obviously getting ready for the beach. She reached round to the wood store latch, opened it and said, 'No time to talk. You'll have to go in now.'

Although he was as expressionless as ever, there was nevertheless something different about him: a new frailty in his appearance or something like that, which made her feel guilty to be getting rid of him so soon after he had been "summoned", if that was what was happening each time.

'I'll try to be here tonight,' she added. 'OK?'

He might have given a nod. He certainly didn't say anything. But he had an air of understanding about him and slipped past her and into the wood store. For some reason she felt it would be intrusive in some way to do anything but close the door behind him but she caught a glimpse through the gap between the frame and part of the door attached to it by hinges and what seemed to see a figure half way in among the wood. Or was he part of the wood? Or was it just wood? Before she could focus more closely, the sound of Fish's voice made her close the door and drop the latch sharply. She looked round but could not see her brother.

Then his voice came again repeating what he had just said. She peered round the corner of the house.

'I'm up here,' he said, and she looked up to where he was leaning out of an open window. 'I opened the window and the dog stopped barking,' he said. 'Must be the magic trick.'

Vic smiled inwardly. A window opening, or a door closing, she thought to herself. Whichever had done the trick, there was nothing else about Fish's tone to suggest that he'd seen anything.

***

After the desperate moments with Apple, Vic was very quiet in the car. Fortunately the others didn't notice because they were preoccupied too. Fish was thinking about his new-found girlfriend; Dad was also thinking about her, trying desperately not to say anything which might embarrass his son. So he ended up saying nothing.

By the time they reached White Sands Bay the silence had become almost something you could touch and Dad, being Dad, just couldn't stay off the subject for ever.

Getting out of the car he looked back in and said, 'Come on you Capulet and you Montague.' Fish certainly recognised what he was talking about. Vic knew just about enough to get the Shakespeare reference.

'*He* might be Romeo but *I'm* not Juliet,' she protested. She glanced at Fish, expecting to see him glowering, but in fact he was laughing. It *must* be love, she thought.

Fish got out of the car and, still smiling, said, 'OK, have your fun. Just one rule: don't do any of this stuff when Grandpa arrives. As soon as he finds out, my life will be a misery, so don't make it worse.'

Dad and Vic, who had both suffered at Grandpa's hands at one time or another, were sobered by this thought and agreed immediately. Vic added, with a mutter that Dad couldn't hear, 'But I want all the Scoob before we leave this beach, right?' And then added, 'After all, I gave you the advice that helped you get started, remember?'

Fish gave her a withering look but sure enough, while Dad was off on a stroll across the dunes behind the beach, Fish told her about his girl.

It turned out that although Vic had not met her, they already had what might be termed a "connection".

'Her name's Sarah and she's an art student, just like you want to be,' said Fish. The job in the chip shop is only for the holidays. It's owned by her Dad.'

Victoria ignored the art student detail as she did not like people planning her life for her. 'Where do they live?' she asked.

'Across the bay, at least she and her father do. Her parents are separated. Her Mum lives quite near us. She didn't say much about her.

Vic said, 'That's a shame,' which was a mild version of what she was actually thinking. She would kill to have a Mum "not to talk to" and she had little sympathy for anyone who took the fact that they had families for granted; and friends for that matter. The she asked, 'Why?'

'Dunno,' Fish replied. I would have said if I knew, wouldn't I?' He spoke in a tone Vic had not heard since they had come on holiday, so she made no answer. 'Anyway,' he went on, 'We were talking about *my* love life so can we stick to the subject of *my* new friend?'

While Vic silently registered the fact that Fish did not yet refer to her as his "girlfriend", he carried on where he had left off. 'Anyway, Sarah's really nice. We talk about art and we stroll up and down the front of Oilslick Bay.'

Vic nearly said, "Dead romantic!" but stopped herself being ironic just in time. Fish read her thoughts anyway.

'Yeah, I know it doesn't sound romantic but we enjoy it.' He went on in this way for some time and Vic realised she wasn't going to get any details about hand-holding and kissing and all that stuff. Maybe this was what caring for someone was really all about, she thought. Just giving a person the pleasure of your company and getting the same thing back. And then for some unknown reason she thought of her mysterious visitor. Maybe that was what Apple needed. Just the warmth of company. If she possibly could, she would find him and spend some proper time with him when they got back to the house. Though how that was going to be possible she could not imagine.

At this point, Dad returned and romantic gossip was suspended while he proceeded to set out the first of his snack treats. Vic's was in a little basket which he had obviously taken from one of the upstairs rooms. It contained her favourite salt and vinegar crisps in a specially made foil wrapper. Dad always used foil to wrap presents.

'I've got a book!' said Fish, with a note of surprise in his voice that it was not food. However, when he opened it he found that Dad had cut out the centres of several pages and three of Fish's favourite Rich Tea Biscuits nestled there in the middle. Like a gun in a James Bond film, thought Vic.

Then she said, reproachfully, 'You shouldn't do that to books, Dad.' Even as she said it she knew this might upset him, but it was one of things people say without really meaning to be critical and he took no offence.

'Agreed,' he said. 'But this is a duplicate copy of one I already have. It would only get thrown out, so I thought it would make a good treat.'

'It does,' said Fish. Vic noticed a tone in his voice that she hadn't heard from him before. I bet he'll tell Sarah about this, she thought. If she's artistic, she'll appreciate it.

Vic's drink, in her favourite flask, was hot chocolate. Fish had tea, made in a small pot from hot water in another flask. 'Very classy!' he said, sitting there on the beach with his little finger crooked under the handle of his tea cup. 'No thank you vicar, no more buttered scones for me,' he added, repeating another old family joke.

After a swim, Vic and Fish returned to find that Dad had laid out lunch for them. It was all in egg boxes, except for the soup, that is, which came out of their biggest flask.

'What sort is this?' asked Vic.

'Leek, of course,' replied Dad. 'We are in Wales, after all.' It was delicious, especially with the rough brown bread he had also brought.

Each egg box contained a sachet of salt and one of pepper, and then each person's favourite things to go with the salad he had prepared.

Vic found curls of smoked salmon, Fish had honey-roast ham.

While they were eating this Dad said, 'So, Fisher-me-lad, are you going to tell me anything about this girl, or will I have to wait until Vic and I are alone so she can pass on the details?'

'Dad!' Vic protested. But Fish continued to surprise her with his calmness.

'Her name is Sarah Clinton,' he began, only to be interrupted almost immediately by Dad.

'Clinton!' he exclaimed. 'I had an Aunt whose married name was Clinton. Does her family have any connections with the North-East?'

'I don't know,' said Fish, adding, with sarcasm, 'It wasn't top of my list of things-to- establish-when-you're–getting-a-girl-to-go-out-with-you.'

Vic could see from her Dad's face that he was preparing what he would think was a witty comeback. She would not let him. 'Honestly, Dad,' she said mock-reproachfully, 'Can't you keep your relations out of this?'

Dad looked in her direction, as if thinking up a good reply for her instead, but something in her expression warned him off and he got the point.

To save his sister the agony of being interrogated by Dad later, Fish repeated a version of what he had told her. There was an additional detail as well: the person who cleaned The Pilot's Cottage between guests also cleaned for Sarah's Mum. She had therefore known a bit about them from her before Fish had summoned up the courage to ask her out.

Vic didn't hear the next part of the conversation. Fish was taking his chance to get back at Dad for his remarks by suggesting that he was being talked about by strange women. But the talk of Sarah's Mum had brought on her sad feelings again and she could only think of her own Mum. She only rejoined the conversation when Dad suggested ice cream to finish off the picnic and she had to tell him what kind she wanted so he could trudge over the dunes to fetch them. As soon as he was gone Fish said,

'You alright, Vic?'

Her reply was a half-hearted, 'Yeah,' which confirmed what Fish had been thinking. He didn't bother to press the point, however. Instead he asked her about another bit of the conversation she had missed.

'What about Granny and Grandpa coming down so soon?' he said.

'I dunno,' she replied. 'When will they be here?'

'To-night!' he said. 'They're on their way even as we recline here soaking up the Welsh sun and rubbing Welsh sand from between our toes. Knowing them, they'll be installed in the Oilslick Bay Hotel by the time we drag our sun-bronzed bodies back. Hey! Maybe they'll invite us to join them for supper!'

Dad came back surprisingly quickly. 'Who's going to invite us for supper?' he asked.

'No-one,' said Vic. 'Fish was just wondering whether G and G will when they get here.'

'Don't bank on it,' he said. 'They will have had a long journey. They'll be tired and...'

'Oh, never mind the old folks' eating arrangements,' Fish cut in. 'What about ours?'

Dad and Vic both looked at him, puzzled.

'You went for ice creams,' he explained, 'And unless they are cunningly hidden in your shorts, I don't think you've got them.'

'Ah! Yes. You see, I forgot my money,' explained Dad. 'I am fairly sure that although the Spanish bloke on the van might call it "gelado frio", they probably don't let you have it for nothing!' While Fish told him that of all the laboured jokes he had ever constructed, this was *the most laboured*. he dug around in the bottom of a bag and found his wallet. 'Won't be long,' he said, ignoring Fish's semiserious criticism, and trotted back up to the car park.

Vic and Fish tidied up while they waited. Dad eventually returned with three large choc-ices and, apparently, unconcerned about his joke falling flat. While they opened them, Fish said, 'I wonder what G and G might like to do? Do you think they would find the invasion tapestry interesting?'

'You never can tell with them,' Dad replied. 'The main concern will probably be the comfort level of the hotel and the quality of the food.'

'Yeah. Have you noticed that Grandpa does all the eating but Granny is the one who comments on the food?'

'Yes. I've never been entirely sure that the food your Grandfather eats makes any significant contact with his tongue or his palate.'

'Or the alcohol he drinks!'

'I know! Yet I have never seen him drunk, you know.'

'Your grandfather knows when to slope off for a nap, that's why! Naps run in the family, come to think of it,' mused Dad, and it was his turn to go quiet. He became thoughtful and Fish, noticing the moment, dragged Vic off into the sea on their body boards. They didn't think they had been in long when Dad appeared by the water's edge waving to them to come in. He looked odd, in the way that people often do on the beach, dressed for sea, sand and sun but carrying personal effects which have to be taken everywhere. When Vic and Fish had finished laughing at the combination of trunks and shoulder bag they took one last ride on the warm waves and followed him up the beach. He had just about packed everything else.

'We're lucky it's warm enough for you not to need wetsuits today,' Dad observed. 'It's one less item to shake and rinse when we get back. And we'll have room for some shopping on the way.'

'We're going shopping again?' said Vic.

'Not exactly. There's a big superstore just the other side of St. David's. I want to get some petrol. It's several pence per litre cheaper here than at the Oilslick Bay garage.'

It was nearly four when they left the beach, and gone five when they finally had a full tank of petrol and pulled out onto the road home. When they reached "The Pilot's Cottage", which Fish always liked to announce in any one of a number of funny voices, there was a note stuck in the letter box, written by Grandpa ('Grandma writes all the letters; Grandpa writes all the notes,' observed Fish.)

Their relations, it seemed, had arrived, checked in, found "The Pilot's Cottage" and gone back to the hotel for their supper. "Join us for coffee?" were the last words before Grandpa's unreadable but unmistakable signature.

Vic set about cooking some pizza and setting the table while Fish had a quick shower. Dad called Grandpa on the mobile and arranged to meet in the hotel lounge in an hour. Vic took her turn showering while Fish and Dad finished off the cooking. Dad ate quickly and took his shower before they all set off down the path, Fish and Dad making bets about what Grandpa would say to them. They agreed that the most likely thing would be "You mean you haven't… " followed by any one of a selection of things about the area that Grandpa would have read about in a book, or on the Internet, or worse still, from the days when he had cycled all the way here in a day when he and his boyhood chum had been lads before the war. The only thing was, his youth must have been made up of more days than existed because he claimed to have been everywhere!

Vic took no part in the conversation; she was too busy looking out for moles, without luck.

The path ended by running parallel with the high stone wall which divided the wooded hillside from the road. A pair of metal bars set in the ground made you go in single file through the gap which took you onto the approach road to the hotel. Later, during an outing, Vic would mention this to Grandpa and, in return for her polite attempt at making conversation, would receive a little lecture about how it was intended to slow down silly kids who would run on the road. Grandpa, in turn, would receive a sharp reprimand from Granny, in the form of his name, hissed sharply and he would shut up for a minute or two. But this pleasure remained in the future. For the present, the three steps and the wrought-iron porch welcomed them into the hotel, where Vic and Fish went and sat down in the lounge while Dad asked the receptionist to send a message up to G and G's room. They were down in a couple of minutes and, although they were both on form, Vic and Fish agreed later that Grandpa had been more bouncy than usual and Grandma had interrupted him whenever he started to ask them how they were doing in the holiday home because, as Fish put it, 'He seemed to be on the brink of saying something beginning with, "since there's only three of you".'

'So, what are you doing tomorrow?' Grandpa asked after they had caught up on the details of the holiday so far.

'Well,' said Dad, 'We're going to be without Fish for the day.'

'Oh? Why?' said Granny. 'Fed up with them already, are you?'

Fish laughed.

Taking this as a good sign, Dad grinned and went on. 'He may be, but that's not why.' He glanced at Fish, who still gave no indication of being uncomfortable with Dad telling them. 'Fish has met a girl. He's been good enough not to dash away from us so far, but he arranged to go out with her for the day tomorrow. So it's just me and Vic.. toria,' he concluded, remembering that Grandma did not particularly like the shortening of her granddaughter's name.'

'That'll be alright,' laughed Grandpa. 'Teenage boys are a pain at the best of times. Let's all of us go off together and leave Fish to his fun with this girl!'

Grandma put a hand on his arm. 'Maybe their Dad would like a break too,' she said, meaningfully. Looking at Vic she asked, 'Has Dad done any of his writing since you got here?'

'A bit,' she said. 'Not much, really. We've been busy.'

'Well, why don't just you come with us tomorrow? That'll give your Dad some time to himself.' Vic didn't quite understand why this was so important and she wasn't mad keen on the idea of a day with the grandparents, who were fun but not exactly brilliant with children. However, sensing that she would be playing some part in something worthwhile, she agreed.

'Grand!' said her Gran. 'Well, I'm a bit tired after that journey and I expect you two will exhaust me tomorrow, so I'm off to my bed. Goodnight.' And, in Grandma's familiar way, she stood on no ceremony but was gone even as she spoke.

Grandpa never went off to his bed until he had fallen asleep in his chair at least once, and even then he might not leave if his chair if a quick surf through the TV channels turned up a trashy film he could half concentrate on. As soon as Dad and Fish suggested a walk, he was instantly keen and in no more time than it took him to fetch his coat, they all set out for the jetty.

Vic and Fish hung back and let the other two make the pace. The chosen route was the ugly concrete walkway and by the time they had reached the end of the jetty Grandpa had told them exactly how the hydrofoil ferry boats worked, the name of the design of several of the smaller boats in the harbour and any number of scraps of information about harbour construction.

'I think he built them all,' joked Fish. He paused for a reaction and, when none was forthcoming, he added, 'Are you going to be OK tomorrow, Vic?'

'What do you mean?' she asked, surprised by his fatherly tones.

'Spending a day with Grandpa, I mean.'

'Oh, don't be silly!' she laughed. 'He's different when you're not there. He doesn't bother to tell girls all this stuff. There's no competition from us, you see.'

'Ah-Ha!' said Fish, secretly impressed by Vic's insight. 'So that's the secret. In that case, you will no doubt enjoy your day at least as much as the rest of us.'

Vic grinned, inwardly enjoying the way Fish talked like a grown-up on these occasions. Her friends couldn't quite relate to him but she loved his slightly-longer-than-necessary sentences. She would give anything to hear him talking to Sarah and see how she reacted to him.

They caught up with Dad and Grandpa, who had stopped and appeared to be talking about an odd square brick building which stood at the end of the path they were following. When they came within earshot, it became clear that they were actually talking about a van parked next to it. The van was painted with distinctive company colours and Grandpa was imparting one of his odd bits of information about it to Dad. When he saw Fish arriving he directed it at him too.

'Hey, Fisher,' he said. 'Do you know what a Livery Index Tracker is?'

Fish tried to muster some enthusiasm. 'I don't think so, Grandpa. Something to do with horses, is it?'

'No, no no!' crowed Grandpa, delighted to be able to fill a gap in his Grandson's knowledge of the world. 'It's someone who provides information about colour combinations used by firms.'

'Why would they do that?'

'Competition, dear boy. It's so one motor manufacturer doesn't use colours that resemble those used by another manufacturer.'

'So this person spends their time checking motor car colours?'

'That's the idea.'

'How do you know?' asked Dad, though all three of them knew from long experience that Grandpa often engaged complete strangers in technical chit-chat, so the answer was predictable.

'I stopped for petrol on the way here. There was a blokey on the forecourt looking at some accident damage on a car and I told him about the respray I had after someone scraped the side of my car and he told me that part of his job was to research colour possibilities for vehicles.'

'So what's the job called again?'

'A Livery Index Tracker.'

'And he looks at colours.'

'That's it.'

'Sound like a job of limited interest.'

'Maybe, but they earn a hundred grand a year.'

'How much?!' exclaimed Fish. 'A hundred thousand pounds? Why doesn't my careers tutor ever tell me about jobs like that?' Then, with an apparent sudden change of subject, he asked 'So, did you figure out why there is this slipway here?'

'It's for unloading fish at low tide,' Grandpa said.

'I can't recall them laying a finger on me,' said Fish, which reduced both Vic and her father to helpless giggles. Grandpa, who had never seemed to understand how jokes work, just told them they were blithering idiots.

It was getting quite dark now and Vic was actually more interested in the strings of lights along the hillside which reflected in the black water.

Dad noticed she was a bit out of the chat and asked whether she was warm enough. Although she said she was, he nevertheless suggested they all walk back. It was quite dark by now and they all felt a bit cold, so quick "Goodnights" were exchanged at the hotel gate, a time fixed for Grandma and Grandpa to collect Vic in the morning, and then they headed up the steep, very dark path and home.

When they got to their front door, Vic realised that she had not thought about apples and strange visitors since they had got back from the beach. She sat and watched TV for an hour, sipping hot chocolate which Dad had made in a big jug for them all, and the dog did not bark, and no fruit made a mysterious appearance in the fruit bowl and no shed doors rattled.

Bed and welcome deep sleep soon followed.

9

FRIDAY

At half-past four in the afternoon, Grandpa swung his car round where the road widened above The Pilot's Cottage and hit the horn to announce their arrival.

'Doug!' said Grandma. While not a full-blown back-seat driver, she had never liked Grandpa's driving habits and always commented. For good or ill he ignored her, a tactic born of years of her attempting to correct his annoying behaviour.

'Here we are, then,' he said, as Vic opened the back door and got out. 'And here's your father.'

Dad came up the path and opened the gate.

'Hello Vic,' he said, giving her a little hug. 'Did you have a lovely time?'

'Yes. Great,' she replied, surprising both him and herself with her genuine feeling.

'Thanks for having Vic for the day,' Dad said, turning towards her Grandparents.

'It was no trouble,' said Grandma. 'We had a lovely time.'

Grandpa leaned across from the driver's seat and called out, 'You'll be coming to eat with us tonight?' His upward inflexion showed that this was a question, but any member of his family knew that as far as he was concerned an arrangement had already been made. The family tended to act as one – Fish had told Vic that he had heard one in-law refer to them as "The Tribe" – so it was always assumed you were going along with what they wanted to do.

Dad, who had spent a large part of his life trying to maintain at least a semblance of independence, hesitated a moment, as if wracking his brains to check whether they had already discussed this possibility. After what he considered to be a suitable pause he said, 'Sounds good to me.' He wasn't really going to say anything else to an entirely sensible suggestion, thought Vic. Thanks to Fish she was alert enough to family politics, even at her age.

Grandma said, 'Will you all be coming?'

'Do you mean Fish... er as well?' Dad asked, remembering once again at the last moment G and G's preference for their grandchildren's full names.

'Yes.'

'Well, I did tell him not to neglect us and, as he's had a whole day in the arms of his new love, I'm expecting him to repay me by being back before supper time.'

'Right,' said Grandpa. 'If that's your long-winded way of saying he will, we'll book a table for five. I'll phone you when we get a time.'

'OK. I'll switch the mobile on just for you!' laughed Dad.

'You mean it isn't already on?' said Grandpa in a despairing tone.

Grandma rolled up her window before her husband could make a remark about that and they drove off down the hill.

'I'm glad I resisted the temptation to make a joke about the booking,' observed Dad, and he explained to Vic that when Grandpa had said "for five", meaning people, he had been about to ask whether that was a little early to eat. 'I saw your Grandmother's frown and thought better of it,' he said and then, in a more serious tone than the one he had used for G and G asked, 'Was your day really fun, then?'

Vic was actually thinking about Dad's shared confidence about his joke and wondering whether she was beginning to look old enough to join in such conversation or if it was just part of some special effort he and Fish were making for the holiday. 'Yeah, Dad,' said Vic, turning and walking down the path. 'They're not monsters, you know.'

Dad followed and pulled the gate shut. 'I never said they were, though now you come to mention it…'

He caught up with her and she bashed his arm as she skipped in through the porch. 'What have you been doing?' she asked.

'Writing, mainly, with a bit of reading, eating and drinking in between.'

'What did you write?'

'Oh, a poem for my Mum and the first draft of an article.'

This was very informative by Dad's standards, and, knowing his boundaries Vic made no further inquiry. If a complimentary letter came back from Dad's parents, or a letter of acceptance from some publication, then they would find out what Dad had really written and they would have an opportunity to react. But he didn't like a fuss being made until he had completed a process. Fish always said his perceived secretiveness was one of the things about Dad that used to infuriate Mum... Vic tried to dismiss that thought straight away. She had had a good day and was pleased to be achieving the secret holiday product of keeping Dad off the dreaded subject.

She paused, and then, thinking she had her focus back, she asked, 'What did you have for lunch?' She instantly regretted the question because she knew that when Dad was on his own in the daytime he tended not to have a proper meal. He would snack, on and off, so as not to interrupt what he was trying to get done in his rare moments alone. He was sure to mention fruit at some stage, so even as he started answering she began putting in distracting extra questions to change the subject, which gave the conversation a rather desperate feel.

'Oh, you know, just bits and pieces I found. I had some fruit with my coffee...'

'I had a jam doughnut with my coffee. We bought them from a garage with some takeaway coffee from this machine that Grandma thought we'd broken.'

'Sounds fun. I finished off that jar of apricot jam on a slice of toast at some stage, though I don't remember exactly when.'

Dad had brought what he called "key provisions" with him on holiday. He had a cake he had baked to go with the first cup of tea on arrival and Vic knew there was a jar of his home made apple jelly in the cupboard too. She leapt in before he could mention it. 'I had Welsh cakes with honey for afternoon tea. Grandpa made us go in this really plastic-looking fast-food place and it turned out they had home-made stuff made by one of the assistants.'

Even Dad could sense that the conversation was becoming forced, to say the least, but, misunderstanding why, and thinking his daughter was desperate to talk for some reason, he ploughed on with their strange exchanges. 'My exotic lunch was a third of a can of left-over baked beans on another slice of toast. Delicious drink of…'

Knowing that there was apple juice in the fridge, Vic leapt in once more. 'Did it rain here?'

Slightly bewildered by their desperate conversation, Dad soldiered on as best he could. 'Not that I noticed. How about where you were?'

'Yeah. We had to change our lunch plans because we went to this National Trust place and they had lovely hexagonal striped parasols set up on this sort of patio thing and then it tipped down for about twenty minutes and we all had to be moved inside. It was still nice, though, because the inside was a sort of converted greenhouse thingy… Oh, what do you call them? One of those things you always say Mum liked.' Dammit, she thought. More distracting emotions.

'A conservatory?'

She was really struggling now. 'Yeah. That's it. And they had all these plants growing inside like grape vines and orange trees and even an apple…'

Vic could have kicked herself. Why couldn't she just have asked Dad if he'd had a nice day and then gone straight off for her shower? Now she had said the very word she had been trying to prevent him saying! She braced herself and, sure enough, the dog next door set up a terrific row of yaps and yelps.

'Do you know?' said Dad, 'That thing hasn't barked all day long. I was wondering why I managed to get so much done... Where are you going?' he added, as Vic suddenly stood up.

Vic had to think very quickly. It had crossed her mind more than once that she ought to prepare for such a moment with a handy excuse for her actions, but she had never got beyond that idea. Now she had to think on her feet. 'I'm going to put the washing line whirligig up and make sure it's all clean. I want to wash a top for tonight,' she said, hastily stepping out of the porch and pulling the door firmly shut behind her to discourage him from following. She just hoped he wouldn't look out of any windows that might give him a view of something he shouldn't see. By luck, the whirligig was actually lying on its side on the second terrace, which would also make a pretty good description of Apple himself. Vic did not actually notice him at first because she was scanning the garden for a standing figure which might be visible from the house and need some explaining. Only as she stooped to lift one of the washing-line arms up so she could continue her pretence by wiping it did she see a bundle of twigs which oughtn't to be there and which she suddenly realised *wasn't* a bundle of twigs. At least, it wasn't *just* a bundle of twigs. It was Apple, and he seemed to be sleeping where he lay, against a shrub between the top wall of this terrace and the patio by the house. Then he made a slight movement and looked at her and something told her was lying down because he couldn't stand up.

'Are you alright?' she asked, impelled to move towards him to help, but unable to do so because she was sure Dad was looking out of the sun lounge.

There was no reply, though Apple was looking at her. Maybe he doesn't know I'm speaking to him, she thought. 'I can't talk properly,' she explained. 'I think someone's looking.'

Apple continued to gaze at her but said nothing. 'Are you alright?' she asked again, remembering to start wiping the next part of the washing line. There was still no reply so she made an elaborate pantomime of lifting the whole thing up, examining it carefully and laying it down again, only this time with the top near to Apple. Now she could kneel down and finish her job and get closer to her visitor.

'Are you alright?' she asked for a third time.

Down close she could hear that he was actually speaking, but very faintly. 'Feel… strange…' came the reply.

'Strange?' she repeated.

'Dry.' he offered.

For some reason, Vic guessed that he was not actually asking for a drink. 'I still don't think I understand,' she said, helplessly.

'Something's missing,' he tried to explain. 'Nothing's coming into me.'

'Coming into you? You're missing something?' she asked. Then something occurred to her. I'm missing something, too, she thought. Or rather, someone. And I've been trying to forget it by not thinking about it. And that doesn't work.

If there had been the time, she would probably have burst into tears right there. But Apple, in a state of collapse, obviously needed immediate attention.

'Drying up inside,' he went on, still saying things that could as easily have applied to Vic.

Hoping no-one was looking out over the garden, she put a hand out and touched him. He did feel different. As if he would snap if she put any pressure on him. Last time she had touched him he had felt brittle but not this bad.

'I wish I could stop and help, but we're supposed to be somewhere else very soon. It's quite possible someone will come along in a minute. If I get you to the woodstore, do you think you will be alright?'

'Probably,' came the reply.

'We'll have to risk it,' she said. 'Look, I'm going to pick up the washing line and take it up to the patio where it's supposed to be. Try to get round the other side of me from the house and we'll just have to hope no-one looks out.'

Vic's plan was based on the notion that someone looking out of the window might confuse the arms of the whirligig with the bundle of animated branches beyond her. In reality, she realised, this was the sort of half-baked ruse which worked in stories but in real life her only real hope was that no-one would be looking out. With her sudden decision to sort out the whirligig and the dog still barking its head off she knew this was highly unlikely. So she took a deep breath and they began their manoeuvres.

And their luck held because no-one did happen to be looking out of a window, or if anyone did they didn't notice anything unusual.

Just about at the end of his strength from their exertions, Apple staggered through the door which she yanked open as she went past, and as she stuck the whirligig in the hole set in the patio she saw him disappear among the wood. He seemed to fall as he went but when she paused to shut the door again on her way into the house she could see nothing but a confused pattern of shadows among the planks.

Suddenly, at the end of a refreshing day with her grandparents, Vic now felt herself terribly drained. The artificial conversation with her father and yet another emotional encounter with Apple left her in no state to do anything other than go to her room and get ready for a shower. Fortunately, luck continued to favour her as Dad was on the phone; presumably speaking to Grandpa about the meal arrangements. While he was occupied, she went straight up to her room. If her luck really was in, he wouldn't notice that she hadn't really washed and dried any clothes for this evening.

He didn't. The next person she saw was Fish who dashed in, told her that they were expected at the hotel at seven o'clock and, yes, his day had been very good – which she could tell anyway by the way he seemed almost to be "glowing". Then he was gone, to have his shower, and when they all met at the foot of the stairs twenty-five minutes later nothing else mattered except hurrying up because they were nearly late.

When they reached the bottom of the hill they found that the metal barrier wasn't the only thing making it awkward to get out onto the road. A huge coach had been parked across the entrance to the footpath and they had to squeeze alongside it before they could walk along to the hotel entrance. Once out, they discovered that the reason it was parked there was because there was another equally large one parked between it and the gateway to the hotel car park. Grandpa was standing in the porch.

'The trippers are in,' he said. 'We only just managed to book a table. They've used up one hundred and twenty places for this lot. Hello Romeo,' he said to Fish.

'Hello Grandfather Time,' replied Fish, light-heartedly. He must be clicking with this girl, thought Vic.

'Well, come in all of you, or your Granny will have drunk all the hotel's gin!' laughed Grandpa, turning and starting back into the hotel. Grandma was indeed finishing off a gin and tonic and gratefully accepted the offer of another as Dad went to buy a round of drinks. "To clear the palate for the meal", as he put it. Grandma and Fish started chatting happily while she went with Dad and Grandpa to choose a drink. Once she had decided on Cranberry juice and fizzy water she went and sat down again.

'Hello, Sunshine,' came a voice from beside her. 'How's the orchard search?'

It was the waiter who had shown her the photographs last time they were here. He had a good memory for conversation.

'Is this your daughter? he asked Grandma, which made her smile. 'She didn't tell me you were coming down here for a holiday too.'

Grandma always made a point of getting to know people by name wherever they went and had evidently made his acquaintance already because she said, 'You've been watching too many films, Reg. Flattery doesn't work with me! We just decided to come and see what they were getting up to on their holidays. My husband's idea.'

'That's nice,' he said. 'Are you having a meal here?'

'We are.'

'Well, try the plaice. It's on the menu as "Local Fish" and I know the man who catches it. He says it's excellent just now.'

'That sounds good. Hope there's still some left when they've finished serving the trippers.'

'Oh, don't worry. We give them a set meal. Roast Beef or Vegetarian Lasagne tonight, I think.'

'Lasagne,' said Grandma. 'That's what my granddaughter's mother used to make.' Then, as if suddenly remembering that Vic had actually come back from the bar, she hesitated. She needn't have worried. Vic had seen Grandpa and her Dad coming back with the drinks and she wasn't listening. Reg, sensitive as ever, let the conversation drop, reminded them all about the plaice and went about his business.

Grandpa only put his drink down long enough to look at his watch. 'We'd better take these drinks through,' he said, picking it up again. 'The table's booked for this very minute.'

They went out of the bar and along a dusty, wood-panelled hallway until they reached an archway leading into a sort of lounge area made up of groups of upholstered benches clustered around small low tables, each partitioned off behind painted glass panels. Grandpa led them through and Vic's Dad pointed out how special the light was. Huge plate glass windows allowed the full brightness of the setting sun to enter the room and the painted panels created patches of colour in it. People were eating light meals in some of the alcoves and Vic thought it looked a nice place to eat. However, Grandpa led them on through it and into a narrow room which felt like an old-fashioned tea shop, with tables at right-angles to the windows and cutlery cabinets against the facing wall. Apart from the door they had come in, there was a partition door which was closed but which could not entirely shut out the sound of the day-trippers, who were evidently eating on the other side.

There were no waiters or waitresses around but Dad suggested they take the table at the end as it was the only one set for more than four people.

As soon as they had sat down a cheery waitress with platinum blonde hair came through a door in the wood panelling which none of them had noticed.

'MacDonald?' she asked, picking up a note pad from a table by the partitioning and ticking off their name on a list. 'My name's Ceris. I'll be looking after you tonight.'

'Will you be doing any more magic for us?' asked Dad and, when she seemed not to understand, he added. 'Your appearance from round the corner. I would never have guessed there was a door there.'

Vic could tell that Grandpa was about to tell them all about the construction of such doors but Ceris, practised in the art of taking orders and not getting too involved, got in first.

She smiled. 'No, that's the last trick. Unless you count feeding the five thousand,' and she inclined her head towards the noise from the other side of the partition.

Fish leaned towards Vic and started to say, 'It's a Bible story...'

'I know. I'm not stupid,' she hissed.

Ceris ignored the little local difference with the ease of someone who has witnessed many in the line of her duty. 'Look,' she said, addressing the three grownups, 'Don't let me rush you, but we are a bit pushed with all the extra people. If I give you the menu now and take your orders for Starters and drinks, I can get the kitchen staff to make a prompt start. I've got a feeling things will get a bit slow soon.'

Usually, Grandpa and Grandma's behaviour in restaurants was absolutely predictable. The former ate whatever was put in front of him, but quickly, not seeming to notice the flavour or the texture; the latter had a very small appetite, possibly as a consequence of being a smoker, yet she would examine each dish as if she were actually going to eat more than half of it, and complain about the slightest thing. On top of that, Grandpa tended to be unaware that restaurant staff were busy employees and he would try to engage them in lengthy conversation as if they were friends who had stopped at the table to say "Hello". Grandma would always stare grimly as he spoke to, or rather lectured, waiters and waitresses, and eventually a sharp "Doug", spoken with a tone of disapproval reminiscent of Miss Jean Brodie would render him sheepishly silent for a moment, long enough for his involuntary interlocutor to make their escape. So far today, things were different. 'That will be just fine,' Grandma said with a smile, taking half of the proferred menus and passing them along her side of the table.

They all ordered quickly – apart from Grandma, of course, who never ate starters – and Dad selected some wine for him and Grandpa and the most expensive Italian fizzy water Vic had ever seen, and Ceris disappeared through what Dad was now calling "The Secret Door". When Ceris brought the drinks, Dad gave in to Fish's request to be allowed a glass of wine when Grandpa surprisingly added his voice in favour and then revealed why by proposing a toast, "To young love", which Fish had to put up with because it was Grandpa who had supported him having the drink in the first place!

Dad put his glass back down and said, 'Right, that's the Grandson-baiting out of the way. Tell us about your day in the Welsh hinterland.'

Fish turned his head towards Vic, and everyone jumped when she barked at him, 'I know what it means!!' Adding 'Only joking!' as he started to protest that he had not been about to explain "hinterland" to her. Smiles and laughter quickly followed – especially from Dad, who recognised his own sense of humour in his daughter.

'So,' Dad repeated. 'What did you do today? So far, all I've heard about from Vic is your eating arrangements. Did you do the Invasion Trail?'

'We certainly did,' said Grandpa, 'And Victoria very kindly put up with going to one or two places she had already been to with you.'

'But we did find the house where the farmer's wife trapped some of the soldiers. At least we think we did, because no-one answered when we knocked on the front door to ask.'

'Very embarrassing,' muttered Grandma. 'He took us all the way up this muddy track, we nearly got stuck in mud part of the way along, and then he knocked on the front door of the first cottage we came to. It's a good job no-one was in.'

'Was there no sign at the start of the track?' asked Dad.

'How do you mean?' replied Grandpa.

'Well, you know, tourist information of some sort, to let people know they are near a significant local heritage site.'

'Come on, Dad,' Fish put in. 'You always expect these things to be totally organised. But the tapestry is still only the hobby of a few keen local amateurs. Their leaflets are still home-produced off a typewriter and a photocopier.'

'Don't knock the hard work of the enthusiast,' Dad replied. 'Anyway, it's not that hard to put up a few signs.' Then Vic interrupted.

'We did get into the walled garden.'

This successfully derailed Dad from his previous train of thought. 'You lucky dogs!' he exclaimed. 'What was it like?'

'Oh, you wouldn't like it. It's not been fully restored yet.'

There was a slightly strained pause, then Fish, himself the most recent victim of a bit of teasing, noticed the glint in Vic's eye and hooted with laughter. 'She got you, Dad!' and they all collapsed in giggles once more while Fish pressed home his advantage. '"Fifteen-All", as they say in the tennis, I think!'

Vic wondered whether the torment of her father was going a bit far but she could see that it suited Fish, whose romantic involvements could so easily have become the butt of everyone's banter. And Dad didn't seem to mind at all. In fact, he raised his glass and said, 'Touché!' while waiting for them all to calm down and tell him what he wanted to hear. Then the Starters arrived. As Ceris put them on the table, Vic realised what a good mood Dad really must be in. He had let one of his pet hates go unmentioned: the word "Starters" would normally get him going on about how common the expression sounded; how it was a sad reflection on the English that they discarded a term like "Hors d'oeuvre" just because they had such trouble with foreign languages; and, especially, how it proved that the English were a sad bunch who didn't understand good food if they could give a meal's first course a name that made it sound like someone firing a pistol at the start of a race. Vic knew the whole script, but today he had let it pass and was now adding his Main Course order to the list Ceris had compiled from all the others, while tucking into his "Starter" without comment. When Ceris had gone, Grandpa and Grandma began telling them all about the walled garden.

Although a mouthful of food was not something he would normally allow to get in the way of talking, Grandpa let his wife tell most of the story while he tucked in. She was more on Dad's wavelength in these conversations and she was happily telling him about the beautifully ramshackle place. Vic, who took after her Grandfather in his respect, devoured her prawn cocktail in about four quick mouthfuls, and then joined in.

'The wall goes everywhere, up and down the hillside, and it looks like it's made out of any bit of stone or brick they could find,' she said.

'It's *very* old. There are branches actually growing through it in places and some of it is so overgrown you have to walk on several metres to find whether it continues.'

'Tell him about the pool.'

'Oh, yes! The place is so full of untrimmed bushes and knee-high grasses that you end up thinking it's all just a neglected wilderness, but right at the bottom there is a huge plant that looks like massive rhubarb.'

'That's probably Gunnera. It's such an impressive plant I can remember the first time I ever saw it. I was with a friend from my Youth Club days. That's forty years ago!'

'Indeed!'

'The pool, Grandma.'

'Yes! Well, you know those big Victorian paintings of palaces and temples and the like? The ones where everyone's skin is like alabaster and you can see every vein in the marble architecture? Of course you do. Well, right at the bottom, almost covered by the plant…'

'The Gunnera.'

'Yes, that. Well, right there, just as you think you're just going to get a view of nothing more than completely neglected waste ground, there's a pool, perfectly oval, stone lined, with four sets of steps leading down into it. It's obviously someone's attempt to create something that looks like Ancient Rome.'

'But it has no water in it,' put in Vic. 'There's actually a plug hole in the bottom like the ones in our baths, only about a foot across.'

'What sort of condition is the pool in?'

'About as good as you could expect. The stone is beautifully dressed and apart from bits of branch and leaf mould it's lovely.'

Unlike the "hinterland" moment, this time Vic turned to Fish with a question on her lips, but he anticipated it and said, ' "Dressed" means that the stone has been cut and smoothed so the blocks fit properly together and the surface isn't unpleasant to touch.' Then he added, 'I have my uses,' which was one of Mum's expressions.

As if realising this could collapse the mood, Dad broke in almost too enthusiastically. 'Fantastic!' he exclaimed, sounding too keen and yet also really sorry not to have been there during all these discoveries. It was a knack he had developed of late. 'We'll have to make time to go back there, won't we?' he said, looking at Fish and Vic. They nodded and he went on. 'Were there many other people there?'

'Not a soul,' said Grandpa. 'But it is in an awkward place to visit. If Victoria hadn't told us it was on the brow of that hill we would have shot straight past with nowhere to turn until much further down the road. Not much chance of people who don't know about it stopping.'

Ceris came back for their dishes. 'I'm afraid things have slowed down a bit in the kitchens,' she said apologetically. 'Could be ten or fifteen minutes before the next course.'

'That's OK,' said Dad. 'Thanks for telling us.'

Ceris smiled and went away but she was evidently still concerned because two minutes later she came back to the table saying, 'I've just spoken to my manager and he says I'm to offer you the bottle of wine "on the house" because of the delay.'

'That's very kind,' said Grandma.

'If we have another one, will that be free as well?' asked Grandpa.

Ceris was obviously on his wavelength because she just grinned and said, 'Try the whole cellar, why don't you,' the phrase bringing out a musical Welsh lilt in her voice. This made them all laugh and Grandpa went to get his camera to help fill some of the waiting time.

In fact, Ceris's fears of a lengthy delay didn't materialise. By the time Grandpa got back – and it took him over five minutes because he had to put a new film in his ancient camera – dishes of vegetables were being put on the table by another waitress and Ceris herself was bringing their orders. Grandma and Vic had taken the advice of Reg and were eating the plaice. Fish was having duck, which he would always have if it was on the menu, Grandpa was having Beef Something-or-Other and Dad had opted for Mushroom Pilaff because one of his teeth had been aching and he didn't want to bite too hard on it.

The conversation meandered while they ate but sooner or later Dad was bound to ask "The Family Question" as it was known.

'What was your favourite part of the gardens?' he said.

'You already know,' Vic replied.

'You mean the pool?'

'Yes.'

'Ah!' he said. 'I should have guessed.' There was a pause.

'Is everyone allowed to answer?' came Grandma's voice from her left.

'Of course!' said Dad. 'What's your choice?'

'The fruit trees,' she said.

'You didn't mention them before,' said Dad.

'True. But they were interesting. I don't know how old they are, but they are so twisted and covered in lichen that you would think they went back to that invasion. They are probably descendants of original trees from that time, but they look as though can't be very far removed from those ancestors. You know, I don't know how they live and produce for so long. And they looked so dried-up. You wouldn't think they could still produce delicious fruit.'

Grandpa then joined in but Vic didn't hear his choice. Something in what Grandma had just said made her think back to her mysterious visitor: "descendants of original trees" and "dry". Did Apple have "ancestors"? He gave the impression of drying up. No, it made a sort of sense but where was the logic? She was pulled back sharply to the table by an exclamation from Dad. He was holding his mouth.

'There's something hard in my Pilaff!' he said with some consternation. He put out his tongue and, putting his fork down, removed something from the tip. 'Wait a minute!' he went on. 'It looks like...' he made a motion with his mouth as if moving his tongue around. 'It's my filling!' he said.

'It's enormous!' said Fish.

'You should feel the cavern it's left in my tooth!' replied Dad.

'Does the tooth hurt?' Grandma asked.

Dad tried a small mouthful of food. 'No,' he said. 'Let me have some of that water, please, Vic. That's usually a good test.' He sipped some of the cold, fizzy liquid. 'Still nothing. Maybe I'll survive without an emergency visit to a dentist. Funnily enough I have got an appointment for the week after we get back. That's never much fun but it's even worse to interrupt a holiday with a medical issue.'

'What are you going to do with filling then, Dad?' asked Fish.

'I think I'll start a rock garden. Lean back Doug.' When Grandpa had complied, Dad flicked the filling with his thumb, straight out of the window and into a flower bed.'

Everyone fell about laughing once again and Grandpa complimented Dad on a flicking technique he presumed he had learned from the kids he taught.

'No,' laughed Dad. 'It's just a natural talent.' A comment which for some reason sent Grandma into such fits that she had to blow her nose when the laughing had stopped. Grandma always laughed about odd things.

She had just recovered her composure when Fish made a remark about what a good choice Dad had made to have soft food and with everyone in a laughing mood they were all set off once again.

Eventually, the giggles stopped. 'I think we've just about used up our amusement quota by now,' said Fish, as they finished off their main courses. But he spoke too soon. They ordered dessert and Dad exercised self-control once again, not commenting on "dessert", which he always said was far better than "pudding", which sounded like something from a school canteen. Ceris took the order but, by the time it was ready to be served she was busy in the other room and another waitress brought them instead. Grandma was having lemon meringue pie with custard and the waitress said, as she put it down, 'You're lucky. It's the last helping.' Her words distracted Grandma and she looked at the waitress to thank her. When she looked back from the waitress's receding figure, everyone else was quiet. 'What is it?' she asked, and looked down at her bowl. For some reason she caught on immediately. They had all noticed that the lemon meringue pie was not the most artistic culinary presentation ever to have graced a dining table. In fact, it was broken in two and upside down. She just had time to say, 'Well, I'm sure it will taste just the same,' before the entire table collapsed yet again in helpless giggles.

Coffee was a relatively quiet experience after all that, mainly because they split up – Dad, Vic and Grandpa going off for a game of snooker while Fish and Grandma sat in the lounge and divided their time between a football match on TV and chat about Fish's girlfriend. He trusted her not to make silly remarks.

When the others had finished their games they came into the lounge and Fish asked, 'What are we all doing tomorrow?'

'Well,' said Dad, 'The weather forecast is excellent so, although it's a Saturday we're planning on going to the beach. Are you joining us?'

'Yes,' Fish replied. 'Sarah is working both shifts, and her Dad wants her to go shopping with him in between, so I was not planning on seeing her until mid-evening.' He paused, but nobody said anything, least of all Vic who was listening to him to see how long he could keep talking without abbreviating a word. He continued. 'I suppose we had better all be away to our beds, then. The bay will be busy on a Saturday, so we will need to make an early start.'

'Well, you can go and save us a space,' said Grandpa.

'It is a bit more busy than that,' Fish began again, but Dad held up his hand.

'I've told him,' he said. 'But he says he has a contingency plan. Don't ask what it is. It's either a secret or the details are still being worked on.'

'OK,' said Fish. 'Still, *we will* have to get up early, so we had better head up that hill, especially as you will probably have to spend an hour or so getting some food ready for tomorrow.'

'No he won't,' said Grandpa, while Vic marvelled at Fish's ability to talk so correctly without sounding odd. 'That's part of my plan. Your Grandma and I will deal with it. You just go and relax on the beach. We'll be there by midday.'

'OK,' said Dad. 'Time to go, methinks,' and he leant over and gave Grandma a kiss on her cheek. Vic did the same and thanked her once again for the day out.

'Enough of that,' said Grandpa, who loved doing things for people but hated anything that remotely seemed like soppiness. 'Get yourselves off now and let us aged ones get away to our beds.'

'Get away with yourself!' said Grandma. 'You know fine well you'll still be awake in two hours' time, flicking through books or checking what's on the TV or radio, just like your grandson.'

Dad ushered Fish and Vic out and back up the hill. 'You know what they're like,' he said, once they were outside. 'They could be there for hours But at least if we're gone they won't be able to blame us for keeping them up!'

When they got home it was nearly eleven o'clock and at least one of them was quite obviously tired from spending long days with family and friends.

'You get yourselves off to bed and I'll set the breakfast table,' said Dad.

Vic came downstairs half an hour later because she thought she had heard the door of the woodshed banging.

She couldn't investigate because Dad had settled with a book, so she made a feeble excuse about needing a drink and went back to bed. There was no more noise anyway and she guessed it must have been Dad closing the porch doors.

10

SATURDAY

Hotel life, even just one evening of it, had its effect. Fish, Vic and even their father all slept very sound and woke later than anticipated the next day. Dad, with a tone of annoyance directed mainly at himself for failing to notice the alarm, announced that they only had half an hour to get a bite of breakfast and stuff the car with whatever they might need for the beach. Give-or-take a couple of minutes they managed his deadline, mainly because Grandpa had removed the need for them to do any major food preparation and they ended up setting off more-or-less at the intended time. Even so, Dad, as usual, fretted that they might not find a quick parking place. Fish chatted away as if he didn't have a care in the world. Vic quietly wondered whether she should have checked for any mysterious happenings before they had come out, but she knew that would have meant some odd behaviour on her part which, given that time was tight, would almost certainly have aroused annoyance, if not suspicion. Mercifully, again with no food to prepare, no-one had so much as mentioned fruit, let alone apples, and the dog had been totally silent. Invisible, in fact, which, apart from Dad oversleeping, was the only remotely strange thing she noticed.

There was something for each of them in their arrival at the beach.

There was a queue, which meant that Dad's fretting hadn't been a waste of his energy. Luckily, it was only a queue of early arrivers just like themselves, so it was moving, and they found themselves in the largely empty car park within five minutes.

Vic discovered that her diary had somehow ended up among the paraphernalia they had thrown into the car and, as she had neglected it for a couple of nights that would give her something to do.

Fish switched on the telephone while they queued, in case Grandpa had sent any messages. Instead, he discovered one for him. He wouldn't say what it said, let alone who it was from, but he had a silly grin on his face for some time after. When Vic and Dad later found a quiet moment without him in earshot they agreed that Sarah must have sent the message. They said nothing further to each other about it, but whereas Dad seemed quite pleased that nice things were happening to Fish, Vic was in two minds.

She spent most of the morning putting this feeling down in writing. After a couple of hours her diary contained just about every imaginable angle on what was happening to her: thinking about Mum; being pleased that Dad seemed quite happy; feeling glad that Fish was even happier; wondering whether she could share her experiences with Apple with anyone; recognising that it was too odd to share with Dad – unless she started to feel threatened – and wondering whether Fish would be available enough to be an audience for her feelings. This last thought was to be answered before the end of the day.

While she lay on the beach, alternately writing and pausing to shift herself or the parasol, Dad and Fish spent a lot of time in the water. The weather was wonderful and the sea just right. It took their minds right away from wondering what Grandpa and Grandma were up to.

They really only started to think about it when they had eaten the small number of what Dad called "nibbles" and were still feeling hungry – especially Dad and Fish, who had the sort of appetite you only get from hours in the sea. Some people would have made their way to the nearest café, ice cream van or whatever and risked spoiling their appetite. Dad, however, could be annoyingly fussy about such things and he would not let them eat.

'Grandpa's bringing lunch, you know that,' he said, at least three times. 'Let's not spoil it.'

When he sensed that Dad was about to say the same thing a fourth time, Fish had actually walked all the way up to the car park, and further, going right out of sight, in order to see if there was any sign of them. Then, as he was half-way back, and steeling himself to insist they had something proper to eat, they arrived.

A taxi pulled up right on the edge of the beach and out jumped Grandpa. This led to a rather comical moment because Dad and Vic stood up and waved to him, and Fish, who was walking towards them, waved back. They kept on waving because Grandpa hadn't spotted them yet. Fish, who had seen them, just mouthed rude remarks because he thought they were messing about, being stupid, or both.

It did eventually dawn on him that they might be waving for some other reason so he looked behind him and spotted Doug and Mary. Another comical waving interlude then took place until they saw him walking back up the beach to meet them.

When he came back with them, he was carrying Grandpa's battered old cool box, Grandpa had a couple of bags and Grandma held some foldaway beach seats like miniature deckchairs.

Dad and Vic, who had found the whole waving episode highly amusing, carried on waving after the other three had arrived. Fish got the joke and grinned. Grandpa looked round to see who they might be waving to, and Grandma told them to stop being "blithering idiots".

Quite ignoring the fact that any delay had been his fault, Grandpa said, 'Well, open the box! We're starving you know.'

Dad had long since got used to how Grandpa talked to people. Vic had once asked Dad why he was rude and Dad had just said, 'He's not rude. Just direct. Anyway, if you think *that's* rude, you should have heard him thirty years ago when I first met him!' But he would not elaborate.

When the box was opened, it contained a real seaside treat. Greasy paper was all they could see, but the smell was unmistakeable: fish and chips!

There was no choice. Haddock and chips five times. Usually, when the family had takeaway food they each chose something different, but today they were being treated and, anyway, at least three of them were so hungry they would have eaten the proverbial horse. In any case, that special sensation that comes from things like hot, greasy food by the seaside removed any chance of fussiness. They all grabbed what was on offer and went about the process of getting food to mouth with their fingers in the shortest possible time.

'What this really calls for is a nice drop of wine,' said Dad wistfully.

'True,' said Grandpa. 'In fact, I nearly bought some but, knowing what a snob you are on the subject I decided not to.'

Vic marvelled yet again at Dad's willingness to let a jibe just slide past him. All he said was, 'Well, as it happens, I am in a position to remedy that,' and, with that look on his face which always appeared when a conversation matched his ideal script, 'Because I did, just in case.' With a flourish, he dipped into his own bag and withdrew a bottle of what had to be good quality French wine – the only kind he drank.

Grandpa's eyes lit up. 'That's my boy!' he exclaimed, in a tone as admiring as his previous utterance had been annoying, and gratefully accepted a glassful. 'Glasses, too!' he said, with mock surprise. He knew that Dad's fussiness about wine extended to what he would use to drink it and he loved to wind him up about it. Just as he had all holiday, Dad just smiled, almost contentedly, poured a glassful for Grandma and one for himself, planting it in the sand "to breathe", as he put it, and returning to his feast.

'What gave you the idea, Grandpa?' Vic asked, as they divided the portions up and helped themselves to sachets of salt, pepper and vinegar.

Before Doug could answer, Fish said, "Er, what about Vic and me?"

"What about you?" asked Dad, deadpan.

"Er, we're thirsty too. At least I am." He glanced at Vic.

'Look in his bag,' said Vic, once again wondering who was the older of the two of them.

As Dad allowed a grin to spread over his face, Fish took a look and brought out two bottles of a local sparkling cordial.

As he did so, Vic said, 'Don't you want any wine? You had some at the hotel.'

'Not now,' said Fish, in a tone that managed to make it sound like a reply and an instruction all in one. 'I need my thirst quenched.' Later, he would take the chance to share with Vic that Grandpa, affable in the restaurant, was quite capable of becoming quite "shirty" as he put it about things like teenagers drinking alcohol in a place as public as a beach. 'You haven't answered Victoria's question, Grandpa,' he added, creating a neat reversion of subject at the same time as making sure the Grandparents' version of their names was used.

'What question?'

'The food,' Fish added.

'Oh,' said Grandpa, directing his response to Vic. 'I didn't want your brother pining on his day away from the chippy,' he said, with a broad grin.

Dad and Vic glanced at Fish, but he was smiling too.

'Away with your blether!' said Grandma. 'It's what there was.'

"Chalk and Cheese" was what Dad always called Doug and Mary. It was at moments like this that Vic knew what he meant. 'Come on Grandpa. Tell us how you did it,' she said.

'I thought no-one would ever ask,' he said, beaming.

'We'll wish no-one had ever asked,' added Grandma, drily. 'Get on with it, Douglas!' she added. It was the way of the family to cause delay or distraction one minute and then accuse everyone else of being the problem.

'Well, we bought them in St.David's,' he began. Dad cut in immediately.

'No, Doug. Not one of your bits and pieces anecdotes. We want to know about this from the moment you had the idea. Come on. Tell us the full story.'

'I'm not taking hours over every little detail,' Grandpa replied. 'You may like to ramble on with your stories but some of us like to get to the point!'

Vic sensed one of the traditional family arguments brewing. Luckily, Fish made one of his strange remarks which always took people's minds off whatever they were about to shout or sulk about.

'I read somewhere that the talkative person is often considered to be just a chatterer. But on the rare occasion that a taciturn person opens their mouth, the one thing they say could be rubbish too!'

There was silence for a moment. Grandma sighed at the sound of what she would call "More blether". Dad grinned. Grandpa, who tended to stop listening if a sentence was more than six or seven words long, pulled one of his blank faces and continued as if Fish hadn't even spoken. 'Do you remember those charabancs at the hotel last night?' He didn't pause for a reply, which was just as well because they had all started on their fish and chips before they became cold and enjoying that specially delicious flavour of hot food in the open air.

Grandpa carried on. 'Well, when we'd got rid of you I went down to the car for my map and one of the coach drivers was there. I told him I drove buses when I was in the army and we chatted for a bit... What are you all giggling about? Am I not allowed to talk to people?' No-one replied. Grandpa's chats were a family legend. He always seemed to have done what the people he talked to were doing and he usually ended up telling people a better way to do their job. He went on. 'Well, he told me that the party was staying in the hotel annexe for the night and they would be off in the morning after breakfast to visit St. David's. And that's what gave me the idea.'

He stopped and stuffed his mouth with enough fish and chips to make up for the fact that everyone had managed at least three mouthfuls already. But when he had swallowed it all he didn't resume.

Dad was the bravest. 'Er, Doug. You haven't told us the whole story.'

Grandpa had been doing very well by the family's standards. It was very unusual for a whole anecdote to be told before someone else interrupted or even completely changed the subject and left it forever unfinished. Numerous family misunderstandings and legends had been built around this habit.

'Oh, yes,' Grandpa replied, searching his memory.

'The coach to St. David's,' murmured Vic.

His eyes brightened. Lucky I'm this week's favourite granddaughter, thought Vic as he went on.

'Well, it gave me an idea. If he had a couple of spare places we could hitch a ride and then come down to the beach and meet you without the worry of queuing for a parking place.'

'I don't know how you had the nerve,' sighed Grandma, with a look on her face reflecting a lifetime of such adventures.

'But how were you thinking of getting to the beach?' asked Fish, wiping some batter grease from his chin.

'All in good time,' said Grandpa, with a wicked grin. 'I was instructed to tell the story from the beginning.' He looked at Dad, who grinned back.

'Lovely Fish,' Doug,' Dad said, refusing to be wound up. He had years of practice at this.

'Good. Not cheap you know,' said Grandpa. Dad ignored this one too and Grandpa went on, happier now that the conversation was more like what he was used to. 'Well, we had breakfast this morning, and Mary asked me the same question as Fisher, and I said we could take a taxi to the beach. That way we could by-pass the queue. That's the story, really. We had a lovely ride with all the old dears in the coach, strolled around St. David's for an hour or so, found a taxi, which took us to the chip shop and then here. The cool box did most of the hardest work!'

There was a pause while they continued to enjoy their food, and then he added: 'And you can give us a lift back to the hotel!'

Very unusually for him, Fish finished his food first. If you didn't include Gran, thought Vic, but as she always chose a small helping, or just left food unfinished, she didn't really count. Telling his story had slowed Grandpa down, Dad had been savouring his wine and Vic was just a slow eater. Fish, therefore, was given money by his Grandmother and went to go and get whatever he could for dessert from the beach café. A couple of minutes later, with no more talking or rude comments aimed at Dad, Grandpa finished too and went up to help him. They returned with ice creams and some surprisingly good coffee. Even Dad, who was very fussy about such things, found it drinkable. When they had tidied up their rubbish, Grandpa lay back for his customary nap, Grandma and Fish settled down to another of their chats and Dad said to Vic, 'Come on little sunshine, let's go for a walk.'

They chose a route which followed the shallow waves as they lapped across the bright sand as the tide turned. This took them to the rocks at the southern end of the beach. They didn't talk much, just pointing out interesting objects in the sea and the pools. Then they clambered up the headland until they found a bench overlooking the bay and sat down to scan the scene and spot the others back up towards the middle of the beach.

'How do you think Fish is enjoying the holiday?' asked Dad suddenly. Vic didn't answer immediately, partly because it seemed like an unusual kind of question to ask, and partly because there was an unfamiliar tone in his voice which she couldn't quite identify.

Trying to catch the right tone for a reply, she said, 'I think he's having a great time.' Then, after a pause. 'Why?'

'Oh, no reason really. I thought he was too. Is it the girlfriend, do you think?'

'Well, she's certainly not making him *unhappy*!' she laughed.

APPLE

'No!' He laughed too. He was quiet for a moment, then he seemed to take a deep breath before saying, 'He's been invited to spend some time with her.'

'What do you mean?' she asked, confused by Dad's choice of words.

'Well, go off on a trip,' he explained.

Vic wondered what the big deal was. What she said was: 'That's not a problem, is it? They've been out for a day together already.'

'Not like that,' Dad said. 'More than one day.' When Vic said nothing he went on: 'Apparently Sarah's Dad hasn't been able to have a proper holiday this year but he has managed to arrange a some time off work so he can take his daughter off for a few days before he loses her to art school.'

'Oh,' said Vic, and then, beginning to understand why Dad had wanted to take her off on a walk, she added, 'Where are they going?'

'Oh, not all that far. He's got a caravan up in the hills somewhere a few miles north of here.'

'Oh,' she said again, this time adding nothing.

Dad waited a moment in case she was going to say something more. When she didn't he went on. 'We had a long talk about it because, well, because we are on a family holiday and he wasn't sure if it was fair on you and me... And to be honest, neither was I.'

'How long is he going for?' she asked, abruptly.

'Well,' he said, hesitantly. 'We don't know for sure that he is. That's why I'm talking to you.'

'That's not fair,' she said, slightly more aggressively than she intended, and then, before he could say anything more,

202

'I mean, you can't be asking me to decide what Fish does.'

Dad understood. 'No you're right,' he agreed. 'But that isn't really why I'm talking to you about it.'

'So why are you?'

He paused. 'I suppose I'm trying to be fair. I mean, how would you feel if I *didn't* ask you?'

Vic, thinking about the sudden appearance of a gap in the middle of her holiday, didn't know how she would feel, and she said so.

'No, of course you don't. To be honest, neither do I, and when he told me it seemed to me that if I said "Yes", he would leave us with a different kind of holiday to manage, but if I said "No" we would have to manage his reaction while Sarah was away. So I told him that no matter what you and I think, he's got to make the decision. He's not a little boy, remember. He's put plenty into this holiday so far and maybe he deserves a short break.'

Vic knew that Dad reminding her about Fish's efforts over the past week was his way of talking about Mum without actually mentioning her. She had to admit Fish and Dad had both done well on that score. They hadn't been moody; they'd talked with her even when there was a book to read or a television programme on that he liked; they hadn't sulked when Grandpa made his remarks.

'You're right,' she said and, although she didn't notice, a different look came into her father's eye; a look of genuine admiration. He didn't say anything but he was thinking how mature her reaction was. And he was right. It was mature, at least from the outside. Inside, she was feeling different. If anyone had asked her a direct question on the subject at this moment, she wouldn't have known how to put it into words, but the truth was that she had gradually been building up to sharing her peculiar experiences at the holiday home with someone. And that someone was probably going to be Fish. Until now, that is, so she would have to hide it. But she was learning how to do that sort of thing on this holiday.

'Come on,' he said, getting up from the seat. You know Grandma won't want to sit on the beach for ever, and Fish deserves one more swim before we go. In fact, so do I! Race you back!'

Vic raced him back, but her heart wasn't really in it. There were limits to being mature, and she thought she might be reaching them.

Grandpa woke up when they got back and Grandma, who had probably been told what was happening by Fish, told him that he ought to give his granddaughter some time while "the boys" were in the sea. So he threw a Frisbee backwards and forwards with her and then when they noticed Dad and Fish were coming back, she went with him to fetch more hot drinks for them all and an ice cream for her.

When everyone was more or less dry, and warm inside from the drinks as well as outside from the sun, they picked up all their belongings and squeezed themselves into the car, just as Grandpa had planned it.

At the bottom of the hill where the road divided to go up the holiday home or along to the hotel, Dad said 'Shall we take you straight back or would you like to come up to the "Pilot's Cottage"?'

'We'll come to your place,' said Grandpa, before Grandma could say no, as she tended to do. 'I'm going to be cooped up in a hotel soon enough, so let's have some home comforts. Anyway, we'll not see you again until you get home. We'll be leaving early to avoid the traffic.'

Vic's feeling were in turmoil as they reached the house and went down the path. As soon as Grandpa had mentioned going home she had thought of days without Fish. On top of the gloom that brought, going to the house meant more chances of someone saying or doing something which could cause her a problem with Apple. For the next hour or two, sitting in the sun lounge, helping Fish do bits of his jig-saw or having her shower, she was tense and quiet. Fortunately, everyone else put it down to Fish's proposed trip with Sarah and her Dad and no-one said anything. Luckily, no-one mentioned fruit – Grandpa lived on crisps when he wasn't eating his proper meals – and when they eventually went back to the hotel nothing of any consequence had happened.

When he got back from dropping them off at the hotel, Dad decided to do pizza for supper. For most people, pizza was "fast food". Not for Dad. Taking them out of the freezer was as close as he got to what most people did. Adding individually chosen toppings to suit each of them was his next stage. After that, he would make a salad and a specially prepared fresh dressing, devised to go with the flavours of the day's toppings.

At least it gave Vic and Fish some time alone in the lounge.

Fish was silent and Vic had a horrible thought that he might say something all slushy and emotional. She was not going to let that happen. She decided to broach the subject and get it out of the way as an issue.

'So where's Sarah's Dad's caravan, then?' she asked, trying to be matter-of-fact.

Fish was genuinely startled. Looking like a man who had been planning a sentence beginning with 'Look, Sis...' or some other line of the kind you hear in films, he said, 'Oh, it's on a farm at the top end of a valley. About five miles back up the road into town.'

'And there's plenty of room for you in it?'

'Er, well, no. Actually, they've got a tent and I'm sleeping in that.'

There was a break in the conversation while Vic narrowly avoided being choked on the orange juice she was sipping. 'A tent!' she said. 'You've never been camping in your life!'

When Dad came up to join them she was still grinning about the idea of her stay-at-home brother sleeping in a tent for three nights. Dad was pleased to see her apparently happy, but she was still feeling gloomy inside. Again, she cursed herself for being "mature" and wished she could just make a scene and get lots of attention. But it was too late for that.

'The pizza's ready,' Dad said, and disappeared back downstairs ahead of them.

There were two deep-pan pizzas ready, One just had extra green olives on for Vic. Fish's also had green olives as well as slices of some sort of Italian sausage. Dad's featured black olives, capers and anchovies.

'I don't think I can eat the whole of this,' said Vic.

'Don't worry,' said Fish. Dad will finish it off before bedtime.'

Dad grinned. It was a family legend that although he was no heavier than he had been at the age of seventeen

– what he referred to as his "birth-weight" – he seemed to eat as much if not more than anyone else. 'Stress and nervous energy burn it all off,' is what he always said. And that was what he said this time. He also added that there was a James Bond film on the TV that evening and that they could play a game and watch it at the same time. That seemed like a great idea to Vic and Fish and they wolfed the food down before dashing off to set everything up in the lounge while Dad did the washing up.

The evening was a good one, in fact it might have been perfect if Vic hadn't kept wondering what she was going to do without Fish for the next three days. The film was entertaining and they played a game of Pontoon which seemed to go on for ever. In between, Dad ate fruit, without mentioning apples, Fish raided the cupboard for a packet of salted peanuts and Vic had a bowl of cereal smothered in milk and sugar, with sliced banana on top.

When the film was over, Dad said he wanted to watch the highlights of a cricket match. Vic and Fish went off to their respective bedrooms but Vic came back after about twenty minutes and, without saying a word, sat down on the sofa next to Dad and, although she had brought her diary to fill in, took the chance to snuggle up for a bit of warmth and comfort. Fish was still in the house but she was already missing his company.

After ten minutes of cosy boredom watching the cricket her eyelids began to droop and she went off to bed again.

Eventually, even Dad went to bed and the house went dark for the night.

11

SUNDAY

Vic slept for a long time and she wished she hadn't. Fish came and woke her up at nine o'clock because he was about to go out to meet Sarah and her Dad.

'Bye,' was the first thing she heard him say as she turned her head and pushed the covers back a few inches. 'I'm off now,' he added.

'Oh. Bye,' she replied.

'See you on Wednesday,' he said. 'Oh, Dad's out buying a newspaper,' he added.

'Fine,' she said, and rolled over. She heard Fish leaving and wished she had said something more affable. But it was too late. 'Who cares,' she thought. 'I've got enough problems. What does one more matter?'

She didn't know how long she had been dozing but the bang of a door woke her. She sat up sharply, thinking it might be the woodstore door but it was Dad's voice, and not the barking of the dog, that came up the stairs.

'It's me!' he shouted and she embarked on a long process of getting up. She saw no reason to hurry, so she made every stage last as long as possible. Eventually, however, she had to stop trying on different socks, applying various creams and adjusting her hair into a style scarcely different from the one she usually opted for.

As she went downstairs a totally unexpected thought crossed her mind. She had just reached the little landing where the stairs turned down to the front door when she found herself thinking, "I wish Mum was here!" It overwhelmed her and she had to turn and go back upstairs. She sat on her bed and cried, quietly but deeply. Then she stood up and looked out of the window until she thought her face would not give away her emotions. Then she went and washed it all over again, and, eventually, she made the journey downstairs again.

The breakfast table was unoccupied, though it was still set. She could see Dad on all fours in the sun lounge with his huge Sunday paper spread out on the floor as he pored over it.

'Hello,' she said, half-heartedly.

He jumped. 'Don't do that!' he laughed, holding his hand to his chest as if his heart was hurting. 'I'm the one who usually makes people jump when I come into a room. Did I ever tell you about Jo at school?' He could tell from the look on her face that Vic knew about his colleague who would shriek as if being attacked if she didn't notice someone approaching – and somehow she never did – and his voice tailed off. Then he asked, 'Are you ready for breakfast?'

'I'm not very hungry,' she said.

'In that case,' he went on, ' I have just the thing for you.' He went to the fridge and took out some fruit. 'Pink grapefruit!' he said. 'Chilled for the summer.' He sliced it in half and put one part in a bowl where she had sat down. As she made a start on what he thought was the perfect breakfast for a person like her at a time like this, he fetched her a glass of milk and heated up a small cup of coffee for himself. When she had finished the grapefruit a slice of toast miraculously appeared and he sat down opposite her with his coffee while she spread some marmalade on it.

'Did you hear about the bloke who wanted some bread with his breakfast?' he asked.

'No, go on,' Vic replied, trying to sound interested.

'He'd run out, so he had toast instead!'

This fell completely flat but, as Dad was used to having his jokes ignored, he didn't complain. 'What are we going to do today?' he asked her. Vic knew Dad's questions. You had to listen to how he started. There were a whole lot of little throat-clearings and breath-drawings that he used to signal what he really meant. This time it was obvious that he had an idea. She followed his lead.

'I don't mind. What do you want to do?'

'Well,' he said. 'Nothing this morning, because it's gone ten o'clock already and I want to finish my paper, which I should be able to do a bit quicker than usual without Fish stealing pages.' He paused. 'You do know Fish has gone, don't you?'

'Yep!' Vic replied. 'He came in to see me before he went.'

Dad didn't want to go any further with this part of the conversation and he quickly switched back to what he had been planning to say. 'How would you like to go and see some art after lunch?'

Vic was non-committal. 'Might do. Have you found somewhere?' she asked, knowing full well that Dad rarely asked such questions without a plan in mind.

'As a matter of fact I have,' he said, with a grin. 'Did you know there's a studio just down the hill? It's owned by a woman who does wood sculptures.'

Vic just managed to stop herself saying "Applewood". Instead, she said, 'Yeah, I think so.' She was remembering the woman who had put a card through their letter box the first day, when Dad and Fish had been out shopping. She didn't mention that, so he went on.

'So, are you interested?' She hardly needed to reply to that one. Dad knew she would be interested because she was artistic by temperament. Not that anyone in the family seemed to notice. She had a cousin who did flashy portraits of family members that attracted everyone's attention and her creations seemed to find their way to the front of everyone's displays of family memorabilia. However, Vic was probably the most creative member of the family because she liked to make things from unexpected bits and pieces that she gathered. Her output was the opposite of flashy, and Dad regularly had the job of disposing of what was left after she had turned the bits and pieces into genuinely crafted objects. He might complain, but really he thought what his daughter made was wonderful, which they were, even if they didn't end up prominently displayed for the wider family to admire.

'So, after lunch, then?' he said. She nodded. 'What are you going to do before lunch?' he asked.

'Don't know,' she said, getting up to start clearing the table. Dad showed willing by putting away the cereal boxes and then, while Vic completed the job he went upstairs. When he came back down she had finished the washing up and was half way through wiping the table. Dad hung around for a moment, trying to make small talk, but she wasn't in a chatty mood and he drifted off to the sun lounge to resume his safari through the newspaper. Vic dried her hands and went back upstairs where she spent longer than she usually would on washing, brushing her hair and generally getting herself ready for the day. Dad wasn't in the sun lounge when she came back downstairs. She knew he wasn't in what they now referred to, fairly obviously, as the TV lounge because she had gone in to check for leftover cups and plates on the way down. The downstairs toilet door was ajar so she knew that was unoccupied. She looked out of the kitchen window to see if he had gone out to the car. No sign. She found him, eventually, in the garden, comfortably relaxing in a deckchair, deeply absorbed by something in his paper.

It wasn't a hot morning, which was why she hadn't looked in the garden straight away. Years of living with Dad had still betrayed no recognisable pattern to his outdoor activities. He would go out and work in the garden on days when everyone else was huddling round the fires indoors. When the sun was high in the sky and the temperature was soaring, he would stay indoors while everyone else was running around in shorts or swimming costumes. He would go for a walk when it was raining. Only the wind really put him off doing anything. This morning, it was still quite cool, yet here he was, out on the patio, reading.

'Where did you find the deckchair?' Vic asked.

'In the, er, what-do-you-call-it,' he replied, waving his arm towards the place where Apple had ended each of his appearances. He was right. What would you call it?

'It's a sort of shed/cupboard combination,' he went on, 'Just after you come out of the porch on this side.'

'It's a woodstore, isn't it?' she suggested, wondering whether there had been any sign of her mysterious visitor in there for him to notice.

'Well, you could call it that because it was a bit of a struggle to get the deckchair out, and it was wood that was getting in the way. Quite a lot of wood in fact. When I opened the door some of it fell over and got tangled with the garden furniture, so I had to tidy it up after I had extracted the deckchair. I had quite a job getting it all back in place. It was almost as if it didn't want to go back!' He paused. 'Maybe there's a story in that…'

'You always seem to get ideas for stories when we're on holiday,' Vic said.

Dad smiled broadly. 'Shame it's only the odd article or poem that gets published. I'd love to have a proper book in print. Imagine how that would feel.'

'It might happen,' said Vic, joining in with enthusiasm as memories of past holidays flooded back.

'I don't know,' he said, ruefully. 'There's a lot of luck to getting published. It helps if you're already famous, too. Business, you see.'

Vic nodded. In spite of feeling low, it was almost impossible not to get drawn into Dad's conversations. He had this amazing way of weaving together bits and pieces which other people would not see as being connected.

However the day was still quite chilly in spite of the bright sun and she soon wanted to go back indoors. She hit on a ruse.

'Would you like some coffee?' she asked.

'That would be nice,' Dad smiled. He had actually guessed that she was cold but he had wanted to chat as long as possible to compensate for Fish being away. Vic turned and went back in. While she waited for the coffee to heat up she looked idly through the kitchen drawers. Finding nothing of interest there she went into the breakfast area where she noticed that the table had drawers too. In one of them she found a bundle of unused postcards. She tucked them under her arm, picked up Dad's coffee, to which she added a biscuit and went outside.

'Thanks poppet,' said Dad, taking the cup and saucer and putting them down on the ground next to his seat. 'What have you got there?' he added.

'Postcards,' she said.

'I didn't know we had bought more,' he mused.

'We haven't,' she replied. 'I found them in a drawer in the table. They haven't been used. Do you think I could have some?'

'Well, I don't know,' Dad said hesitantly. 'They're not ours. What are they of?'

'They're all local pictures,' Vic said, showing him one or two. 'We could replace any we use.'

'I suppose that would be alright,' agreed Dad. 'Maybe the house owners left them for guests to use.' What he was thinking was that whether they had been or not it would give his daughter something to do. 'Who do you want to send them to?'

'Some of my friends,' she said.

'Good idea,' he said, with a rather forced tone. Vic could tell he was trying desperately hard and forgave him for sounding artificial.

'Have we got any stamps?' she asked.

'Should be some inside my cheque book cover.' Vic looked around quizzically. 'In the pocket of my coat,' he added, and then, when she still seemed uncertain, 'In the cupboard under the stairs.'

'OK. I'll get them on my way up,' she said and went away, leaving Dad to wonder what she meant by "up". The explanation was that Vic had always liked to turn things she did into projects. Most people would have gone indoors, sat at the most convenient table or desk and quickly written out some traditional holiday messages. This wasn't good enough for Vic; even a Vic who was thinking sad thoughts about her Mum; even a Vic who was feeling sore about her brother going off with his new girlfriend in the middle of their holiday. No, Vic had an idea, as usual, and she would pursue it, happy or not. Just like her father, as she would realise one day.

What she had decided to do was to turn her cards into a little story. Each one would contain a "chapter", which could be read individually, but would also fit together with the others to form a complete message. It was really an idea that had occurred to her some time before but this seemed to be her chance, especially as she now had so much time on her hands…

What she now added to the idea was that she would go up to top floor of the house and begin writing her cards there. Then she would go into a different room for each one and work her way down to the sun lounge. Each room would be a "chapter" of her story.

Nearly an hour later, Dad was in the kitchen, thinking about what they could have for lunch when his daughter arrived, looking quite perky, he thought.

'What have you been up to?' he asked, as she sat down at the dining table and spread out her writing materials and cards.

She explained what she had done and Dad smiled with genuine delight. Although he didn't often have the spare time to do such things these days, he could see that Vic had inherited something from him. The difference was that his life was littered with half-completed projects whereas Vic had what his own father called "stick-to-it-iveness" and usually got to the end of anything she began.

When Vic finished recounting her postcard-writing stages he said, 'What? You even wrote one in the upstairs bathroom? I hope you signed off with "Toodle-oo"!'

Vic didn't get it. By the time he had finished explaining that it was an old expression meaning "Goodbye", which he had also learned from his own father, and how it sounded like "To the loo", the joke, if there had been any, was long dead. He changed the subject.

'Do you think you could write the last three in the sun lounge while I...' he began.

The sentence went unfinished. Even before her facial expression began to change, he remembered the lesson he should long since have learned: Vic had to do things "properly". Being in the same room you were writing about was part of the event. She was not even prepared to do the dining area first so he could get on and set the table when she had finished. The kitchen was the next room you went into after coming downstairs and turning into the house rather than out through the front door – she left out the downstairs loo and shower because they were both no bigger than cupboards and didn't "feel" like rooms – so it had to be done next. He worked around her until she mooched off into the sun lounge to seek inspiration for one last card.

She had already decided that this one would explain what she had done so that the person receiving it, who was her best friend Emma, would go and see the others and work her way back through the message.

"So," she began. "As I said in the third card, Fish has been great, UP UNTIL YESTERDAY, when he decided to go off with his girlfriend FOR THREE DAYS. Now I'm here with Dad. He's doing his best, but he's got things he wants to do as well. Anyway, we're off to see an artist's studio after lunch. Oh! Nearly forgot: Having a lovely time. Wish you were all here! Love Vic"

'I wonder if I'm the first person who ever really meant it when they put "Wish you were here" on a postcard?' she mused as she re-read it. When she had finished, she checked one or two of the others, to make sure each one contained a clear enough clue so that each of her friends would know to put them together. Then she tidied up her materials because lunch was now ready. It was somosas and salad. If her friends *had* been there they would have turned up their noses at the spicy, filo-pastry vegetable parcels, but *she* loved them, though not with mayonnaise, which was how Dad and Fish ate them.

When they had finished their lunch, Dad said, 'Is that the time?' He was studying the clock over the kitchen door, which it had taken him most of the week to master. It was a novelty clock with the numbers on in reverse, a fact which had taken him the first few days of the holiday to understand. It had already caused one or two moments of confusion and Dad was now momentarily uncertain of whether they were ahead, behind or bang on time.

'Does it matter?' asked Vic. We haven't made an appointment, have we?'

'Oh, no, not really, no,' replied Dad, which seemed to suggest that he had. 'Haven't you got some cards to post? We might catch the midday collection if we go to the post box first. Anyway,' he added, 'We haven't generated enough dirty plates and stuff to be worth washing up right now. Let's leave it soaking and do it later after we've been out. There might be some tea things to add by then.'

'Alright,' said Vic, cautiously, in case this was some kind of trick. She was not at all used to the washing up being left while they went out. She remembered the mass family holidays when everyone would tumble out of the house in a huge hurry to get somewhere, leaving stuff lying around. And Dad always hated it. But on this occasion he really did turn his back on unwashed dishes and cutlery, went and got ready to go out, and five minutes later they were walking down the hill together. Ten minutes after that they were on their way back up the hill, chuckling over the fact that Dad had forgotten that, as it was Sunday, there was no postal collection.

'I really must be getting old!' he said

'Yes, you are,' replied Vic.

'Thanks! Anyway, you didn't think to point it out to me, so, although I hate to tell you, you're getting old too!'

'I think you mean "older" ', Vic said with mock-feeling.

'Oooh! Twist the knife a bit more won't you!' Dad laughed. 'And here we are,' he added. And he stopped by an old iron gate that was so decrepit that it didn't need opening so much as lifting and carrying because it had obviously been a long time since the hinges and catch had worked smoothly together. Vic actually had to help him close it again as it threatened to fall off the post completely.

When they turned to go up the path the front door was already open and a woman Vic recognised from their first day at the Pilot's Cottage was standing there, grinning. She spoke as if they already knew each other and were just picking up the thread of an on-going chat.

'Ah! That gate!' she exclaimed. 'All my life I have promised myself that I wouldn't turn into one of these people who's always meaning to get things fixed, and here I am, already "one of those people who…" ' she said, putting on a sing-songy voice for the expression.

There was a brief pause as Vic and Dad came up the steep stone steps to her door, then Dad said, 'Hello,' in a voice that sounded almost like he knew the woman. Vic had put the woman's way of addressing them down to a personal characteristic of some sort. Now she was slightly surprised. She was even more surprised when the woman turned to her and said,

'So you must be Vic…' Her voice trailed off as she waited for Vic to confirm her identity, but Vic was turning to her Dad with a "How-does-she-know? You-told-me-we-hadn't-made-an-appointment!" look on her face.

Dad ignored it as best he could. 'Yes,' he said. 'This is Vic. Victoria, really, but only the Grandparents dare call her that!'

While he spoke, the lady was ushering them through the front door, saying 'I promised myself I wouldn't turn into the sort of person who said things like, "You must be…." Makes me sound like someone's great aunt!'

Vic had a feeling that she was having an early introduction to someone's catch-phrase and it distracted her a moment from pursuing her unspoken question. By the time she was ready to say something about it the adults were ahead of her, making their way through into the passageway that led towards the back of the house. They went past two rooms: a lounge and a sort of study, both of which contained wooden sculptures like the ones in the front room window that could be seen from the road. As they went through the kitchen, Vic noticed that the table was set for tea. There were buns on a plate and, although none of the china seemed to match, there were three place settings of cup, saucer, plate and knife.

Dad didn't seem to have noticed. 'If he gets talking the way he can, then I'll have to find a way to let him know that she's expecting guests,' she thought, and then had to hurry up because they were disappearing out of the back door. Through the door she found a semi-circular patio of light brown bricks. It was bordered by a low wall of flint slabs with a gap in the middle from where a path wove through overgrown flower beds across to a long, wooden building. This turned out to be the woman's workshop.

It had a sliding door which she opened to the width of about two people but which could obviously slide much further. The woman noticed Dad looking and said, 'The biggest problem for artists is that we stand in our workshops, absorbed in what we are making, and when we finally step back and look at what we've made we discover it's too big to get through the door!'

'Yes!' agreed Dad. 'Like in that Tony Hancock film… The… er… The…'

'The Rebel,' said Vic.

The lady turned to her. 'I'm impressed. That was a bit before your time, wasn't it?'

'Dad drags us off to see his favourite old films in London,' she said.

'You poor thing!'

'Oh, it's alright. Some of them aren't bad and we go to eat pizza afterwards to make up for it.'

'That's a good deal. By the way, I don't think you know my name. I'm Hannah.'

She held out her hand and Vic shook it. It was a remarkable hand. Her fingers were very slim and long but her grip was exceptionally firm. And the skin was really rough, which Vic guessed was caused by all the wood she handled.

'So,' she said. 'Do you want the grand tour or are you happy just to browse? Vic looked at her Dad, who already seemed to have become absorbed by a large book he had found lying on a long workbench that ran the length of the workshop's back wall. While she still had a nagging suspicion that this had all been prearranged, with her dad it was difficult to decide. When he was at home he tended to be restless, moving from job to job, a sort of permanent multi-tasker, but when out he could easily become so absorbed in something that he would forget who he was with, or they would forget him. It was not unusual for the family to have reached the tea shop of a gallery or stately home, had a drink and browsed the gift shop shelves before he caught up with them, having stood for ages gazing at a painting or a view, or talking to a room steward. She tried to catch his eye, but he was either ignoring her or just typically lost in what he had found. Hannah either sensed what Vic was thinking or would have said something anyway.

'Oh, come on!' she said, crisply. 'Your Dad's found something he likes, so come and have a look at some of my rejects round the side of the shed.'

"Rejects" did not sound especially promising but Vic went along with it. They'd be going home again soon, anyway, she thought. But what she got was another surprise. Although the finished articles she had seen, were polished and mounted and very impressive, the ones which had had only been begun were somehow even more interesting. Vic was immediately fascinated by the way that some of the carvings and sculptures seemed to grow naturally out of the wood and others looked more as if they were just sticking awkwardly out of a big, plain block of wood.

She wasn't sure what to say, so she asked an obvious question. 'What type of wood is this?'

'Apple,' said Hannah, and for a moment Vic experienced a shiver of anticipation that her mysterious visitor might appear. When nothing happened she relaxed again, remembering that it only seemed to happen in their house. Hannah saw her expression and took it for one of pleasure. 'Most people are surprised to learn that I use apple wood,' she went on. 'I don't know why. Maybe the fruit is so important that they think the wood is nothing more than a means of growing each year's harvest.'

'Or,' said Vic, 'Perhaps they think that apple trees just have thin branches and twigs!' Unconsciously she was relishing the pleasure of being able to say "apple" without worrying about something weird happening.

Hannah laughed. 'Could be,' she said and turned her attention to the rejected work. 'You know,' she added thoughtfully, picking up one of the smaller objects, 'I hardly ever look at this lot unless I'm showing it to a visitor, and when I do I begin to regret setting some of them aside. I nearly always end up finding something I might have another go at.'

Within a very short time the two of them were rummaging through the pile together, pointing out which ones they each thought might have some potential. Eventually, they decided on one, which was too large even for the two of them to carry. 'I've got a barrow in the workshop,' Hannah said. 'I'll just go and fetch it.'

While she was gone, Vic occupied herself by getting the partly-worked piece of wood they had selected out from among the rest by leaning it over and rotating it on its base. Then she pushed a couple of other pieces into the space she had created. She was just finishing this job when Hannah returned with a very clever looking device which had bits on the front and sides which could be raised or lowered to help you get objects onto it and the option of using two or four wheels.

'You've been busy!' said Hannah approvingly, at which point Dad came round the corner of the building. "Ah!' she said, 'So you've finished your reading. You know, your daughter is very industrious. I only left her for five minutes and she's already done some tidying up I've neglected for months. And I didn't even have to ask her to do it!'

APPLE

Dad looked at his daughter with evident pride. 'Vic always finds something to do,' he said. 'Our home is full of the evidence of her busy-ness! So is my office at work, come to that!' he added wryly. 'Need any help?' he asked.

'I'm not sure *I'm* even needed,' laughed Hannah, seeing Vic already making a start on levering the sculpture towards the barrow. 'Maybe you could steady the barrow,' she added, seeing it begin to shift awkwardly as she and Vic put the weight of the sculpture on its edge.

Dad held the handles and said, 'What is it, anyway?'

'The sculpture? Well, it's apple wood and, as I was explaining to Vic, it's not often used for sculptural carvings. It's more likely to be part of a tool or machinery, so I had this idea of carving a big piece into the shape of something like one of the tools I use, like a mallet, or at least the handle, only, you know, many times larger.'

'Hmmm,' Dad said reflectively. 'I didn't know you could do anything with apple wood.'

Vic and Hannah exchanged looks. 'Well, that Adam and Eve business gave the fruit some pretty bad press, you know! But the wood can be very special. It's very dense, you see. If you can get a piece to dry evenly it turns into something more weighty than most hardwoods.' She paused, pulled a face and laughed. 'Now, what am I doing? I've sworn before not to turn into someone who sounds like a tour guide. I'm sure this isn't really all that interesting.' She looked at Vic. 'I think we'll concentrate on the creative stuff. There are plenty of books back in the workshop if your Dad's interested in the technical details!'

Vic was quite pleased to hear this. She was the member of the family who most liked getting her hands dirty doing projects. Dad liked to read about things before doing them and even when he was doing a job he would spend ages thinking things out. Fish was even worse. If he had his way, no jobs would get done at all because he would never get past what he called the "research" stage. Then she remembered that he was away camping, just about the most practical thing she could remember him ever doing. She grinned at the thought and it gave her some satisfaction as revenge for him deserting her.

The sculpture was on the barrow now and as Dad began to manoeuvre it round towards the workshop Hannah said, 'Could I just leave you to wheel it round for me? I really ought to go and put the kettle on.'

While she did this, Vic, steadying the sculpture while Dad pushed, said, in a low voice, 'I think Hannah's expecting guests. There's a whole table set in the house with cakes and things and I think putting the kettle on is a little signal to us.'

Dad grinned. 'I think the cat has struggled enough!'

Vic held the sliding door open and looked at him blankly. She was used to what Fish called his "gnomic sayings" but she didn't get this one.

'The cat,' he explained, wheeling the barrow into the workshop and grinning at her over his shoulder, 'has nearly forced its way out of the bag.' When his daughter still looked blank he began to explain the saying, at which point, as she would have with Fish, she told him she was quite familiar with "Letting the cat out of the bag" but she didn't see what it had to do with whoever Hannah was about to have tea with.

'It's us,' he said. '*We're* the guests,' he added, leaving the trolley standing in the middle of the workshop and walking back out to the garden path. 'It was supposed to be a surprise.' As he said this, Hannah came out of the back door and met them by the workshop entrance. 'Vic has just found out about tea,' he told her. Hannah's face took on a perplexed expression.

'Tea?' she asked, with a conspiratorial glance in Vic's direction.

It was Dad's turn to be confused. 'Yes,' he said, clearly unsure about whether he had got the arrangements right. 'Didn't we arrange... ?'

'Of course we did!' she said. Vic hooted with laughter and bashed Dad's arm.

'Very funny,' said Dad. 'I thought if I got rid of Fish I might get some peace. If you two are going to gang up on me I'm going camping too! Is this just about where you wanted the wood?' he added.

'Fine,' said Hannah. They followed her into the workshop and after they had stood it in a convenient place she showed them some of her finished and nearly-complete pieces. Most of them were quite small. 'It's because applewood is very hard,' Hannah explained. 'It takes a long time to work through. People mainly make things like musical instruments, flutes and whatever, or bowls, little toys, kitchen items. Each of my special pieces takes a long time to complete, so I also make clock casings and supply them to a local firm that fits them with the clock mechanism and they're sold in one of the gift shops across the bay. Helps to pay the bills!'

'Dad always tells us that's why he does his writing. He claims that the money he earns helps to pay for what he calls our treats.'

Hannah's expression showed interest. 'So you write?' she asked, and Vic suddenly wondered whether she should have mentioned it. Dad could be quite secretive about his writing. To change the subject, she pointed to an object on Hannah's workbench. It was a device for burning patterns into the wood which Vic thought was wonderful, especially when Hannah showed her things like spoons and egg cups with patterns burned into them. She also spotted the label on the side of the box it was kept in, and made a mental note of the word "Pyrograph" in case Dad, or even Fish, were to try and teach her what the device was called.

'We ought to have that tea,' Hannah said after a while, and she led them out and back through to the kitchen where the cakes had been joined by an enormous brown teapot. 'I hope you don't mind tea leaves,' Hannah said. 'I can't stand teabags and I like to make my own blend anyway.'

'Suits me,' said Dad. 'What do you put in your blend?'

'Oh, it's not some magic formula,' Hannah said modestly. 'I just add a new bag of whatever I fancy when I get near the bottom of the caddy. There's all sorts in it by now: some Earl Grey, a lot of Ceylon and even some herbal stuff, camomile and whatnot.'

'Never heard of that ingredient,' he said, with a look of interest.

'What? Camomile?' asked Hannah.

Vic knew what was coming. 'He's going to say, "No. Whatnot"' she said. 'It's Dad's idea of a joke.'

Hannah still looked as if she didn't understand but Vic noticed a twinkling glance in her direction.

Dad walked straight into the trap. 'Yes,' he explained. 'You said "Camomile and whatnot," so I was going to say... Oh, that's not fair!' he protested, as Hannah and Vic grinned again. 'That's twice you've caught me!' Vic laughed and he said, mock-seriously: 'I might not be able to win against the whole monstrous regiment, but wait until we're home alone. I'll have my revenge.' He cackled like the villain in a James Bond film and added, still with a villainous accent, 'Enjoy these cakes while you can, Miss Darwin.'

'Before she has to meet her terrible fate,' said Hannah. 'While I'm pouring the tea maybe you can put your poor daughter out of her misery by telling her what's going on.'

'Going on?' said Vic.

'Oh, it's no big deal,' said Dad, quickly. 'I just thought it would be nice for us to get out of the house.'

'This is supposed to be one of your surprise treats, isn't it?' she asked.

'Well, I suppose so. Yes.'

'You're not getting very far with your explanation,' said Hannah, putting the big teapot down and topping it up with more boiling water. 'What your Dad is failing miserably to tell you is that he came past while I was out at the front of the house yesterday. I was trying to see whether my cat had climbed up and got stuck on the roof again. He asked if needed any help and once we had decided that it wasn't the cat but some bit of greenery blown up there after the men had finished clearing the old laurel from over the road, we had a chat. When he found out about my artistic activities he asked whether he could bring you round to see my studio.' She paused and, to avoid a strained silence, she added 'And I agreed...'

Dad interrupted. 'You also said that the word "studio" was a bit grand and told me you called it a workshop.'

'True,' Hannah smiled. 'Tell me,' she said to Vic conspiratorially, 'Does your Dad always make three conversations out of one?'

'Yes,' said Vic and put her tongue out at her father, who was pulling elaborate "Who me?" expressions.

'So there we have it,' said Hannah. 'Quite easy, when you know how.'

'Agreed' said Dad. He looked at his watch and remarked. We have been imposing on you quite a while now...'

'Nonsense!' said Hannah. 'Anyway it's nice to have company.'

'Do you live here alone?' asked Vic and Dad pulled another face, this time a typical grown-up one to show disapproval of asking personal questions. Hannah was unconcerned.

'Well, I suppose I do, but my daughter is here quite often. She would normally be here on a Sunday afternoon but my ex-husband has got some time off work and he's taken her away for a few days before she goes to college.' She stopped. 'What?' she asked, noticing Vic and her Dad exchanging fairly obvious questioning looks.

'Er... what's your daughter's name?' Dad asked.

'Sarah,' Hannah replied uncertainly. 'Why do you ask?'

'Well, it's just that my son has gone off for a few days with his new girlfriend and her father and...'

'Not *Fisher!*' Hannah exclaimed.

'Actually, yes,' said Dad.

'We call him Fish,' Vic put in.

'Well,' said Hannah. 'I know this is a small seaside town

and there aren't many eligible young men and women, but that's still one heck of a coincidence! Well,' she said again, 'I've heard a lot about your brother, Vic. My daughter thinks he's the best thing since sliced bread.'

'He's pretty keen on her, too,' replied Vic.

'Well!' It was Dad who chose the word this time. 'I think I'm beginning to learn more than I wanted to hear. Anyway, now you know why we're here, Vic, what do you think?'

'About Fish and Sarah?'

'No! About coming here.'

'It's been fun.'

Hannah interrupted. 'No, Vic. Your Dad, who may be an expert at taking conversations in all sorts of interesting directions, has forgotten that he hasn't actually told you about our idea.'

'Idea?' said Vic.

'Yes,' said Hannah. 'Your Dad told me that you love art and craft and asked if he could bring you to see mine. I have to confess that it was my suggestion that if you were interested you could come here and do some, as long as you earned your keep by helping to keep the place tidy. There's free tea and cakes, if that's an incentive.'

Vic was torn between being cross with people for trying to plan her life for her and pleased with the chance to do something interesting with a person who could also tell her lots of "scoob" about her brother's new girlfriend. She decided the benefits outweighed her annoyance.

'I think I would like that,' she said.

'Good!' said Dad with a very obvious note of relief in his voice. 'Tomorrow morning, then? The weather forecast for the next couple of days is cloudy with showers, so we won't be missing any beach action.'

It was agreed, and after one more cup of tea Dad and Vic strolled back up to the Pilot's Cottage.

When they got in, Dad immediately had another idea. 'How about going to see a film?' he asked. This was another family tradition. For as long as Vic could remember, Dad had organised holiday film trips. No matter where they had gone, and there were usually large numbers of aunts, uncles, nephews, nieces, cousins and assorted in-laws on the big family holidays, he managed to load most of them into the cars at least once for a trip to the local "flea pit", as he called it. It was always fun to see what cinemas were like in other towns, especially small seaside ones. Some of them really were "flea pits" but Dad had usually treated them to piles of junk food to make up for it.

'OK,' said Vic. 'What's on?'

Dad went and fetched the free local paper which had come through the letter box the previous week. He scanned through. 'There's a cinema across the bay that's showing "Grease". Have you seen that?'

'Not the whole thing,' said Vic. 'Just the famous bits they show on those sort of... you know... those television programmes which put clips of other programmes together.'

'I know what you mean,' said Dad. 'What *do* they call them? Well, whatever it is we ought to continue your film education. Let's go and see that, shall we? When does it start?' He ran a finger down the list of times. 'In an hour. Right. Tell you what. Let's walk there. We don't need anything to eat after all those cakes and biscuits. Let's buy a burger or something while we're out. We're bound to find something in or near the cinema. How does that sound?'

Vic thought it sounded fine. All they had to do was equip themselves with some extra money and some warmer clothes for the walk there and back.

The outing was a treat. Dad loved it because the cinema wasn't one of these huge, gleaming multiplex places, which he hated. Instead, it was a square brick building, painted to look like an iced cake. Vic loved it simply because they went straight to it. Dad had a tendency to improvise these journeys and get lost. On this occasion, they were comfortably in place watching the adverts only forty minutes after leaving the house.

The film was wonderful. The audience was even better. Dad said it reminded him of when he used to go to the cinema as a boy and the place was always full of young lads trying to impress groups of giggling girls by throwing things at them when the lights went down. Sure enough, that was exactly what happened, until the cinema manager came down and stared at them. Vic thought this was great. So different from their local cinema back home where the naughtiest thing that happened was someone's mobile phone ringing.

'Must be the effect of the seaside,' Dad said.

When the film ended most of the audience stayed right through to the end of the credits, which put Dad into an even better mood. He always moaned at the cinema when people got up as soon as the last scene faded and Vic had lost track of the number of times he had told them about when he had watched the credits to the end and there had been a scene after them. He would make them both sit there and watch until the very last detail had rolled past. Sometimes it was worth it. There might be an extra scene and Dad would crow about the people who had missed part of the film. Most of the time, though, it was just boring lists. After "Grease", however, there was more singing and dancing action, and, apart from the one or two people who had dashed out even before the credits began, they all watched, and even clapped along at one point.

When they came out Dad was in such a good mood that he suggested they eat in the burger bar next door. Vic was astonished because it looked like a hut leaning against the side of the cinema – all pine panelling and cheap plasterwork. But when they got inside it turned out to be a bowling alley – and Dad loved ten-pin bowling, even just watching. The café inside sold really huge burgers packed into big, soft buns. Vic's veggieburger was amazing and Dad said so.

'Who would have thought,' he said, with the voice he used for one of his rehearsed sentences. 'That here in a cheap and cheerful temple to greasy fast food, you could find a vegetable burger that is actually more vegetable than burger? I almost wish that I had ordered one myself, except that this cheeseburger is not far short of the best one I have ever eaten too!'

Cheeseburgers were Dad's holiday fast-food treat, so as soon as he saw it on the menu the veggieburger didn't have a hope.

Once filled, they wandered home, swapping lines from the film, punctuating them with high-speed falsetto bursts of "You're the one that I want!"

They both had a lovely feeling of seaside tiredness when they finally wandered down the path to their front door.

'I don't know about you, but I fancy an S.T.B.,' said Dad, yawning. "Straight To Bed" was another family saying.

'What, without setting the breakfast table?' said Vic, astonished that Dad could think of such a thing.

'No,' he said, ironically. 'Some things go without saying.'

'I'll help you, then,' Vic said.

Five minutes later they were both preparing for bed on their respective floors and five minutes after that the house was silent and dark. It occurred to Vic that she hadn't had a chance to gloat about knowing what a Pyrograph was but she dismissed the thought because it would have taken the edge off a good day and a lovely evening.

Next door, the small dog pricked up its ears once as it heard the wind gusting across the hillside, but it did not bark.

Vic didn't hear the gust of wind. She was already asleep.

12

MONDAY

The next morning Vic woke feeling refreshed by a good sleep without barking dogs and mysterious visitors. She lay there wondering what the day would bring. Her first thought was that she would have to manage without Fish being around. That thought was chased away when she remembered Hannah and her studio. It had seemed a nice idea yesterday. Hannah was a likeable person and she was glad that something was going to take her away from the things that made her anxious at home. But she wondered now whether she was going to be any happier with her brother's girlfriend's mother than she would be mooching around with Dad.

Her thoughts remained mixed as she went downstairs struggling with one inside-out arm of her dressing gown. It didn't help that she had to go past Fish's bedroom door and her thoughts did turn a little grey for a moment. She decided to get on with things and hide her feelings. "I'm getting good at that," she thought, ruefully.

There was no sign of Dad, which was a bit surprising as it had gone seven o'clock and he was usually up by this time, even on holiday. She remembered Fish once telling her how Mum would see holidays as a chance to sleep for half the morning and for a moment the thought of her brother and her mother nearly overwhelmed her but she remained determined to make a good start, so she held back her feelings, and switched on the massive old radio, the one Dad said reminded him of the one he had listened to when he was a boy.

She poured herself some cereal and wondered what time would be reasonable for her to arrive at Hannah's. She had forgotten to ask Dad, so she would just have to wait until he emerged from his bed.

She had just put a slice of bread in the toaster when she heard a sort of scrabbling noise in the front porch. 'Oh no!' she thought. 'Not another apparition. Not now!' She walked out of the kitchen and into the hallway and as she went she said, 'App...' and then, hoping she had stopped herself in time, said instead, 'Is that you?' in a low, urgent hiss, which might be heard upstairs but would not be understood.

'Hello, Vic. Yes, it's me,' came the reply, but it was only Dad, taking his key back out of the lock and stepping in through the front door. 'What's up? Were you wondering where I'd gone?' I did leave a note by your bear.'

'I didn't see it,' she said. 'I didn't even know you were up.' She was forming a strategy in her mind as she went along. Had he heard her begin to say "Apple"? Had she said enough of the word to start a whole new episode? What would happen if she had? So far there were there no noises from outside; not even the dog barking.

'Did I scare you?' Dad was saying, evidently quite concerned and having no idea that the consternation on her face was about something quite different. As they went through to the kitchen together he added, 'I just woke up very early and couldn't go back to sleep, so I went for a walk up to the end of the road. You know, there was a ferry coming in belching black smoke. I could have sworn it was on fire but it came into the harbour in the usual way and there's no smoke showing now. I only came back this soon because I could see clouds over the next headland that looked as if they were full of rain. Still, I think I might have got a poem out of it all. Something to do while you're out.' The expression on Vic's face must still have troubled him because he was evidently forcing the conversation. When Vic's toast popped up he grasped the chance of a change of subject. 'Ah Ha!' he exclaimed. 'I'm hungry now. Is there any bread left?'

Vic shook her head.

'Never mind, then. I'll just have toast.'

His joke was the same old one but it always seemed to get a laugh. This time was no exception. She grinned and said, 'You can have mine if you like. I've got something else.'

'Only if you're sure,' Dad replied, then, when she indicated she had her large bowl of cereal, he added, cautiously, 'Are you all set for your day with Hannah?'

'Yeah,' she said. 'What time am I expected?'

Dad's voice relaxed a bit with her apparently positive reply. 'Well, she said "Anytime you're ready, but I don't suppose she meant "dawn"! 'Even if she's an early bird like us it probably wouldn't be fair to be there before about nine, to be on the safe side. Now, where's the apple juice?'

Luckily, Dad did not want an actual answer to his question. Even if he had, Vic couldn't have answered as her teeth were gritted as she braced herself for what she was instantly sure would happen. But nothing did happen. No door slammed. No dog barked. If anything, this was worse and she felt even more tense than if something dramatic had occurred. The thought crossed her mind that, as she was actually desperate to share her experiences with someone, what better way for them to discover what was happening than for the source of her anxiety to make an appearance there and then, in front of them? It would be the oddest of all odd things, but the one thing she would not have to do would be to explain it, "sight unseen" as one of Grandpa's favourite sayings went.

But nothing went on happening and Dad had found the apple juice and was getting himself some coffee, so Vic realised she would just have to get properly dressed and take a look outside, casually, if that was possible. As she stood up, acting casually became that little bit harder when she noticed another crisp green apple *had* appeared in the fruit bowl. She grabbed it and took it upstairs with her. She could always eat it on the way to Hannah's as it didn't look as though she was going to get much more breakfast. She shot upstairs as fast as she could without making a noise to attract Dad's attention. When she came back down Dad was doing a bit of Fish's jigsaw and hardly even seemed to notice her reappearance, which suited her. She slipped through the hallway, across the porch and out into the back garden.

She made her way slowly down each terrace, looking carefully along each level but finding nothing unusual.

As she reached the lowest one she realised that she hadn't looked to see whether the dog was there. It was. But it was just looking. Its little pink tongue hung out of its open mouth, but it did not bark, it just looked. 'That's even more strange than the barking,' she thought. At the bottom terrace she glanced around and then leaned on the boundary wall and scanned the hillside and the bay. And then she found him. Something which looked like little more than an old scarecrow now was lying crumpled at the foot of the wall. But it had to be him because nothing like that had been there the previous day and she could not believe that some random country person had chosen a Sunday night to visit this plot and discard a scarecrow.

'Apple!' she hissed, for the second time this morning. The figure did not move. She glanced back up the garden to check that she was still alone. There was no-one in her garden but she couldn't be sure about any neighbours, and what if someone happened to be in the old orchard grounds? She had little choice. 'Do something if you can hear me,' she said, as loud as she dared. Then, knowing how stupid this would sound if she were overheard, 'Sigh, or something.'

The figure made a noise like a dozen leaves swirled in a gutter by the wind. 'That's good,' she said. 'Hang on. I'll be right back.'

She went briskly back up to the house and found that Dad was no longer downstairs. She went half way up the stairs, ascertained that he was now having a shower, and ran back down and into the garden. She scrambled over the wall and in one easy movement, because Apple was by now very light indeed, she put him over her shoulder and climbed back over the wall. Then she eased him down and, cradling him in her arms, she walked straight back up the garden, leaned on the shed catch until it fell open and let Apple down in among the wood. As she did so, he seemed to gain a little substance. Then, before she could say or do anything more, he sort of collapsed down between the pieces of wood. She thought he might have hesitated a moment and looked back at her, perhaps with gratitude, but, then again, she might have been making that thought up to reassure herself.

When she got back into the house Dad was still upstairs. Her pulse was racing and she had a nagging throb in the back of her neck. She stood in the kitchen grateful for a moment or two in which to compose herself. After about five minutes she made her way upstairs. Dad wasn't in the shower now, nor was he in his bedroom. She found him in the TV lounge plugging in his word processor.

'There you are!' he said. 'I thought you might have gone to Hannah's already. Do you want me to come with you?'

Vic was not in the mood for a long conversation. She was worried about what had just happened. 'No,' she replied. 'I think I know the way.'

Either Dad did not notice her rather short tone, or chose to ignore it. 'Fine,' he said. 'Just one thing, though,' he added. 'Put on what my grandfather used to call "stout shoes".'

'Why?'

'Well, my experience of workshops is that things can get knocked over or dropped. You don't want something heavy or sharp on your toes, do you?'

'I guess not.'

Vic put on the most sensible shoes she could find but she also shoved her trainers into a bag, just in case.

'I'm off now!' she said from the doorway as she came back downstairs.

'See you for lunch! Have a nice time!' he called back, and she went off, slowing down as she went, wondering what to make of her latest encounter with the mysterious Apple. She was very tempted to go back and look, but she realised that there was nothing she could do there, especially with Dad in the house. Of course, he might say the word which seemed to conjure up all the trouble, but again, he was more likely to do that with her there. The day, she decided, was going to be a strain either way, so she had better get on with it as planned.

As forecast, it the rain had begun to fall since she had been out to retrieve Apple. She considered taking out her kagoule, which was also in the bag with the trainers. In the time it took to make up her mind she was under what was left of the trimmed laurel bushes and nearly at Hannah's house anyway. The front door was ajar, so instead of knocking she shouted 'Hello!' and tried to push it open so she could step in. Hannah's instant reply came from somewhere down near her knee and she hesitated. Hannah's face came round the door, still at knee height.

'Come in, Vic.' She said. 'I'm fixing the hinge. This door was replaced a year ago and I think they must have put the hinge on upside down. There's a metal rod that holds the two parts together and it slips out every so often.'

Vic smiled and edged in, taking care not to step on the cat, which was also behind the door.

Hannah gave the hinge a crisp tap with a hammer and stood up, shooing the cat back down the passageway.

'Right!' she said with a broad grin on her face. 'That's the DIY over and done with. Time to do some entirely different work with the hands!'

Hannah could be a chatty person, that Vic already knew, but she also knew when to get on with things. Her assignment, as agreed with Dad, was to help occupy Vic while their respective relatives were away together. She already knew that Vic had been attracted by the patterns burned on the clock cases she had shown her so she led her straight through to the workshop and gave her an instant lesson in how to use a pyrograph. While she plugged it in to warm up she said, 'You're supposed to wear protective clothing in a workshop. I see you have some stout shoes but you also need... What's so funny?' she broke off as Vic grinned broadly.

'Sorry,' she said hastily, 'But you've just repeated one of our family catch-phrases. Apparently my great-grandfather always used to talk about stout shoes, and Dad just insisted I wear some!'

'My family too!' laughed Hannah. 'Small... Oh, I nearly said "small world". I promised myself I wouldn't turn into the sort of person who says "small world". She paused and scratched her head. 'Now where was I?'

'Protective clothing,' said Vic.

'Of course! Now you also need to wear an apron or overalls. I've got both. Which would you prefer?'

Vic chose overalls. She was thinking to herself how refreshingly matter-of-fact Hannah was. Most adults either talked down to you about safety or were ever-so-cautious because they thought that as a young person you might be touchy about good advice from adults. Hannah just spoke as if certain things were true and got on with it. Like an improved version of Dad.

What she didn't notice until later was that Hannah's directness drove her immediate troubles away. She had already relaxed somewhat and Apple didn't really cross her mind for the rest of the morning.

She watched as Hannah demonstrated the basic pyrography technique. She made a few lines of varying shapes on an off-cut of wood. Then she handed the tool to Vic. She impressed her student once again by trusting her straight away to handle it properly.

'Here's another piece of wood to practice on,' she said. 'Have a go while I make a couple of phone calls.'

It turned out that Hannah was not going to leave her entirely to her own devices with a very hot tool. A moment later she reappeared in the workshop doorway talking into a cordless phone and, whenever Vic looked up, she was keeping a distant but careful eye on what was happening.

When she had finished, she took the phone back to the house, came back in and said, 'Good lines! Now see if you can draw something,' and she went off to the other end of the workshop to move some objects which were sitting in vices, half-finished. She picked up some other prepared bits of wood. When she had finished sanding and shaping them a bit more she glued them to the pieces in the vices and Vic vould see instantly that they were all small clock cases.

Hannah came back and said, 'You *have* got the touch. Usually, when I get proud parents telling me their offspring are artistic I take it with a pinch of salt, but your Dad was right.'

Vic grinned, and then she stopped grinning because Hannah added. 'Why all the apples?'

Vic had genuinely not realised what she was doing, but when she looked at her designs she saw that they were mostly apples, and those that weren't looked like twigs and leaves from apple trees.

'Oh, it just seemed like a good idea,' she said hesitantly. Then she thought of the obvious answer. 'Apple designs on applewood!' she added.

'True!' agreed Hannah, and then, in her customary no-frills manner, 'Actually, that offcut is just a piece of softwood, but I see your point. How about a cup of coffee?' and she disappeared off towards the house.

Vic carried on practising. While she did so, she kept thinking about Hannah's easy way of speaking to her, pointing out what the wood was as if she was just a person, not a child or a teenager who had to be instructed or corrected; or worse still: handled with kid gloves in case she got upset!

She finished off her design and switched off the pyrograph, as instructed. Then she walked out of the workshop, speeding up when she realised that it had actually continued raining, gently but steadily, since her arrival. The cat was standing by the back door, not keen on going out among the raindrops. It mewed and turned as she stooped to tickle it behind the ear.

'If that's you,' came Hannah's voice, 'Then come in. The coffee's ready. If that's not you,' she added, 'Then get your hands off my cat and go away!'

Vic laughed and went in. 'How did you manage to make the coffee so quickly?' he asked.

'It's the real deal,' Hannah said. 'I keep it warm all day. Can't stand instant coffee. No flavour. Is that alright for you?'

Coffee wasn't Vic's automatic choice of refreshing drink. However, for some reason it seemed like a nice idea. 'Yes,' she said, adding, 'Just a small cup, with milk, please,'

While the coffee was being poured, Hannah said, 'I wonder how your brother's getting on with Sarah and my "ex".'

Her comment came just as Vic took her first sip of the coffee. She didn't reply immediately because she was surprised to find that it was it was delicious. She thought she might have some more in a moment. By the time she did reply, saying, 'It's Fish's first time camping,' Hannah had almost forgotten what she had originally said.

She hesitated, then, having retraced her thoughts, said with a grin, 'Really? Well, let's hope my daughter's keeping him warm and dry,' then, evidently remembering Vic's age, she added, 'The rest of the time, I mean, of course!' Then, changing the subject like Dad did, she looked at Vic's already empty cup and said, 'Would you like some more?'

'Yes, please.' said Vic. 'Dad always drinks real coffee but I don't like it when he makes it.'

'Well, I do make my own blend. Perhaps he would like the recipe? I wonder how he's doing without you this morning. It is just you, Fish and him on holiday, isn't it?'

And at this point the floodgates opened.

Hannah was startled by this reaction to what she had intended as only a casual bit of conversation. 'What's the matter? What is it Vic? What did I say?' she asked urgently as Vic's tears rolled down her cheeks.

She made as if to get up and come round to try to offer some comfort but Vic waved a hand towards her and said, through sobs, 'No… It's alright… Wait a minute…'

So Hannah sat there and waited as the young girl across the table gradually calmed down. It took quite a while and it occurred to Hannah more than once that she ought to do something. But what? Go and fetch the girl's Dad? Or try and get him on his mobile? He had given her the number. In the end the cat solved the problem. It jumped up on the table, which it was not supposed to do, and pushed itself under one of Vic's arms, forcing her to stroke it. And that helped her calm down.

When she was quiet again and only her red eyes and cheeks suggested she had been upset, Hannah said. 'Feeling better now?' Vic nodded and blew her nose, which startled the cat but did not drive it away. 'Let's talk about something else,' Hannah added. She was surprised by the reply.

'No, please,' said Vic, quite urgently. 'Can we talk? I want to.' She didn't actually know what she wanted to say but she just did not want to hold things in any longer, and she told Hannah so.

'Well, alright,' said Hannah with caution. She was aware that this was not her daughter and she should not do anything which might cause someone offence. 'What's the matter?'

Vic hesitated for quite a while, composing her thoughts, and stroked the cat which had started purring again after recovering from Vic blowing her nose next to its ear. 'Everyone's been so nice,' she began uncertainly, and she looked up at Hannah, who decided that saying nothing was the best policy for the time being.

Vic took a very deep breath so she could get through the sentence without her voice cracking. 'My Mum was killed in an accident...' She paused again. She realized that she hadn't said that sentence for a long time. Hannah decided that she should now say something.

'When?' she asked.

'I was five. I was in my first year at Primary School and Dad came to get me before school finished that day. He was very, very upset and even before I knew the reason I decided that I would keep my feelings to myself so as not to make things worse for him.' She paused again, but just as Hannah was framing another question she added, 'And I haven't really said anything about it ever since. Not even to Fish.'

'What did you mean when you said "Everyone's been so kind"?' Hannah asked.

'Well,' Vic sighed, 'Ever since it happened the whole family has organized things to help make up for Mum not being there. Every summer we've gone on a big holiday with Mum's sister and brothers and their kids, and sometimes their kids' friends. And then Dad makes sure we never have a half-term holiday without going somewhere interesting and, well, you know...'

'Misplaced helpfulness,' said Hannah.

'What?' Vic asked.

'Well, it's an expression,' said Hannah. 'It doesn't quite fit the situation but it's near enough. It's when someone thinks you need something and they offer what they think you need but it's actually at the wrong time, or in the wrong place or the wrong kind. You know...' It was her turn to run out of explanation. 'Look,' she said, 'I'm not the best person in the world at offering advice. I haven't exactly got a normal family myself and I prefer to be doing things. Let's get on with our work and talk as we go. OK?'

'Yes,' said Vic. She didn't mind one way or the other but she did appreciate, not for the first time, that Hannah talked to her in an adult way, and that was making her feel better.

They left the dirty mugs and went back out to the workshop. Neither of them said much while they got on with their work but after a while their conversation resumed and by the time lunchtime came around Hannah knew all about Fish's attempts to fill in for their Mum, Dad's efforts to do all the things Mum might have done, like teaching Vic some cookery skills and so-on. Also how Vic's grandparents were helpful but she didn't feel she could cry on any of their shoulders.

'Is it unusual?' Vic asked suddenly while they were sweeping up before she went home.

'Not at all,' replied Hannah, misunderstanding. 'You have got to keep a workshop tidy.'

Vic laughed unexpectedly. 'Our English teacher taught us about that. It's called talking at cross-purposes! He was teaching us about comedy on the TV and how it usually only happens there to make things funny.' She paused. 'Situation comedy. That's what he said it was called. Sitcoms. I can't wait to tell him it happens in real life!' Then she looked serious again, realizing that her nervous chatter had taken them completely off the subject. 'I meant not talking about things that really worry you, like my family seems to do.'

Hannah's expression turned cautious too. 'I understand. But I don't think anything is quite "usual" where emotions are concerned,' she said. 'My family has always been very ready to shout when they don't feel too happy about something and now we don't all live together. There's no magic formula. Sometimes you shout, sometimes you ask, sometimes you listen. And speaking of listening,' she added, looking at the clock, 'It's just about lunch time. Your Dad will be expecting you.'

She was astonished when Vic suddenly gave her a big hug, said, 'See you after lunch,' and was away down the path and up the hill.

When she got home, Dad instantly had a plan. 'We're going to eat up on the headland,' he said, not even pausing to ask whether she had enjoyed her morning.

'A picnic?' asked Vic, eying the showery weather sceptically.

'No way!' he snorted. 'We're going for a pub lunch!'

He pulled the front door shut, locked it and within ten minutes Dad had a half of the local bitter in front of him, Vic had a huge glass of fizzy water full of ice cubes and slices of lemon and they were eagerly anticipating cheese omelettes.

'So, how was the art, then?' Dad asked.

'Great!' said Vic, wiping stray drops of fizzy water off her nose. 'Hannah glued her clock cases and I practised pyrography. She's going to finish her job while I'm here with you and then she's going to teach me how to turn some objects. Then I can decorate them tomorrow.'

'Poor old Hannah, having to miss her lunch for you,' Dad said with mock-seriousness.

'Oh, she told me she doesn't often have a proper lunch. She snacks through the day instead.'

'Ah!' said Dad, archly. 'Typical artist, eh?'

'She is a bit,' Vic agreed. 'But she has routines. We have to sweep up before coffee, and before lunch. She says a tidy floor is the definition of good workshop.'

'Sounds fair enough to me,' Dad nodded. 'Here come our omelettes.'

The next few minutes were spent in silence. Dad was silent because while he was eating he was flicking through some local papers which had been left on the window sill. He had some idea that there was going to be a firework display in the area and he wanted to take Vic as a surprise if it was on that night. He hadn't been able to find anything about it at home so this was his chance. Vic was silent because she was preparing a question for him.

Dad got up and fetched more drinks for them. As soon as he came back Vic said, 'Tell me something about Mum.'

Dad looked at her briefly. Then he took a sip of his drink. And then a rather bigger sip. Just as Vic was beginning to think she had been too direct, he surprised her by equalling her directness.

'One of the things I really loved about your Mum was how she got expressions wrong. You know those old "Carry On" films that you and Fish liked so much when you were younger? Well, you know how whenever a character said something which could be rude in one of them, someone would say "Ooooh, Matron!" Well, Mum would always say "Ooooh, Doctor!"' He paused. 'I used to laugh because I knew what she meant, and everyone else would just look, which would make us both laugh.' Vic was just looking at him, saying nothing. 'Well, that proves it,' he added. 'You had to be there, I suppose.'

They didn't say anything else until Dad had paid and they were on their way down the road again. Then she held her Dad's hand and when he looked at her with surprise she just smiled at him. At the gate, Dad said, 'I suppose you won't be coming in then. Got work to do haven't you?'

Vic smiled again, 'Absolutely. See you about five.'

She walked on down the hill and it was only when she was a few yards from Hannah's house that she remembered that she had not done what she had planned, which was to go in and check that Apple was alright. Or at least that he hadn't appeared while she had been out.

But it was too late now and she would feel stupid going back, so she took the pathway round the side of the house and found Hannah in her workshop. She was packing away the bits of clock case that she had said she would do while Vic was with her Dad.

'Hello,' she said. 'How was lunch?'

'Fine,' said Vic. 'We went to the pub at the top of the road.'

'Ah! The Old Spit and Sawdust.'

'No,' said Vic. I think it's called The Port In A Storm.'

Hannah laughed loudly. 'That's the one! It was "re-branded", as they say, when the brewery put a new manager in and tried to attract "a better class of customer", as they also say. But anyone who's lived here for a while calls it "The Spit and Sawdust". Term of affection, I suppose. How was it? I haven't been up there since they went up-market.'

'Fine. We had omelettes.'

'Don't tell me,' Hannah interrupted. 'The kind that don't have much flavour but look more like the omelettes in recipe books than anything you can make at home!'

Vic was amused. 'Yes!' she exclaimed, laughing. 'That's just how Fish describes them!'

Hannah grinned and then remembered that she was supposed to spend some time demonstrating wood turning, which Vic picked up quite quickly. It was nearly an hour before the conversation resumed.

'And how's your Dad managing without you?' Hannah went on, with cheerful disregard for any possibility that she might strike an unhappy chord in Vic. Vic didn't mind. In fact, she was enjoying the direct conversation and it occurred to her that it was this, as much as the art work, that was making her like coming to Hannah's place. She would probably never have let the tears flow if Hannah hadn't been such straightforward company.

'He's fine too. I don't know if anything does trouble him. He thinks so much. His mind is so active that he never switches off. I sometimes wonder whether his emotions are there at all, and then his eyes will stream with tears at unexpected moments, during a film or when he's listening to some music. Just at the moment I think he's planning a treat of some sort. He spent half of lunch ferreting through the local papers.'

Hannah thought that was sweet, and, while she gave Vic some tuition in more advanced pyrography she found out about a few more of the treats and surprises that Vic's Dad had been known to plan.

While they were having a tea-break, Vic said, 'According to Fish, Dad's always been a planner of treats.

At least since Mum died. He tends to fill your time up with things to do and adds little details to ordinary daily routines like meals. You always feel with him that whatever you're doing has to be done on time so the next plan can be carried out. It's great, really, because you can end up doing some really interesting things, but it's hard to get a serious, quiet word with him, like at lunch.'

Hannah looked up from the biscuit crumbs she had been cleaning off her plate with a licked finger. 'At lunch?'

'Yes,' said Vic. 'I did what you suggested. I asked him to tell me something about Mum.'

'*I* suggested that?'

'Well, sort of. Yes. You know, when I was upset this morning.'

Hannah remained puzzled but she decided to let it pass. She could tell that Vic was sorting out some things in her young mind and anything she found helpful in that process had to be a good idea. She could only remember frantically trying to think of what to do or say which might be helpful while a teenage girl sat at her table in floods of tears. She hadn't noticed herself being wise or giving advice. Still, she decided not to pry. If Vic wanted to tell her more about her conversation with her father she could do so. And she had just mentioned her mother's death quite comfortably, which was interesting.

'If you've got the hang of the pyrography,' she said 'I'll teach you how to cut shapes out with the jig-saw, then you can plane and sand them ready to burn some patterns into them.'

By the end of the afternoon Vic had several shaped pieces of wood prepared and she told Hannah that she would spend some of her time in the evening sketching out some designs to put on them with the pyrograph. This did not happen immediately, however, because when she got home her plan was interrupted by Dad's schemes, which included fetching a takeaway meal from the local Chinese restaurant. The silver lining to this was that the takeaway generated virtually no washing up, so while Dad dealt with the few dishes Vic managed to squeeze in an hour or so of sketching. This was in turn interrupted by the trip along the coast to see the fireworks that Dad had mentioned at lunch time.

When he had suggested it earlier in the day, she hadn't felt all that keen. Now, apart from her sketching plans there was a good film on the TV that evening and there was still rain in the air, which could spoil a firework display. However, she did go, because Dad pointed out that as it was going to be cloudy, it would be dark early enough for the display to happen reasonably early and then they would be able to get home so Vic could complete her sketches.

And it did turn out well because as well as being cloudy and dark, even though showers did keep blowing down the coastline there was something Dad called an offshore breeze which carried most of them away from where the display was held. And as soon as some of the fireworks started bursting over the sea she began to get some design ideas for her pyrography, so the evening was definitely not wasted.

13

TUESDAY

In the morning, Vic was up quite early but Dad, as usual, was up even earlier. He was sitting in the lounge writing and, after a slightly distracted "Good morning", stayed there while Vic got herself some breakfast.

While she was waiting for the kettle to boil, Vic thought about Fish and wondered whether he had tried to contact them. She went round to the foot of the stairs and shouted,

'Dad!?'

Dad did not normally like being shouted to through the house but on this occasion he replied.

'What?'

'We haven't heard from Fish, have we?'

'I don't know. There might be something on the mobile. I haven't checked.'

Vic did check. She found three messages: two from Fish and one from Grandpa. This last was just to let them know he and Grandma were home safely, and one of Fish's was only a similar "Let you know everything's alright" kind of message. The other one caused a problem.

Although it was a bit garbled, Vic could make out something about him going on foot with Sarah and her Dad to the walled garden. That was all she could make out. At that moment Dad called downstairs, 'Are there any messages, then?'

'Yes!' she called. 'Grandpa says they're home safely. Fish says he's been on a hike. Can you imagine it? Fish of all people!'

Dad's reply showed why he disapproved of shouting through houses.

'What?'

'A hike. He's been on a hike. To the walled garden.'

'A hike to where?'

'The walled garden. You know. The one with the old apple tr…' And she stopped.

Nothing happened, but she knew from last time that that did not mean nothing *had* happened. She wondered how long she might have before Dad came downstairs. She went through to the sun lounge and looked across to the neighbours' shed. The dog was there but just like last time it wasn't barking. However, unlike last time it wasn't even standing. It was flat down on the roof with its head in its paws like dogs do when they sense a bad atmosphere.

But there was another green apple in the bowl, so something was happening.

Dad had still not come down so, hoping he would not be looking out of one of the upstairs windows, she headed for the garden. As she reached the porch she noticed a red vehicle stopping up by the gate. It was a postman. He got out and took some letters to the house next door and then, as he walked back up the neighbours' path, he looked down at the letters in his hands and then across at the Pilot's Cottage as if he had something for them.

'Oh no!' thought Vic. 'Not another person. Not now.'

She quickly unlocked the front door – Dad always left the keys in the lock in case of a night time emergency – and went up the steps to meet him.

'Morning!' said the postman, as if they had known each other all their lives. 'Mainly junk mail, but you have got a card.'

Vic muttered a "thank you" and took the handful of paper without even looking. That was the limit of her conversation because over the postman's shoulder she had seen a familiar form beside the path. This time it really looked more like a bundle of twigs than a living creature, which is probably what had saved it from the postman's interest. In fact, without the scraps of material to suggest clothing, it might have passed unnoticed but she was taking no chances. She said goodbye to the postman, walked down the steps, dropped the mail on the table by the downstairs shower and checked that Dad was not in the vicinity. Then she re-opened the porch door and walked swiftly across the tiny square of grass cut into the hillside and below the level of the road that made up the front lawn. She could tell immediately that she was going to get nothing out of the inert bundle so, without even the precaution of a glance up at all the windows which overlooked her, she scooped it up. This time it really did weigh next to nothing as she cradled it in her arms. She went through the porch, not even pausing to see if Dad was there by now, and turned towards the wood store door and...

Dad was there!

The woodstore door was open – he must have been looking in it – and now he was standing beyond it making friendly noises towards the dog.

He wasn't actually looking in her direction so she took a deep breath, walked the three or four paces to the woodstore and nudged the door further open with her foot. Then she turned smartly and carried Apple to the back. She didn't have time for niceties. She found a corner where she could place him, partly obscured by some garden canes, and put him down. He didn't seem to move as she did so, but as she stepped back out and began to shut the door she thought she might have detected a slight stirring.

Dad turned as she shut the door. He had not noticed her until now and she just hoped against hope that he had finished looking in the woodstore. 'There you are!' he said. 'You know, this dog's funny. Wouldn't stop barking last week. Now it's gone all quiet and won't even respond when I make my world-famous dog-attraction noises. Vic tried to respond to his everyday good humour but she felt out of step with it because of Apple and the tension of hiding what she was doing.

'I think someone must have left that door unlatched,' Dad said, indicating the one Vic had just firmly shut. 'It was slightly ajar when I came out to find you. Where have you been? I thought you'd gone off to Hannah's without telling me.'

'The postman came,' she said, half-heartedly. 'I saved him a journey.'

Her story was entirely credible and anyway, Dad was not the sort to push for every last detail and just asked, 'Anything for us then?'

'I..er.. I'm not sure. The postman said something about a card but then I heard you out here,' said Vic a bit feebly, 'And I put the stuff down by the shower room to come out and see what you were doing.'

Either Dad didn't notice her air of distraction or he just ignored it. He continued, 'Well, let's go and see, shall we? Maybe there's something from Fish.'

Sure enough, Dad knew his son well. Fish had always woven little messages into holidays, just like Dad enjoyed making little treats for picnics and things. Typically of Fish, even though they were all on holiday and he was only a few miles away, he had sent them a postcard, as if The Pilot's Cottage was their home.

'It'll be just my luck if it's from the walled garden,' thought Vic, but it was actually a card with four shaggy Welsh sheep on it. Each one had a sort of bemused look on its face which made Dad laugh helplessly. Vic would have laughed too, because it was a genuinely silly picture, but she was preoccupied by thoughts about Apple, in a turmoil over the state in which she had found him.

'See the message on the back?' said Dad. '"Weather here. Wish you were lovely!"' It was an old joke, but, combined with another look at the soppy sheep, it reduced him to giggles once again. Vic put on a good act once more but even Dad noticed enough to stop laughing and change the subject. He was assuming that she had become mopey at the mention of Fish. He paused and looked at the reverse clock.

'I'm still not used to that thing,' he said, 'But I'm pretty sure that you're nearly late for your second art day.'

He was right. Five minutes later, and having gathered her things and herself together with remarkable speed, Vic was on her way down the hill, hoping she would be able to put her thoughts to the back of her mind for a while. But it was becoming more and more difficult.

There was no rain so far, but the clouds were heavy and there was a cold wind with them. Hannah took a while answering the door because she had been out in the workshop switching on a heater.

'Oh, it's you!' she exclaimed. 'You could have come round the side. You know the way by now.'

Vic didn't say, but she realized that she had been thinking so much about the latest Apple encounter that she had forgotten that knocking was no longer really necessary.

Hannah noticed the look on her face and immediately tried to cheer her up.

'Come in. You've *got* to see what the postman has brought me,' she grinned. She closed the front door and picked up something from the hall table. When she turned back Vic could see it was a postcard. When Hannah held it up she saw that it was the same one Fish had sent to her and Dad.

'It's from Sarah,' Hannah began. 'It has the corniest message you can...' She stopped. Knowing the message well enough not to need to read it, she was looking instead at Vic, who once again had large tears rolling down her cheeks.

'Oh, I am sorry,' she began. 'I didn't mean to...' But Vic waved a hand to indicate that she needn't say anything.

She sniffed hard and said. 'No. It's not the card. We got one too. It's very funny. It's just… Oh, I can't explain.' She paused and then said, 'Would it be alright if we had some coffee?'

If Hannah was surprised by this request she didn't show it. 'Of course we can,' she replied, and they went through to the kitchen where the inevitable pot of coffee was already simmering.

Consciously or otherwise, Vic's request for coffee was an attempt to find a restorative of some sort. Adults liked it and most members of her family insisted on drinking the "real" stuff rather than the instant variety. Having fixed on this as a drink that might be strong enough to knock out her troubles, Vic decided to go the whole hog and drink it black, like Dad did. When she took her first sip the heat and strength nearly took her breath away. But it seemed to clear the tears too, somehow or other.

Hannah didn't say anything until Vic was calm enough to notice the cat and make little clicking noises to encourage it to come and be stroked. Then she said, 'They'll be back tomorrow, you know.' She was referring to Fish and Sarah.

'Oh no!' Vic exclaimed. 'I'm not upset about them. I'm enjoying myself here.'

'Oh,' said Hannah, though her tone really said, "So what is the problem?" But she didn't say that bit and sat finishing her own cup of coffee instead.

Vic took a deep breath. 'I've got to try and stop someone from dying,' She blurted out suddenly.

For a moment, Hannah thought Vic's sadness had got the better of her and that this was something to do with her mother, or even her father. If this was the case, she thought, then she really did not feel qualified to express a view. She was about to say that perhaps Vic ought to go home and talk to her Dad when the girl said something that seemed be another confusing change of subject. 'What do you know about apple trees?' she blurted out, almost aggressive with emotion.

Not sure whether this was a good or bad direction for their conversation to take, Hannah cautiously followed the lead. 'How do you mean?' she asked.

'Well, you work with applewood. Is it special?'

Hannah had, of course, no idea of the turmoil of meanings that was prompting Vic to say these things, nor how there could be any connection between them and "saving someone's life", so she tried making small talk to give Vic a chance to explain.

'Well, it is pretty special stuff,' she began. 'And of course it's got a bad reputation.'

'Bad reputation?'

'Yes. You know. Adam and Eve. The Garden of Eden. Apples are still called "the forbidden fruit" because of all that. And it's not fair, you know. It doesn't say "apple" in the Bible and they don't grow naturally in the Middle East anyway. It was probably a pomegranet or some such fruit.'

She paused. Vic said nothing. 'Was that what you meant?' Hannah asked.

'No,' said Vic, clearly at a loss for any further words. Hannah cast around for some other line to pursue.

'OK. Do you remember when you first came here with your Dad?'

Vic nodded.

'Well,' continued Hannah, 'If I remember rightly, on that occasion I said to your Dad that the wood itself is very different from what people expect. It has...' But Vic took a very audible deep breath, which made her pause mid-sentence. She looked hard at Vic. She could see that she was wrestling with her thoughts so he waited. When Vic eventually spoke, her words didn't make much sense for all the effort she had put into them.

'How does it feel?' she said.

Hannah couldn't conceal her puzzlement. 'The wood, you mean? Its texture?'

'Yes. Well, no. I mean, in a way. Oh, I don't know what I mean!'

'Look, Vic,' said Hannah, more firmly than before. 'You're confusing me. Yesterday you cried and the reason seemed clear. Today you're crying again, yet you tell me you're not upset and you're asking me questions about applewood...'

'Does it seem like it's alive?!' Vic blurted out, cutting across Hannah's words.

'Well, I always think of it that way, and it was before it was cut. It twists and warps very easily as if it were squirming. In fact you tend not to hear fans of applewood talking about "drying" or "seasoning". People have told me I sound a bit strange when I talk this way, but my favourite word is "coaxing" because if you don't look after it – if you turn your back on it and don't pay it enough attention – it goes out of shape and it might as well be dead.'

'Might as well be dead,' Vic echoed. 'That's how he looks.'

'He? Who's he?'

Vic took another deep breath. '"Apple".'

'Apple? What apple?'

'The one who keeps appearing,' said Vic and, as if realizing that she would have to tell the rest, she poured out the story of the last ten days. When she had finished it was Hannah's turn to struggle for words. She knew that Vic's feelings were still rather fragile and she would need more than just one holiday to recover from several years of pent-up feelings about her mother. On the other hand, the things she was telling her sounded like just the sort of imaginings a young person would use to try and cope with just such feelings. In the end she decided that as she was the person Vic had confided in she ought to respond as helpfully as she could.

'Why do you think this... er... Apple, appeared when you arrived?'

'I don't think he did,' Vic said thoughtfully.

'Don't think he did what?'

'Appear when we arrived. I think he was there before we were.'

'What makes you say that?'

'Well, he was already very vague when I first met him. You know, already fading. And right from the start he would look out at where the old orchard was, at the bottom of the garden, and I know that was uprooted some time before we came here for our holiday.'

'That would seem to fit,' said Hannah, and she paused because she sensed herself being dragged into Vic's story. But on the other hand, she didn't really mind. She knew applewood was an odd choice to work with and she had never been able to fully explain the attraction. There were any number of types of wood which would have made her working life so much easier, yet the stuff seemed to have a hold on her. She tried to dispel her own odd thoughts by suggesting that they should get on with their work and talk at the same time. Vic agreed and surprised Hannah by working with a will at her plaques, key rings and coasters. If this was a depressed girl, or one suffering from some other serious mental distraction, she nevertheless managed to work very hard and she had some beautiful designs – exploding firework shapes, some of them with reflections from the sea which had given her inspiration.

'Why did they have to uproot that orchard behind our holiday house?' asked Vic at one point.

'I don't know why that was done,' said Hannah. 'I do know why they didn't do it before. There was a covenant.'

'A what?'

'A covenant. A legal arrangement to make something happen, or not happen. The land that the houses are built on over on that side of the road originally belonged to a lady whose son was killed in the First World War. She planted the orchard in his memory. She also presented a sapling to every householder in the town.'

'Every one!' exclaimed Vic. 'She must have been well off.'

'Well, it was a much smaller town in those days, but yes, she was pretty well off. Her family had a big property in the countryside with lots of fruit trees in a...'

'Walled garden!' exclaimed Vic.

Hannah was surprised again. 'You know it?' she asked.

'I think we've been there, with my Grandparents. The same one I think Fish and Sarah hiked to. You know, it says in their card.'

Hannah looked puzzled. 'Not in mine, I don't think,' she said, hesitantly.

'Oh,' said Vic, with disappointment. Then, after a moment's reflection, 'No, it was a voicemail he sent us. They went for a hike there because I told him about it after I went there.' She described the pool and the neglected plants.'

'That sounds like it,' Hannah agreed. 'Well, that's where all the apple trees came from.'

'Is there one here?' asked Vic.

'Well, there is an old apple tree down among the shrubs at the bottom of this garden and there are a few more like it in some of the other gardens around here.' A distracting thought must have come into her mind because she paused for a moment and then said, 'Hang on a minute. I must check the time.' She went over to the house and came back almost immediately, saying, 'Look, I'm supposed to walk someone's dog for them in a minute. Why don't you come with me. I can point out the apple trees I know as we go.'

Even though Vic was obviously in a strange mood at the moment, Hannah could hardly believe that a youngster like her could be interested in spotting a few old trees, but she knew she would like the dog. Sure enough, when they got to her old neighbour's house a middle-aged but still frisky Labrador was waiting at the gate for what it seemed to know was coming. Vic was immediately lost in the delight of an animal that nuzzled you affectionately and responded ecstatically to tickles behind its ears. The dog's owner was very old and came very slowly down to the gate with them.

Hannah greeted her and introduced Vic. The old lady smiled vaguely at her through glistening eyes and stood looking at them as they strolled away with the exceptionally well-behaved dog.

As they walked away up the path behind the house, Hannah said, 'She's on her own, you know, and she still does her garden. She just can't walk any distance.'

'The dog must really matter to her, then,' said Vic. 'What would she do if she lost it?'

'The same thing she's done the other two times, I suppose,' said Hannah.

'Two times?'

'Yes. This isn't her first dog, you know. They don't live as long as us. She had two others. They both died. She was sad, I know that, but she got on with things just the same.' While she was talking, Hannah was actually thinking hard about where the apple trees were. It did not occur to her that there might be any connection between what she was saying about the old lady and Vic's life. But Vic made the connection, even though she said nothing. Somehow, this simple piece of information about a person she had never met before and who she would probably never meet again after today, was making her think quite seriously about her own experiences.

The path they were walking along was another steep one, like the one up from the hotel, except that it was among houses and gardens instead of overgrown bushes and trees. Vic held the dog's lead and just followed. He or she – for some reason its name hadn't been mentioned when they had picked it up – knew the route and pulled her along. Hannah walked behind because the need to spot old apple trees slowed her down.

An hour later they had been to the top of the hill and seen several trees which looked about the right age. They had actually stopped next to one and a woman who must have been even older than the lady whose dog they were walking had come out and spoken to them. She obviously knew Hannah, because her face lit up when she saw her. But that was nothing to what happened when the subject of apple trees came up. Then, her face changed completely and she seemed suddenly to be half her age as vivid childhood memories returned. Looking at Vic all the time, as if picturing herself when she had been her age, she told them that when she was young everyone knew about the trees. 'None of us youngsters was allowed to climb one,' she said. 'They say it was out of respect for the lady's son but we just felt there was something strange about them. Ah, the things children imagine!' she laughed as they took their leave and walked on down the hill.

When they got back to Hannah's house there was a large van outside and a man was in the process of taking a lot of boxes round to the back of the house.

'Colin!' Hannah exclaimed. 'I'd forgotten you were coming this morning. I am sorry. Vic, this is Colin Goodwick. He sells the stuff I make in his shop.'

'He also brings the materials for making the next lot, at no extra charge!' added the man in a heavily serious tone. He winked at Vic to indicate that this was just part of a little wind-up aimed at Hannah. 'You must be Hannah's talented new apprentice,' he added, holding out his hand.

Another grown-up who speaks to you like one of them, thought Vic as she took his very large hand. He was also one of those people who doesn't just shake your hand but keeps hold of it for longer than you expect. She usually found this annoying but this Colin Goodwick was nice. 'I've got a daughter about your age,' he said. 'You'd like her.'

'Why don't you bring her up later?' asked Hannah.

'Sorry, no can do,' he replied. 'She's gone off for a week to France with the wife. I can't get away this time of year,' he added, for Vic's benefit. 'Can't leave all you lovely tourists with nowhere to spend your money, can we!'

Hannah had meanwhile been taking one of the boxes round to the workshop. She came back with another in her arms for Colin to take away and said to Vic, 'Have you looked at the time? Your Dad will be expecting you.'

'Oh! Right!' said Vic. 'I'll go now. Have I left anything in the workshop?'

'It won't matter if you have,' said Hannah. 'You can get it this afternoon.' She glanced towards Colin, who looked as if he was hanging around for a chat, and added, meaningfully, 'We can finish our conversation later, if you like.'

'OK,' said Vic. 'I'll get back as quick as I can to try to finish off my designs. Unless Dad has planned another special lunch break! Bye, Mr. Goodwick!'

'Call me Colin!' He shouted, as she headed for the gate. 'And don't forget to come into my shop! You can't miss it! And bring money!!'

When Vic got home Dad had two surprises for her. The first was a picnic lunch, but spread out in the sun lounge so they would get the benefit of the view without being in the cold wind, which was still blowing even though the rain had gone and the sky was now bright. The second was that he knew Colin Goodwick's shop. At least, he presumed he did because Fish had told him about a gift shop he and Sarah had been in which was piled to the rafters with what the family called "Clart" and everybody else called "Trinkets" or "Ornaments".

Vic found out about that when she decided to ask him for another detail about Mum. She had digested the previous day's information and this time she wanted to hear something new and real. She had thought very carefully and decided to ask Dad to tell her something that wasn't all "pink" as she put it, not just a selection of carefully chosen nice things.

'Well, I'll do my best,' Dad had said cautiously. 'In a relationship you can't choose all the things you would like in a person. We change, so there's no point in getting wound up about whether things are good or bad. But if you want "warts and all", as they say, and as we've just used it in relation to Mr Goodwick's shop, your mum did use the word "clart" a lot. To me it sounds like another word for "rubbish", but your mother's family also used it to mean what my own mother would call "bits and bobs". And she especially used it to describe any object that was in her way, especially if she was doing the hoovering, when everything seemed to be in her way! And that used to upset Fish because the things that were in her way were almost always his precious things that she was trying to hoover around. I often had to patch things up between them after he had run off crying because he thought she was calling his precious models and pictures "rubbish"!'

'She took after Grandma, then,' observed Vic. 'I've heard her use it if Grandad brings any of his tools into the house.'

'True,' said Dad. 'Though in his case I think soldering irons on the dining room table and bits of wood with nails sticking out of them on the living room floor really do qualify as "clart"!'

They both laughed at that, Dad with especial feeling because he was secretly delighted that Vic seemed increasingly able to talk about things to do with her mother without becoming upset. He had waited some time for this to happen and it made him feel that this holiday was what the family might call "VFM", short for "Value For Money", although financial transactions were the last thing they ever described that way!

While they finished off the picnic, Vic had told her father as much as she wanted to reveal at the moment about her pyrography designs. She wasn't going to tell him everything because that would give away surprises she had planned. Luckily, she also had the dog-walking to tell him about, though she left out the details about the apple trees.

'So you'll need to be getting back to make up for lost art time,' he said, understanding, as he often did, what she needed. They were finishing their picnic by now and Dad said he would tidy up if Vic wanted to go. She gave him a hug, which rather surprised him, and dashed off back down the hill.

Hannah was on the phone by an open front door when she arrived and she just waved Vic through. By the time she joined her in the workshop Vic had warmed up the pyrograph and finished one design – a Catherine Wheel-inspired pattern on a drinks coaster.

'Hello,' she said. 'I hope I didn't make you jump.'

'No,' said Vic. 'How does this look?'

'Very good!' said Hannah, and Vic knew she meant it. She wasn't one of those adults who praised you just because you were a child.

'Do you think I'll have time to finish them all today?' asked Vic. 'I've still got five coasters to do and a couple of key rings. The only things I've finished as a set are the name plaques.'

'Well, you can come back before the end of the week if necessary,' said Hannah.

'I don't know,' said Vic. 'I suppose Dad will have Fish with him. Maybe a morning or an afternoon.' It occurred to Hannah, who by now had a reasonable picture of Vic's life, that this hint of being a little less dependent would warm her father's heart – and Fish's, come to that

They worked on quietly for a while until the inevitable coffee break came round. Vic came in with the cat. It had tried to get into the workshop, something it knew was not allowed as it could do itself harm on some of the equipment.

'So that's where the moggy went!' said Hannah, grinning.

'Yes,' said Vic. 'This annoying thing stopped me working, didn't you?' She held the cat up and stared into its face, her smiling expression and gentle arms making it plain that her words were not seriously meant.

'All fine at the holiday home?' asked Hannah, casually.

'Yeah,' said Vic. 'Dad's getting masses of writing done and he's making plans for when Fish returns.'

'Oh really? What sort of plans?'

'Oh, I've no idea. Dad can be very secretive. You just learn to pick up little clues. Maps lying around, that sort of thing. It's an art observing my father.'

'And how about Apple?'

Vic was amazed how unfazed Hannah seemed to be about this. Surely she should really be wondering what I'm going on about, she thought. Yet she takes me apple tree hunting and asks about mysterious apparitions as if they were commonplace. She found herself wondering whether there was something some grown-ups know which they don't speak about in most company.

'Nothing,' she said. 'I didn't mention fruit of any kind. I even had a natural yoghurt for pudding, which I hate!'

Hannah dropped the subject and they both got on with their work until Vic's arms and legs ached. 'Am I meant to ache like this?' she asked.

'Well, workshop work is more demanding than you think. Even if you sit down all day you spend so much time on hand-eye coordinated tasks that the strain tends to build up. It doesn't help either that you often find you have been holding your hands or arms in a fixed position for longer than usual. Does your neck ache, too?'

Avoiding transferring the dust and dirt on her fingers to the back of her neck, Vic rubbed it instead with the face of her wrist. 'Yes, it does,' she said with a grimace.

Hannah smiled knowingly. 'Thought so. It's strain. Either that or you're getting the flu!'

'Oh no! Not on my holiday!'

Hannah reassured her. 'Relax. Like I said, it's normal. So, what have you got left to do?'

'Not too much. But I will need another hour or two.'

'Well, we'll have to find a way before the end of the week. Unless you want me to finish them off for you. No!' she added hastily, remembering how possessive she was about her own work. 'Forget I said that. I must respect your artistic integrity. Oh dear, I promised myself after I left art college that I wouldn't turn into the sort of person who came out with pretentious arty sayings like that! Well, there you go. In fact, there you do go. It's time you were back with your father. Time to find out what treat he has planned for tonight.'

Vic was rather hoping that Dad hadn't planned too much for the evening and, sure enough, he seemed to have realized that she might need a quiet night in. He had planned one of her favourite meals – pasta baked with tinned tuna and cheese sauce – and a relaxing evening watching TV and playing cards. She took a long luxurious bath which disposed of all her workshop aches, and enjoyed the evening no end. It also gave her a chance to get her diary up to date, something she realized she had neglected for a couple of days.

Half way through the evening they checked the mobile for messages. There was no news. 'I'll leave it on in case Fish wants to tell us about tomorrow,' Dad decided, sounding more disappointed than Vic.

'Didn't he know when he would be back?' asked Vic.

'Yes. Just after lunch, or so he said. Sarah's got a shift at the chip shop tomorrow evening, so it can't be any later than that.'

Vic decided to take the direct route. 'What have you got planned for him when he gets back?' she asked.

Dad's eyes widened in mock innocence. 'Plans for tomorrow? Me? How could you possibly suggest such a thing?!'

Vic threw a cushion at him, laughing. She stopped laughing immediately because she could hear the dog barking, but when she investigated it was just someone teasing it in next door's back garden.

As she sat back down, Dad said, 'I've been thinking about your mother today.'

'Uh-huh,' was Vic's non-commital reply. She was beginning to cope with her own feelings but she wasn't sure she was ready to deal with Dad's emotions just yet.'

'Yes,' he went on. 'She would have really loved this place. There's plenty of room, you see, and corners for everyone to go off into. She wasn't really a great outings person, you see. She saw holidays as times for longer lie-ins. This house isn't like some we used to stay in, where we were crammed together and needed to go out visiting things at all hours of the day. She would have tucked herself away in a new corner every day."

He stopped there and Vic was glad that he had left it as an observation, especially as it sounded to her as if he was telling her something about Mum that might not have been one of his favourite things. Dad was, after all, an early bird and even a holiday didn't make him vary his time of getting up because he liked to get at least one worthwhile thing done in the morning. If Mum didn't like getting up Vic imagined that he must have spent a lot of time hanging around waiting. She would not really have liked discussing that with him. She looked in his direction and was glad to see that he was already half absorbed in a book.

'I'm going to bed,' she announced.

'Hmmm? Oh yes. Goodnight,' he said, distractedly.

She went off to bed and found she couldn't sleep, not because of the dog but because she was excited about Fish coming home. She realized that she had given him very little thought and, feeling a bit guilty about that kept her from sleeping for a while.

14

WEDNESDAY

Ironically, Vic overslept in the morning. At least she overslept by the standards of their household. It was nearly nine o'clock when she rolled over and picked up her bedside clock where it lay flat on its back. It wasn't meant to, but the folding stand was also the mechanism for illuminating the face, and that had snapped about three days after she had got it.

She went downstairs to find Dad standing looking out of the sun lounge at a blazing blue sky.

'Good afternoon!' he said, seeing her reflection in the glass as she tried to sneak up and make him jump. 'Look at that weather. I can't remember there not being at least one cloud dashing across that bay since we came here. I can hardly get used to it; normally you'd think they grew out of the landscape naturally. If Fish was home he would insist on us going to the beach.'

Having seen the local clouds since her spectacular

introduction to them on the very first day of the holiday, Vic knew what Dad was talking about. She also liked his appreciation of the clouds and remembered what one of her aunts had once said. "Why doesn't anyone in our family notice things and put them into words the way you do?" she had asked Dad. "All our family does is shout a lot and talk about ourselves!" He hadn't replied, just smiled, proudly or with embarrassment. You never could tell which where Dad was concerned.

'What *are* we going to do until he gets here? Vic asked.

'Well, it's nine o'clock now and if he's due back around lunchtime we can't do too much. How about visiting that sea centre down in Oilslick Bay?'

'Why not?' said Vic. She was actually thinking that she knew perfectly well why not. It was one of those buildings which looked very stylish from the outside – all curved white walls and no sign of anything looking like a window but it also bore no obvious sign of an entrance or any staff. There was always at least one place like this wherever they went on holiday and it usually became "The place we never went to during our holidays." She said this to Dad and he promptly told her one of his favourite things about Mum.

'She started that idea off,' he said. When we first met she worked near this park where office workers and students went at lunchtime. One of those islands of greenery in between two busy roads going in and out of the city. Well, she got off the bus next to it every day and, when we bought our first car we would sometimes drive past it on the way to the coast. And she always used to say we should visit it. And we never did. "Finch's Field' it was called. And ever after that, anywhere we didn't seem to get round to visiting was called a "Finch's Field", or a "Finch" for short.'

'Like Cockney slang,' said Vic, and realized that they were having another normal conversation about Mum.

'Yeah, a bit like that,' he replied.

So she ate her breakfast while Dad made himself a small flask of black coffee to drink down by the bay later. While he did so he gave her another snippet of information about Mum. Apparently she had disliked flasks. She always said they gave drinks a strange flavour, he explained, adding, 'Wherever we went for an "explore", even though I always took a hot drink in a flask, I always ended up buying her tea or coffee from a café or bar.'

While Vic was digesting this latest snippet of family history, he also explained that Mum had invented the family expression "an explore", but then promised to stop reminiscing, which Vic was grateful for. Even though she was pleased to be talking about Mum at long last, she felt that there was a limit to what her emotions could cope with all in one go.

Their outing did turn into a "Finch", however. The place was as shut as it looked, even though the opening times on a small board outside seemed to match the time on Vic's watch. Dad half-heartedly skimmed a couple of stones into Oilslick Bay and then Vic suggested that they go and sit by the flagpoles and drink their coffee. When they got there, Vic realised that she and Fish had never told Dad about their last visit to this end of the bay. He loved the story of the crabs and he chuckled for several minutes at the thought of a foreign visitor's vehicle nearly demolishing something paid for with European money.

The hour or more that they might have spent in an open museum had not really been used up by coffee and chatting but, the coffee gone and nothing else of interest presenting itself to distract them, they decided to walk back up to the house. No matter how slowly they walked they were still far earlier than they had planned to be. They both kept glancing round, hoping to be met by the sight of Fish coming up the road behind them and thereby making them feel as if something was going to happen. But all this hoping to get back to doing something together was a fairly pointless exercise because they had no idea when and how he might arrive. Dad tried turning it into a game which he called "Fishappears".

'He will arrive on foot, on his own after a passionate but private parting from the love of his life at the foot of the hill,' he said.

'He will sweep up to the house in a taxi, exhausted by failing to sleep in a tent for three consecutive nights,' suggested Vic.

'Sarah's Dad will drop him off but we will get no glimpse of Sarah who will have stopped off to see her Mum,' Dad offered.

They were still making up scenarios as they turned through the gate and descended the path to the front door and both jumped nearly out of their skins as Fish's voice reached them from where he sat, on the front garden seat. Vic probably jumped more than her father as the last thing that had occupied the seat had been the crumpled figure of Apple and for a moment she had thought it, he, or whatever, was making a reappearance.

'So this is your idea of welcoming me back!' he said.

'Your welcome depends on how extravagant you've been with the presents you have no doubt brought us,' Dad replied as Vic gave her brother a hug. They made their way indoors and Dad put the kettle on. 'Have you been here long?' he added, not waiting to be told about, or given, an actual gift. There were members of their family for whom such things were a priority but Dad was always just happy to see people and have a chat.

Fish looked at his watch. 'Five minutes,' he said. 'In fact, I'm surprised you didn't see Sarah's Dad's car go past you on its way back down the hill.'

'Maybe they stopped off to visit Hannah,' suggested Vic.

'Could be,' agreed Fish. 'So, you've found out the connection too, have you?' He didn't wait for a reply. 'How's the art coming along? Are you ready to put on your first exhibition?'

'You missed it!' Vic came back as quickly as Fish would.

'Oooh!' he said, in mock surprise and disappointment. 'You artists are such prima donnas.' He paused. 'Want to know what that means?'

'Not fussed,' said Vic. 'Takes one to explain one!'

Fish turned to their Dad. 'Blimey! What have you been feeding her on? Razors?'

Vic noticed that their conversation was different from the normal type of chat they usually had. She put it down to the fact that Fish had been away with his girlfriend. What she didn't know was that similar thoughts were crossing Fish's mind, except that he was putting the change down to Vic's artistic days with Hannah. Either of them might have been right, but the third person in the room – their father – was wondering whether Vic's seemingly new-found confidence had anything to do with them opening about her Mum over the past couple of days.. Fish got an inkling of this when Dad asked him how he, of all people, had been persuaded to go rambling.

'Oh, you know,' he replied. 'When your girlfriend says you have to go for an explore, you go!'

'That's Mum's word!' Vic interjected.

Fish paused, glanced at her and at Dad. Whatever he expected to happen didn't because Dad just grinned and said, 'Right!' and added, 'So another member of the family has now seen the famous walled garden.'

'Yeah,' Fish said. 'That's where I got the sheep postcard, which I am pleased to see has pride of place.' He reached over to the shelf above the gas fire and picked the card up. 'How do you like it?' he said. He held it up. Vic looked at Dad. Dad looked at Vic, and they heaved with laughter. 'I know!' said Fish. 'We laughed until we cried in the caravan. And to think that I was disappointed when I couldn't find anything to send you that was connected with those ancient apple trees.'

Dad carried on laughing but Vic stopped. Her listening re-tuned from the room to outside. The dog did not seem to be barking. She stood up and walked past the fruit bowl where there was now definitely a new green apple. 'Back in a minute,' she said over her shoulder. She found what she was looking for very quickly. A stack of twigs was slumped in what you could just about call a sitting position by the dustbin at the bottom of the path from the road. She knelt down and could scarcely tell whether it was Apple or just some bits of wood. She found herself feeling that nothing, not even a postcard of some silly sheep, could make her feel happy at this moment. She didn't even have to put her hand on the figure to tell that it was brittle to the point of snapping at a touch. Somehow, she knew that this was the last time she would see Apple, one way or another. She decided to take action. Turning on her heel she went inside.

'I've just got to go and see Hannah,' she announced to the others. 'Forgot something.' And with no more explanation and pausing for only a second to see whether either of them objected, she left, scooping up the squatting twig figure by the door as she went. She had no time to conceal it. She just had to hope no-one would see her or ask any awkward questions. The one saving grace was that it weighed nearly nothing.

As far as she could tell no-one saw her. When she reached Hannah's she went straight round the back and called into the workshop, 'Hannah!' She wasn't in there but she heard Vic and came out of the house.

She surprised Vic yet again by needing no explanation, or at least, not asking for one. She just looked at the shrivelled figure in Vic's arms and said, 'I have an idea. Come round the back.'

Vic followed her to where the old apple tree grew on the edge of a bank behind the workshop. 'Put it... er... him... down there,' she said, indicating a hollow where a couple of big roots came near the surface.

Vic did as instructed. 'OK,' Hannah added. 'My guess is that you've come away in a hurry. Right?'

Vic nodded.

'Well then, I've got a freshly baked cake in the kitchen. Take it back with you and tell them it's from us, for them to eat with their coffee, or whatever. Come back after lunch to finish your pyrography.'

Vic was in a daze, either from the latest episode with Apple or Hannah's astonishingly quick-witted solution to problems she hadn't even mentioned. She followed her through to the kitchen, took the cake and was back home to the huge and greedy delight of her father and brother less than ten minutes after she had dashed out. The alibi worked and when she said that she would like to go and finish her pyrography that afternoon, Fish said he was going to take a long bath. After holding his nose and expressing agreement for Fish's decision, Dad said he didn't have anything planned until the evening, but, typically, he wouldn't be drawn on what he had in mind.

Over lunch Vic did her best to look interested as Fish told them one or two things about his time with Sarah and her father. It turned out that the caravan was quite luxurious and the tent had been pretty comfortable too.

'Wasn't the ground hard?' Dad asked. 'This is Wales, after all. There's not a lot of soil on top of the local rock, you know.'

'I had a camp bed,' was Fish's reply. 'Not that it was especially comfortable, but the air between me and the ground was better than the ground!'

Apparently Sarah's father was especially keen on barbecues and that had occupied a large amount of their time.

'We've been all over the place hunting for ingredients,' Fish said. 'We've been up endless farm tracks to buy prime cuts of organic beef. We've been into the gardens of people he knows from his shop to select the best home grown onions and potatoes. It's filled at least half our waking time each day but he was kind enough to refuse my offers of help so I got to spend some time with Sarah while he prepared the feasts.'

'If that had been Grandpa he would have made you do the barbecue so he could tell you how you were doing it all wrong!' said Vic, trying to make an effort.

Dad agreed. 'We've all been there!' he said ruefully. 'But we've had rain here most of the time you've been away. Didn't the weather spoil it?' he added.

'No chance! He's got canopies to go over everything. Even a couple of those big outdoor heaters they use on café terraces when it gets chilly in the evenings.'

'It will have been chilly in the mornings, too, I imagine,' Dad commented.

Fish pulled a rueful face. 'Yeah, it was. And Sarah's Dad's other little ritual was porridge for breakfast.'

'Ah! Porridge. One of Mum's favourite things,' said Dad, grinning.

'Really?' said Fish, hesitantly. He had still not got used to the fact that Mum could now be a topic of conversation.

'No, not at all, actually. But whenever I made it, according to my favourite recipe: soaked overnight with a pinch of salt, gently simmered with milk in the morning and a scattering of sugar over the top, Mum would always say: "You can't make porridge like that. Salt and water, that's the way. It didn't make any difference that I was enjoying my deliciously creamy concoction, nor that she never actually ate porridge herself. In fact, I'm not sure there is any record of your mother ever having eaten porridge. But she had an opinion on it!"

Fish had obviously only been half-listening to Dad's explanation because he asked another question which made Dad frown with confusion. 'Why did you say "not at all"?

'Hmmm?'

'When I asked whether it was one of Mum's favourite things.'

'Oh, well, I've learned over the years that you don't have to have done something to have an opinion about it. That was Mum and porridge! Never touched the stuff but she was an authority on how to make the best kind!'

And so the chatter went. At least the chatter between Dad and Fish. Vic was suffering agonies of her own, not just because of Apple but because even in her present state she was actually beginning to enjoy the conversation. Any other time she would have loved to hang around, especially if the conversation should turn to the woman in Fish's life rather than the woman from Dad's life. But she knew she needed to get away back to Hannah. And Apple. If he was still there...

To the astonishment of the others she had virtually finished her food while they were still organizing theirs on their plates – another of her Mum's characteristics, which Dad would surely have told her about if she had not announced her sudden departure. 'I think I'll pop down to Hannah's now,' she said, abruptly.

'Oh, yes. Sure. Bye,' said Dad, glancing at the clock. He had just about got used to its reverse face by now, so he said with some confidence, 'Be back by five o'clock.' And then he added, in response to Fish's quizzical look, 'You'll find out why in good time.'

Vic hurried back down the hill and walked straight in through Hannah's front doorway.

'Is that you, Vic?' Hannah's voice came from the front room, one that hardly seemed to be used except as a vantage point for the cat to watch the road.

'Yes,' Vic replied. She looked round the door and saw that Hannah was picking up some sheets of paper that she had spread out on the floor. She looked up.

'I'm just filing some invoices and stuff,' she said. 'Go on through if you like. I'll meet you by the workshop.'

Vic made her way out to the back. She looked around for Apple but there was nothing to see. She ventured over to the workshop door and looked in. Still nothing. Stepping back out she heard the cat miaou and as she looked in the direction of the sound she saw it disappearing round the end of the workshop towards where the unfinished sculptures were kept. She followed and, as she reached the sculptures, Hannah also appeared.

Vic turned and said, 'Is this where I'm meant to be looking? I just followed the cat.'

'I don't know whether the cat knows what is going on,' Hannah smiled, 'But if you keep walking you should find what you're looking for. They walked past the sculptures, towards the old apple tree.

When they were about ten feet away Hannah stopped, motioning to Vic to keep going. Vic stepped forward and then turned and said, 'Where is he?'

Hannah said nothing but put her finger to her lips and looked upwards towards the middle of the tree. Vic turned and looked, still seeing nothing, but as her gaze searched the branches she could sense a certain movement at the heart of the tree, different from that caused by the breeze, and the more she looked she could see that a figure made up of branches was in there, at rest but shifting occasionally.

'He's alright!' she exclaimed.

'For the moment,' Hannah agreed, cautiously.

Vic's face fell once more. 'What do you mean?' she asked.

'Well,' said Hannah, searching for the words. 'It's not exactly a family, is it?'

'A family?'

'Well, I don't know what he looks like to you, but to me he's young...' she paused to see whether Vic was following her line of thought. She could see she still wasn't getting through properly. She tried another tack.

'Look. It's like your life and my life. Just because I've split up with my husband doesn't mean we can't be civilised to each other, and my daughter means everything to me, even though the arrangement is that she lives with her father.' She paused. 'And correct me if I'm wrong but you told me yourself that even though you hardly knew your Mum you need some memories of her.' Vic's expression changed as she began to grasp Hannah's train of thought.

'Apple's missing his family?'

Hannah smiled.

'But where are they?' Vic asked, looking round at the tree and its occupant. 'Oh!' she exclaimed. 'The rest of the trees! The orchard! The one they grubbed up.' Then her face fell. 'But it's gone. Apple's Mum and Dad and brothers and sisters, or whatever he would call them, aren't alive any more.'

'Yes, but his Grandparents probably are.'

Vic looked bemused once again.

'The walled garden. Where you went with *your* Grandparents when they were filling in for your Dad.' She paused and then added, 'Where the person who set the trees in this town grew them as saplings.'

Vic's thoughts suddenly tumbled over themselves. 'Of course! They're his nearest surviving family! We've got to take him there. Have we got time? Will it be open? Where will we find transport?'

Hannah let her talk and only when she sensed that Vic had exhausted her thoughts did she say, 'We'll drive him there in my car.'

'*Your car?*' asked Vic, failing to conceal the astonishment in her voice. 'I didn't think you had one.'

'Well, it's not a major subject of conversation for me!' Hannah laughed. 'But yes, I do. I don't need it much but it's there, in one of the garages you walk past every time you come up the hill.'

'That's why I didn't think you had one,' said Vic. 'You have no drive.'

'Deductions can be false,' Hannah said with a gentle smile, 'But that's a conversation for another time. However, the drive detail is important. If I had one we could do what needs doing without too much risk of being observed. The neighbours are used to seeing me lugging lumps and bundles of wood back and forth but it would be just our luck to bump into someone who might stop and then notice we were doing something, shall we say, "odd". So we'll have to be on the lookout while we get him down the path and into the car while it's out on the road. We can't walk him down to the garage. Apart from anything else, it's one of a row and someone else could easily drive up while we're there.' Hannah paused and then added, 'So… We'll just have to give it a go and hope for the best. I'll lock the house and fetch the car. You climb the tree,' said Hannah.

'What?' said Vic, puzzled once again.

'Well, someone's got to let him know what we're doing. He knows you, doesn't he?'

'I suppose so. I'll try. I'm not very good at climbing trees,' she added as Hannah walked away, but her words went unheard, or ignored. She went up to the tree's base and pulled something which might have been a sculpture up against it to help her reach the lowest strong branch. She pulled herself up and scrambled into the crook of the lowest branches, just below Apple. He spoke first. She had actually been composing a sentence to start her explanation with, so it surprised her considerably to hear what he said.

'It's a good idea.'

'What?' she asked. 'Bringing you to this tree, you mean?'

'No. The orchard.'

Vic was nonplussed. 'You know? How do you know? Did Hannah tell you?'

'I can hear more than you think. Your friend knows about the apple. She's in touch. I can sense it.'

'Well, you know what we need to do, then.'

'Yes.'

'You don't sound happy about it.'

'It will be good *if* I can last long enough.'

'Are you still weak?'

Hannah's voice suddenly interrupted them from below. '*Of course* he's weak. He'd almost completely dried out when you got him to me. He needs more than just this tree. Come on. The car's ready.'

Vic had turned away from Apple to speak to Hannah.

When she turned back he was no longer there. She felt a momentary sense of panic and then noticed movement below her and when she looked down he was leaning against the trunk below her. 'There are some advantages to being related to trees!' she muttered as she scrambled down, rather more slowly.

The walk to the car was a challenge. At first, Apple declined Vic's offered hand. Then he wobbled as he walked and by the time they rounded the workshop he was leaning heavily on her. From there, she could almost see him getting smaller as they staggered step by step, down the side of the house. Hannah was waiting with the car door open and she shielded him as best she could as Vic did what *she* could to help him into the back of the car. It was like pushing several awkward broomsticks, but eventually she managed to get him in before anyone came along. Then she got in the front with Hannah.

As they drove off, she exclaimed suddenly and Hannah nearly swerved with astonishment.

'What's the matter?' she asked, half turning her head in case it was something to do with Apple.

'I haven't told Dad where I'm going.'

'Taken care of,' smiled Hannah. 'I called him on my mobile as I was walking down to the garage. I've told him you're helping me fetch some wood. Or rather, I told your brother, who now has your mobile switched on permanently. I think it must be something to do with my daughter. "Only three days left", as she put it when they got back!'

'Is that how she sees it?' asked Vic.

'What do you mean?'

'Well, a holiday romance. One that ends in two weeks.'

Hannah paused thoughtfully for a moment. 'Actually, no. I don't think so. I think she's quite smitten. Sarah's not like me.' She looked at Vic, apparently uncertain for the first time exactly how she should talk about this to a girl of her age. She chose directness. 'What I mean is, I fell for the first man I met and then regretted it later. Sarah's more cautious. But she likes your brother.'

'That's nice,' said Vic, with feeling.

Hannah smiled very broadly indeed. 'Yes, it is, isn't it?'

The walled garden was only about two miles out of town and the conversation about Fish and Sarah took them half way there. Apple was not stirring in the back and whenever Vic glanced over he seemed more and more frail. Eventually, they pulled into the lay-by and, as Vic went to open her door, Hannah said, 'Hold on a moment. I'll just go and check the lie of the land. Heavens,' she added with a grin, 'I promised myself I wouldn't turn into the sort of person who sounds like a character in a film, and there I go! You stay here, in case anyone comes along who might notice what we have in the back.'

She pushed the car door open. 'What will I do if someone does come along?' Vic asked anxiously.

'To be absolutely honest, I haven't the faintest idea. I'm afraid you're on your own with that,' Hannah said, without apology. 'You'll have to improvise.'

As soon as Hannah got out of the car, Vic began trying to think what a passerby might say and how she would reply. It proved unnecessary, however, as Hannah came back very quickly.

'We're in luck,' she said, pulling the rear door open.

'There's no sign of anyone. Let's go.'

Getting out of the car and into the garden was a reverse repeat of getting in. Apple's limbs were now so brittle that they seemed likely to snap as soon as they were touched. Once they had got him upright it took both of them to support him as they passed through the gateway and down the zig-zag cinder path which led to the screen of bushes beyond which was the orchard.

As they went, Vic found herself wondering how this could all be happening. She had had enough experience of Apple to get past the strangeness of his existence but the fact that Hannah, an adult, could be helping her to walk a figure which looked like a bundle of branches and twigs into a garden in the Welsh countryside just bewildered her. She looked across at her helper, wondering whether to ask, but there didn't seem much point and, a moment later, when they cleared the shrub area and stepped tentatively across the open strip of grass in front of the orchard, she was too focused on looking out for other people to do anything but support Apple and walk.

A moment later, as they passed between the first two trees, any thoughts of discussing the matter with Hannah were dashed from her mind as she felt a sharp stabbing sensation in her arm. She yelped out loud and looked down. As she did so, Hannah, who had glanced across at her when she heard the yelp, drew her breath in sharply and pulled her hand away from where it was grasping Apple. 'Something dug into my hand!' she said.

'And my arm!' added Vic, rubbing the spot where the discomfort had been felt.

These distractions had brought them both to a halt to investigate their injuries. Before they could do more than rub their skin they looked up in astonishment to see Apple walking on in front of them. He was upright and appeared not just to be growing in stature but actually growing. And not just walking; he had gained what could only be called a stride. And he seemed to have forgotten them.

'He's sprouting!' said Vic. 'That's what dug in to us.

For once, Hannah didn't seem to know what to do or say. She watched silently as the figure of Apple walked, grew more upright and even took on a fresher, shiny brown hue. And he was definitely sprouting, gaining bulk in all directions even as they looked. Then she touched Vic's arm and said, 'Time to go. We mustn't draw attention to ourselves.

'But I haven't said goodbye,' said Vic, resisting Hannah's efforts.

'He would have said it if he wanted to,' replied Hannah wisely and led her up the cinder path.

Half-way up, Vic stopped and turned. She thought she could see Apple moving slowly from tree to tree and then she wasn't sure. And then she couldn't make him out.

'That's it, then,' said Hannah, who was peering at a plant next to them and trying not to draw undue attention as she noticed a car pull up by the gate..

'Oh,' said Vic.

'You may have noticed that we adults don't know everything, but one thing I do know is that goodbyes aren't always as special as we may wish…' Hannah began, and then she stopped.

Down around the orchard a breeze had stirred and although the apple trees themselves were unmoved, the waving of the willows and beech and other tall trees around the perimeter was clear. As they looked, a dusty cloud swirled up from the orchard as if disturbed by the wind.

'Butterflies!' exclaimed Vic.

'Or moths,' said Hannah. 'They like dry old bits of wood, and there's plenty of that here.

As they looked, the cloud rose a few feet above the trees, spread out, seeming less and less to flutter and more and more to just hang. Then it settled back down.

'It *was* a special goodbye!' said Vic as the wind dropped.

'Indeed,' Hannah agreed, glad to be proved wrong 'Now, I think it's time we went and finished what we told your father we were doing. It's always best if an alibi is actually true.'

They didn't talk at all on the way back. Vic helped put the car away and it was only as they walked up to the house that Hannah said, 'I'll make some fresh coffee while you warm up the irons.' Then they went about their tasks and made little further conversation until the coffee had been drunk. It was when Vic had finished off her designs, something she managed quite quickly, that she did something which made Hannah chatty once again. Vic had found time to do one more than previously planned. It was a key ring fob which Hannah hadn't seen her making so she was genuinely surprised when Vic presented it to her. The design made her exclaim with delight.

'An apple with a moth on it!' she said with genuine emotion. 'That's what art should do, you know,' she added and, seeing Vic's quizzical look, she explained. 'It's a way of making a creative record of our experiences. At least, that's what they told me at college. And this proves it, don't you think?' It was Vic's turn to smile very broadly indeed. Hannah saw this and said, 'Oh, and I told myself I wouldn't turn into the sort of grown-up who tries to pass on wise snippets to children… What?' she added, as Vic laughed out loud at the latest use of her friend's favourite expression.

Although Hannah was a very open person, Vic decided not to explain what had really amused her. She had learned with her father that people have characteristics which they themselves don't necessarily notice and that even if they strike you as fun it is not always fair to point them out. Luckily, the cat came out to have a fuss made of it and that put a stop to that bit of conversation anyway.

Hannah helped her put all the things Vic had made into a spare wooden box from the workshop and accompanied her to the front door. 'I won't say "goodbye" just now,' she said. You're not going home until Saturday so our paths will probably cross.' She held the front door open for Vic and then pushed it slightly shut in that way people have of saying, "Hang on, I've thought of something".

'Tell you what,' she said. 'Why don't you and Fish and your Dad come here for supper on Friday? I don't imagine you'll have much left in your own cupboards the day before leaving and you can have a restful evening before your long drive home on Saturday.

'You don't know Dad!' laughed Vic. He times everything up to the last minute. And I've got a feeling

Fish might want to spend his last evening with Sarah. But I'll ask anyway.'

'I might have a way of getting round that last problem,' said Hannah. 'Ask your Dad to give me a call when you've all talked it over.'

'OK. Thanks. Bye,' said Vic and she went back up to the Pilot's Cottage to resume her holiday, or what was left of it.

***

Back at the house she decided not to make the presentations or pass on Hannah's message immediately. Dad, it turned out, had booked a lane at the bowling alley and they were then going to a restaurant he had found. 'You'll love it,' he told them.

'He means he'll love it,' sighed Fish with mock-weariness..

'No, you will,' Dad insisted. 'There's a bar downstairs, done up to look like something out of a Western movie. And upstairs there's a sort of family area on a kind of balcony which runs right round the first floor level. You get up to it by a wide staircase that you can just imagine some glamorous film star descending and making all the customers' jaws drop.' He gave up at that point because Fish and Vic were making a very bad job of seeming to be seriously interested.

When they got there, it turned out to be every bit as good as he had said, better even. What Dad had neglected to mention was the cheeky bar staff who flirted with everyone and the huge quantity of film props which had been used to partition off the sections of the eating area.

Vic spent the whole meal thinking the waitress had come back to their table because opposite her, behind Dad, was a life-size model of an American Indian. Every time she lifted her eyes from her food she had to remind herself there wasn't a person there. "And just when I manage to move Apple out of my life," she thought.

And the food! It too was just like something out of a Western movie and they ate the most enormous burgers and banana splits until they were stuffed to the gills.

When they got home, Vic made her presentations. She gave Dad a set of coasters with fireworks pyrographed into them. Fish received an egg cup with the words "Barbecue Boy" on one side and something which he generously agreed looked like a tent on the other.

As they were going to bed, Dad said, 'Something strange happened today. The dog next door barked furiously for a couple of minutes but when I looked out of the window it was gazing up at me with its tongue hanging out and its tail wagging nineteen to the dozen. I went down to get the washing in later and it actually let me reach up and tickle it behind the ears. I thought I'd lost my touch with dogs. Amazing, eh?'

Vic just smiled but, as she went upstairs she thought. 'Yes. Really amazing'.

As she got into bed she had another thought, "Botheration!" she said to herself.

She had forgotten to pass on Hannah's supper invitation.

15

THURSDAY

She forgot the message in the morning as well because breakfast was a bit of a rush. Fish had obviously been missing his comfortable bed because it proved exceptionally difficult to prise him out of it. Dad was preoccupied with getting food and drink ready for a trip to Whitesands Bay and Vic was packing the beach stuff, which had all thoroughly dried since the weekend, except for one or two items which had stood, forgotten, in the rain, and had to be put in plastic bags for the trip.

Finally, when they were well over half-way there, Vic yelped.

'What?' said Dad, alarmed, taking his foot off the accelerator.

'It's OK,' said Vic, and then, 'Sorry!' as he gave her a look which meant "Don't distract drivers". 'It's just that I remembered something that I was supposed to ask you.'

'Which was... ?' Dad inquired.

'Hannah says would we all like to go and have supper with her on Friday night.'

Dad was surprisingly agreeable. 'Well, I did have one or two ideas about Friday, but I don't see why not.'

Fish, who was sitting in the back for this journey, was quiet for a while. Eventually he said, 'Is anyone going to ask me what I think?'

Dad looked genuinely puzzled. 'Ask you what you think about what?'

'The supper invitation.'

'Er..OK…' He glanced at Vic, who had suddenly found the contents of the glove compartment deeply interesting. 'What do you think about the invitation?.'

'Well, Sarah and I were planning to see each other before we go home,' Fish stated, baldly.

'I see,' Dad replied. 'Well, I suppose Vic and I could go on our own.'

'Now you're making me feel as if I'm breaking things up again,' said Fish, surprisingly aggressively.

"He *must* be in love" Vic thought and decided to keep out of it.

Dad said, 'Not at all.'

There was another lengthy silence which lasted until they had parked and carried their things down to the beach, which was as warm and bright as the first time they had seen it. When they had put everything in place, Fish suddenly broke the silence by saying, 'Can I have the mobile phone?'

'Certainly can,' said Dad, digging it out of his pocket.

'Thanks. I'm phoning Sarah,' he added, by way of explanation, and started to walk away for privacy. Vic and her Dad exchanged looks but said nothing on the subject. Fish walked a little way up the beach, looking at the phone. Then he stopped and studied it for a minute or so and then turned and came straight back.

'That was quick,' said Dad in as good-humoured a way as he could, knowing he was likely to get his head bitten off.

To his surprise his head remained on his shoulders. Fish grinned sheepishly and then said, 'There was a voicemail for me. From Sarah.' He hesitated.

'And... ?' asked Dad.

'She wanted to tell me that she had heard about the invitation for supper and that it's a great idea because her Mum has something planned. For her and me, I mean.'

Vic now realised what Hannah had meant when she had said that she might have a way of getting round the problem. She didn't bother to share her thought, in case it got rid of the pleasant atmosphere which had only just returned. Instead she threw a towel at Fish and challenged him to a race into the sea. This didn't last long as Vic had forgotten how early it was and the chill in the shallow water chased them back up the beach to put wet suits on. Then they spent the best part of an hour letting the waves carry them the length and breadth of the bay. Neither actually admitted it, but they had missed each other and it was nice to just relax together.

Fish noticed that his sister didn't seem tense any more and she noticed that he had relaxed and made fewer "smart Alec" remarks as Grandad called them. Neither of them actually mentioned this either. But they did listen to each other.

Fish listened while Vic told him about Hannah's workshop, the fireworks, going to the cinema and putting up with Dad. Vic listened as he told her about having damp socks in the morning because he left them outside the tent, walking miles across the Welsh countryside and... putting up with Sarah's Dad!

Eventually, the real Fish did reappear, as he tipped her off the body board she was floating on and said 'Race you back to up the beach.' He was furious, again just like the "old" Fish, when Vic won because he got the cord of the body board tangled up in the Velcro fastening of his wetsuit and had to sit down in the shallows and disentangle it.

Dad had brought a flask of hot drinking chocolate, which they consumed very quickly indeed.

When they had drunk it all, Dad said, 'You know, I've never been to see what's round the Northern headland of the bay.' He glanced at Vic, remembering that the only reason that he had been to the Southern headland had been to break the news of Fish's camping trip. He needn't have worried; she betrayed no concern as she got a book out of her bag and left Fish to "volunteer", as they knew one must, to accompany Dad on his walk.

'Back in a while,' Dad said, as they trudged off. Fish gave her a grin, which she did not notice, absorbed, as she already was, in her book.

She was so absorbed that she did not notice when a shadow fell across her and stopped. Then it moved away but, when it made a second appearance, about ten seconds later, she did notice it. She looked up.

'It *is* you,' said a man who was largely in silhouette

against the bright sky. She sat up, cautiously and then, when she no longer had to squint against the sun, she recognized him.

'Mr Goodwick!' she exclaimed.

'Colin, please,' he replied. 'Good day for the beach.'

'Yes, it is. But…'

'I know,' he smiled. 'I'm not exactly dressed for the beach am I? This is business. I'm just taking a break. Had a delivery to make to the house over there.' He gestured towards the direction in which Fish and Dad had walked. 'There's another of those artist people living there, too. Place is crawling with them.' He waved an ice cream that she now noticed he was holding. 'Getting into the spirit of the seaside with this, though,' he grinned. Then he added, 'So, I'll be seeing you tomorrow night, then.'

Vic looked at him quizzically.

'At Hannah's,' he explained.

Vic was just about to say how nice that would be when Dad and Fish returned. Dad looked slightly concerned about Vic's unexpected adult company but when she introduced him, he relaxed and shook Colin's hand.

'He's coming to Hannah's tomorrow, too,' said Vic.

'Thank goodness,' Dad said, with mock relief in his voice. 'That means the men won't be outnumbered!'

'Unless Hannah's invited anyone else,' observed Fish.

'Oh dear, yes,' said Colin. She has a habit of adding people onto her list. 'I may not be the only one to have got an invite. Anyway,' he said, looking at his watch. 'Time I made my next delivery. Nice to meet you. See you tomorrow.' And off he went.

'Good way to beat the beach queue,' observed Fish,

watching him trudge over the sand. 'But he must be roasting in his work clothes!'

Dad was looking pensive. He began to unpack the picnic things and said, 'That was one of Mum's words.'

Vic looked at Fish to see whether she had missed something. Fish's face was blank.

'What was?' she asked.

'Eh?' said Dad.

'What was one of Mum's words?'

'Oh! "Invite". She never said "invitation". Scottish habit, I think. Picked up from her parents. I wonder whether your friend has Scottish ancestry?'

'Welsh… Scottish…' put in Fish. All Celts, you know.'

'Yeah,' Dad smiled. Normally, he loved talking about words but this one seemed to have brought back serious memories. He seemed happy enough, but from the way he busied himself with the bags they could tell he was reflecting on something. When he had finished, there in front of them were a platter of cold seafood, some soft continental bread, jars of pickles, a bowl of salad and two very smelly pieces of cheese.

'Where's the ginger beer?' Asked Fish.

'Why should there be ginger beer?' asked Vic.

'So we could be like the Famous Five,' Fish explained. 'You know. In the books. Their picnics always included "Lashings of ginger beer" after a long list of picnic foods.'

'Voila!' cried Dad, triumphantly 'Great minds think alike!' And he flourished a large bottle of ginger beer which he had just taken out of the cool box.

Fish was impressed, and said so, but Vic's emotions suddenly caught up with her and she had to blow her nose long and hard until her eyes stopped watering. The other two pretended not to notice and instead finished unwrapping the food, which this time had been bought.

'I wondered when you would find time last night to prepare one of your spreads,' observed Fish. 'You've hit the delicatessen counter with a vengeance!'

'Well, why not,' said Dad. 'It's nearly the end of the hols after all.'

This time it was Fish's turn to react. He didn't become tearful but he did go silent for a while, something which he carefully tried to conceal by eating slowly and thoughtfully. But you could tell what his real feelings were. Vic hoped he wasn't too smitten with Sarah. One of her friends had had a "holiday romance" the previous year and she had taken ages to get over the fact that the boy never contacted her.

Then the mobile phone rang. At first no-one reacted because they usually kept it switched off. Then Fish realized, and grabbed it eagerly.

'Hello? he said. 'Yes. Oh, hello. Just a moment, I'll pass you over to him. It's for you Dad, he said, adding meaningfully, 'A woman.'

Dad looked quite concerned for a moment but then he listened to the voice at the other end and all became clear.

'Hannah,' he said, kicking sand in Fish's direction with one foot. 'We were just going to phone you. We've just bumped into your friend, er...' he looked towards Vic for help.

'Colin Goodwick,' Vic said.

'Yes, that's right. Mr. Goodwick. Yes, Colin. That's right.'

'He reminded us that we haven't accepted your invitation yet. Yes. We would love to come. Yes. Even

Fisher.' He deliberately used Fish's full name to get back at him for the "woman to speak to you" joke. Fish ignored the jibe but quietly moved Dad's drink behind a bag while he wasn't looking. 'Yes,' Dad went on. 'Seven-thirty will be fine. See you then.' He handed the phone to Vic to put in the bag next to her and looked around for his drink. Without hesitation he put his hand behind the bag and retrieved it with all the practiced art of a parent used to children's tricks.

'Nice try, Fish-face! Let's eat!' he said, and, when they had finished all the prawns, clams and assorted fishy bits, and the cheese, he produced from the depths of the cool box two small cakes. For Vic, there was a pastry case filled with delicate French-style custard and topped with Kiwi fruit. For Fish, a traditional English custard tart with cinnamon sprinkled on top.

'What are you having?' they asked him.

'I have decided to pay tribute to the memory of your mother,' Dad said, in a voice which suggested in some way that he was deeply happy that they all seemed to have sorted out their feelings on the subject. 'I have chosen a French-style apple tart. Apples always were her favourite,'

'Ah ha!' said Fish. 'I thought as much.' He paused, with the air of a detective solving a crime. 'Those apples. The green ones that kept appearing in the bowl. It was you. You were playing one of your clever games, weren't you? Mum's favourite fruit.'

'*Me*?' said Dad, with genuine surprise. 'I thought it was *you.*'

They both looked at Vic. For some reason she now found herself laughing. The others thought her reaction was one of amusement but it was actually the laughter of relief. The mysterious appearance of the apples had caused her no end of trouble. She had been sure that for every one she had spotted they must have found two more. Now she knew they had, but the dread she had felt over the subject being raised was dispelled in that moment. There were to be no awkward, unbelievable explanations.

'I think we have found the culprit,' said Dad, while she offered no further reaction than to continue giggling stupidly. Then she had to have a drink because laughing had made her cough, by which time the conversation had moved on and Dad and Fish were talking about playing with the frisbee after lunch. So, no further explanation was necessary. As she was sure that Hannah would say nothing, she at long last felt she could relax.

When Dad had drunk his customary cup of coffee – as a *digestif*, as he always described it – he did go off and throw the Frisbee back and forth with Fish. Vic used the time to get on with her diary. The sun was now high and hot in the sky so she put up the parasol and wrote in its shadow.

She usually didn't bother with the traditional beginning to diary entries. "Dear Diary" was what Fish would call "naff", so she would just begin with whatever had been happening. However, when she began to-day's entry she found herself writing "Dear… " She paused for a moment before adding "Mum". Then she continued as if she were writing a letter. "We've had an interesting holiday so far. The friends we have made are kind and quite unusual. And they live here by the sea all the time! Fish seems to have found a girl he really gets on with and I have sorted out the Apple problems. I don't really understand what's been happening – I still cannot quite believe it has happened – but it all seems to have worked out. Dad is much more relaxed now and he doesn't seem as unhappy as he was."

She paused and re-read the entry. Yes, the bit about "Apple" could easily mean the fruit, so if someone else read her diary they wouldn't guess what she really meant. She decided to finish the entry later, which was just as well because Fish dashed back up the beach and challenged her to "Long-distance body-boarding", which was a grand title for "Let's see who can go more than a few yards in these pathetically small waves".

After almost half an hour of them doing that, Dad came down to the edge of the waves.

'Who's winning?' he asked, looking down at Vic as she eked out a few more inches in water which was no more than a foot deep.

She stood up, feeling strangely wobbly as her mind adjusted to the fact that the water she had just been floating on only just covered her ankles.

'Me, of course,' she grinned, as Fish finished his latest attempt. 'It's cheating to use your arms,' she said. 'Isn't it, Dad?'

Dad held up his hands. 'Leave me out of this,' he protested. 'I'm on me break.' He said, using one of Vic's favourite family sayings. 'Come on. Time to go now.'

She grinned and asked, 'Why? What are we going to do?'

'You'll see,' Dad replied mysteriously, turning to head back up the beach. Vic tagged along.

'Why do you say "I'm on me break"?' she asked.

'Oh, wow!' he said, with a huge laugh. 'That saying goes back a long way. Before even Fish was born. Your Mum and I went to visit my parents one time. There was an old school friend of mine who had recently moved back into the area – he worked on the railway and my Dad had bumped into him in the station car park. Well, they invited him round because they knew I was coming down. Now you have to remember that when I was a teenager my friends and I used to go to each other's houses on Friday nights after Youth Club, and again on Saturdays. We would always play cards on those occasions but my Dad used to love talking to us and we would often get into some deep discussion and not finish until one or even two o'clock in the morning. Many's the time your Grandmother had to ring round everyone's parents at about midnight to tell anxious fathers and mothers that, yes, their son or daughter was at our house and quite safe!'

They had reached their spot on the beach now and Dad paused to begin packing up.

'You still haven't explained,' Fish observed.

Dad frowned. 'Explained what?' he began. 'Oh! Yes. The saying. Well, my father always had very fond memories of those evenings. He said they were what kept him young while all his friends were becoming middle aged and boring! Anyway, when my friend Cliff came round, one of those long, serious conversation began, just like old times. Dad and Cliff were having a grand old time but I have to confess that I was having some difficulty getting into the swing of things. Anyway, Dad must have noticed I wasn't saying anything. He turned to me and asked what

I thought, obviously hoping for a long, detailed reply just like when I was a very serious-minded youngster. Instead, I just used an expression I had heard in some film, or play or whatever, so, in a Scouse accent – the way I had heard it – I said "I'm on me break!" Well, Dad and Cliff smiled, but your Mum, who knew the source and also, I'm sorry to say, rather enjoyed occasions when my father's pretensions were undermined, collapsed with laughter and repeated it endlessly all the way home. So it became a family catch-phrase. So there you have it. Everything ready now?'

'Yep,' said Fish.

'OK. Let's go.'

He wouldn't say what he had planned and Fish and Vic knew him too well to bother pushing him. Not that either of them wanted to because they were each, in their way, reflecting on the family anecdote they had just heard. Fish had found it interesting because he liked good long serious conversations just like his father and grandfather. Vic was interested because it was a further sign that Dad was opening up about Mum, and in doing so he had revealed one more detail about what she had been like.

They got home. They unloaded the car. They had showers. They watched some early evening TV. Dad wouldn't tell them anything but pottered about downstairs. Then, at seven o'clock, they heard someone knock at the side door. A moment later, Dad called up to them to come down. When they got there, he had the dining table set and a huge bag which he was unpacking. The smells were unmistakable.

'An Indian takeaway!' said Vic.

'Wicked!' said Fish.

'With any luck, you've got our favourites in there somewhere,' Dad told them, slightly anxiously.

'Prawn Korma!' Vic almost yelled. 'Love it! What did you get, Fish?'

'Tandoori Chicken,' said, Fish, maintaining his cool a bit more successfully. 'How about you, Dad? You like Korma too, don't you?'

Dad nodded. 'I do. But today I've gone for Prawn Biriany. It was your Mum's favourite.'

They made a quiet start on the meal but it wasn't the awkward silence which usually accompanied references to Mum. Later, when he got the chance for a chat with her, Fish said to Vic that it had felt like a special moment of "remembrance": serious but reassuring. Normal family conversation began again when Fish broke the silence with his customary well-timed joke.'

'Did you get any seaweed for Vic, Dad? He asked, straight-faced.

'Seaweed?' Vic asked, perplexed. 'I thought that was with Chinese food.' Then she noticed Dad and Fish exchanging grins and said, 'Oh, very funny! **Not**!!' She had always had a habit, when younger, of confusing Chinese and Indian meals and Fish always mocked her for doing so. She got her own back by hiding his knife and fork while he disposed of the wrapping.

'Ha! Ha!' he said, sarcastically as he retrieved them from where Vic had put them on the spare chair. 'Where did all this come from, Dad? How did you get it delivered?'

'There's a restaurant the other side of the bay, next door to that supermarket we went to when we first came here. They don't actually do deliveries but I offered to pay them a bit extra and they obliged.' He looked around. 'There should be another bag,' he added.

'There's one over there, by the apples,' said Fish.

Vic was suddenly anxious. 'I'll get it,' she said, jumping up. However, when she got to the fruit bowl there was nothing new in it and she could not hear any dog barking. 'It's got bottles in it,' she said, returning to the table feeling as if she was walking an inch above the floor. She took the contents out. There were two bottles of beer and one of 7UP.

'It's that Indian beer you like,' Fish observed. 'Not like you to drink two, though,' he added.

'One's for you,' said Dad. 'Drink it slowly. You're not used to it.'

Vic laughed. 'Yeah! Sure!' she said. Fish glared at her, but held up his beer triumphantly.

'I'm a big boy now!' he hooted.

The meal was delicious. Vic was especially pleased because although Korma was her favourite, she had never before found one that tasted half as good as the one they usually got from the Indian restaurant back home. This one was nearly its equal however.

When they had finished, they went up and relaxed in front of the TV until quite late.

'What shall we do tomorrow?' Fish asked, peering at the clock at about eleven o'clock.

'Well, we're invited out for the evening and you're going to see Sarah in the morning, so...' Fish butted in.

'How did you know?' he said, incredulously. I wasn't going to say anything until I knew what you wanted to do.

Dad laughed. 'It was pure guesswork,' he admitted. 'I just guessed that you would not be satisfied with spending an evening with her only a few yards from where we'll be eating, so you had to have thought up something. Call me Sherlock Holmes, why don't you?'

'Do you mind, then?' said Fish, cautiously.

'I would be more disappointed to have been wrong,' Dad grinned. Vic and I can go souvenir hunting and begin the packing. Just be back by lunchtime.'

'I'm bound to be,' said Fish. 'Sarah's working at lunchtime.'

All this time, Vic had been sitting listening. Dad suddenly looked at her with a slightly concerned expression on his face. 'I'm sorry, Pops,' he said. 'We're leaving you out of the planning.'

'It suits me,' she said. She stuck her tongue out at Fish. 'Anyway, I don't want Fish around making sarky remarks while I'm choosing things for my friends.' She didn't add that hearing her Dad use a nickname that she hadn't heard him say for ages was what really had made her happy to go along with anything. She just hoped she would have a chance to chat with Hannah the next day and tell her one or two of these things. She would write them in her diary, of course, but some things needed to be shared with more than just a few sheets of paper.

'Well, great,' Dad said, getting up from his armchair. 'Ooh, these soft seats give me backache. I'll just set the breakfast table.'

He went downstairs and Vic and Fish exchanged grins as they went off to their bedrooms.

Half an hour later the house was dark, apart from three lamps glowing by three beds. Dad was scribbling a few late-night thoughts for a poem; Fish had selected yet another book from the house's shelves; Vic, of course, was completing her diary for the day.

Outside, everything was quiet. Including the dog.

16

FRIDAY

The first thing they all did when Friday dawned was to allow themselves a lie-in. Even Dad was slower to rise than usual. It was as if they were all trying to hang on to the holiday for longer by preventing the last full day from starting before they were ready.

But it couldn't last long.

Dad was incapable of lying around in bed unless it was to sleep. Fish had his assignation with Sarah to get on with. Vic was still not quite able to dismiss the holiday's strange occurrences from her thoughts and she found herself getting up and going downstairs before the others, just in case anything else strange was going to happen.

Nothing did. Fish disappeared out of the house by 9.30 and they didn't see him until noon. Dad made a start on tidying things in readiness for packing. He always liked to make as prompt a departure as possible and, knowing they would be out that evening, he wanted everything packed by the end of the afternoon. Victoria, as he insisted on calling her on days like this when there was business to be done, had the job of cleaning one last time and making sure that everything they had moved around the house went back to more-or-less where it had been when they had arrived. She would normally have resented taking the lion's share of the duty while Fish was swanning around somewhere else, but today she felt oddly happy just to be pottering around the house with Dad.

Fish came back just before noon and tried to help with the preparation of lunch, which his sister and father had largely accomplished before he appeared. Again, and unusually, there was no banter directed at him for this.

'You're just in time for a house speciality,' Dad said.

'What's that?' Fish asked, even thought he had a pretty good idea he knew what was coming.

Vic beat Dad to it. 'Whatever-we-haven't-eaten-already!' she said.

'Yum! My favourite!' said Fish, in a half-sucessful imitation of Dad's voice. 'Let me finish that peanut butter!'

'You'd better,' Dad warned him, grinning. 'If it's not eaten now it goes in the sandwiches for tomorrow's journey.'

Vic made an expression of disgust in Fish's direction. 'I don't think he's joking,' she said.

'As if I didn't know!' Vic replied. 'Grandpa calls himself a survivor of the Second World War. I call myself a survivor of Dad's sandwich concoctions.'

'OK. Joke made and appreciated,' Dad cut in. 'Let's eat up, see what's left to do and then I propose that we all go for a walk.

Vic had a terrible feeling that he was going to suggest the walled garden. She felt she had said goodbye to a lot of things there and she did not feel like going back. Not during this holiday anyway.

'Where to?' asked Fish. Vic sensed from his tone that he didn't necessarily want to go out at all. They were both relieved when Dad said he wanted to go up to the top of the road, turn left, do a bit of the coastline they had ignored so far and then come back over the hillside past all the old houses Vic had seen with Hannah. Fish actually confided to Vic during the walk that he had dreaded Dad suggesting going out on the harbour jetty.

'I know it sounds stupid,' he said, making Vic think that this version of Fish was very different from the one she had been used to. 'I just didn't want to have to wave through the chip shop window to Sarah when I had just said I would see her tonight.'

Vic didn't comment. She was thinking how like Dad he sounded.

They got back from their walk at four o'clock, all dying for a cup of tea, even though Dad had made his customary flask of hot drink and packs of "nibbles", which they had also devoured. Then, all that was left to do was "mooch around" as Grandma would say, trying to find odd things to do to fill the time. Eventually, even the reverse clock couldn't deny that it was time to change and walk down to Hannah's house.

When they had arrived at Hannah's they soon found themselves standing around in her kitchen-cum-dining room in that slightly uncomfortable way people do when they arrive for a meal. The experience provided Dad with his first conversational gambit. Dad could embarrass them sometimes, but you could always guarantee that he would step boldly into an awkward silence and ask a question or make a remark which got people talking for the next half-an-hour.

'Is it just holidaymakers, or do people who live by the sea all year round also feel thirsty all the time?' he asked no-one in particular.

Sure enough, half-an-hour later, and with the additional contribution of Colin Goodwick who joined them ten minutes later, they were all debating holidays they had been on, food and drink they had had in those places and, of course, Dad's original question. They only stopped because Fish, who had been surprisingly quiet, suddenly said, 'Isn't Sarah due by now?'

Hannah smiled broadly. 'She's already here, actually.'

Fish was disconcerted. 'What?' he said, quite sharply, drawing a fatherly look from Dad. But Hannah took no offence. In fact, she was still smiling after she had looked at her watch and told him to wait five more minutes and then go out to her workshop.

When the time ticked round and he could finally go, Hannah gave a hint of what was going on.

'I've not been allowed to look,' she said. 'But Sarah's taken over my workshop for the evening. I know she's got a table and chairs in there because I had to supply them. Whatever else she's planned is her secret. Anyway, let's start to eat. Does everyone like French onion soup?'

They all sat down and made appreciative noises as she dished out the home-made soup and placed a slice of garlic-rubbed bread on the surface of each bowlful.

'Vic sipped hers and said, 'It's just like the soup Grandad makes.'

'I hope that's a good thing,' Hannah said, frowning hopefully.

'It's the ultimate accolade,' said Dad. 'My father's home-made soups are legendary.' Is there any more?'

Vic was embarrassed and Colin made a remark about throats of leather, but Hannah took it as part of the compliments about her cooking and cheerfully ladled out another bowlful for him.

***

And so the evening passed. Every now and then Hannah would disappear out to the workshop with the food for Sarah and Fish.

'What's going on out there?' Colin asked Dad the second time Hannah went out.

'No idea,' Dad replied. My son and Hannah's daughter have been having what I suppose you would call a holiday romance. I was astonished when Fish agreed to come tonight. Sarah must have given him some hint that he wouldn't have to spend the evening with boring adults.'

Colin grinned knowingly. 'So, it's only Vic who has to suffer!' he laughed.

'I don't mind,' said Vic. What she didn't say was that she was actually enjoying adult company that wasn't just her relations. She loved all her grandparents, cousins and the rest but she had spent so much holiday and weekend time with them since Mum died that she was relishing finding out how different people behaved. They were certainly calmer and quieter than most of her family!

Hannah came back and removed the main course from

the oven. When she put it on the table, Dad said, 'Is that Salmon en Croûte?'

Hannah was impressed. 'Very good!' she said approvingly. 'I hope you haven't eaten any recently.'

'Not at all,' Dad replied. It was one of my wife's specialities. 'I've never dared try to make it.' He sensed a quiet moment and, assuming it was because he had mentioned his wife, he quickly added, 'I thought I recognized it when you took the small version out of the oven for Sarah and Fish.' He glanced at Vic. 'You're going to love this,' he said. One of the finest dishes known to mankind.'

Colin had assumed the duty of dispensing wine for the adults and, as Hannah sliced through the pie she said, 'Vic, that jug of juice on the side there is for you. Help yourself to ice from the fridge if you want.'

Hannah had placed some potatoes and vegetables on the table too and while Vic sorted out her drink the plates were filled with food which smelled quite delicious. As she sat down, Dad lifted his glass and said, 'I would like to propose a toast.' He paused, and looked at Vic for a moment. 'To absent friends,' he said.

Vic picked up her glass and looked straight back at him. 'To absent friends,' she said, wholeheartedly. Hannah and Colin echoed the toast and when Vic glanced in Hannah's direction she noticed that she had what could only be described as a huge smile of conspiracy on her face. Vic grinned back. Would Dad ever know just how significant his toast had been?

***

The final course was, Hannah said, 'Especially for Vic.'

They had heard the mixer going round the corner in an alcove but she had prevented them from seeing what went into the oven. Now she fetched Sarah and Fish back in.

'I've told them to be sociable for a little while,' she explained. 'They can get back to the workshop when we've eaten the dessert.

Vic tried not to stare at Sarah but she couldn't help realizing that she had only ever glimpsed her before, and then he had been dressed for work at the chip shop. She wasn't what you would call glamorous and she was quiet by comparison with her mother. Nevertheless, she could see why Fish liked her because she had the most genuine laugh she had ever heard.

By now, each one of them had an individual dessert in front of them. Small pots, which Fish annoyingly explained to Vic were called "ramekins". She was very pleased, however, to notice Sarah tap the back of his hand quite sharply to indicate that he was not to tease. The ramekins seemed to be full of meringue but, as she dipped her spoon in, she discovered why they were "especially" for her. Under the light layer of meringue she found... apple! It also had some bits of cinnamon in it, which Dad loved, but the apple for Vic was perfect. She grinned at Hannah even more broadly than before and Hannah winked back.

***

When they had finished dessert Fish and Sarah retreated once again and Dad turned to Colin to remark, in what he thought was a whisper, "Back to the workshop!" Colin hooted with laughter, but his whisper turned out to be quite audible because Hannah laughed equally heartily, and even Vic grinned broadly, leading her father to say, semi-seriously, "That wasn't for your ears, young lady!"

The chatter over dessert revealed that Colin and Hannah were big card players so, after the table had been cleared, they embarked on a game of Pontoon. Hannah had a box of various shaped plastic counters which she said she had bought years before in Switzerland. There was one missing.

'I always blame that on my ex-husband!' she remarked. Dad volunteered to have the colour which was accordingly one short.

'After all,' he joked, 'I'm about to take you all to the cleaners!'

They played until gone ten o'clock. Dad had still not succeeded in winning all their counters but he decided that home and bed would be a good idea if he wanted to avoid falling asleep at the wheel the next day.

'I'll leave our spare key for Fish,' he said to Hannah. 'Send the lovebirds home when you can't put up with them any longer. Fish can always doze in the car. Thanks for the excellent meal. You know,' he added, looking at Vic, 'When I said we'd have a proper family holiday of our own I never imagined we'd end up sitting down to a meal with some new friends. Did you?'

Vic shook her head and gave Hannah a hug. Colin, who had made a start on the washing up, called, 'Safe journey! See you again one of these days.'

As they walked back up the hill, Vic said, 'Who's going to navigate if Fish dozes in the car?'

Dad took her hand and gave it a squeeze. 'Before you go to sleep tonight practise your map reading skills.'

Vic laughed but, instead of writing her diary that night she got the map out and took a look at the notes Fish had made for the journey, just in case...

17

SATURDAY

Dad, as always, free-wheeled away down the hill.

'In honour of your Mum.' He grinned. 'She always hated me doing this. Quite right, too. It's illegal!'

Vic, sitting in the back for the return journey, took one last look at the house. It still looked ugly, but she noticed for the first time in the two weeks that the green of the exterior was similar to the green of the apples which had played such a part in her time there. Then they passed Hannah's house, whose colour could only be called "nondescript". All three of them looked towards it with interest. None of them saw anything they might have hoped for, which was just as well, thought Vic.

Fish cut across her thoughts. 'We never finished that game, did we?'

'Which game?' said Dad, puzzled.

'The one we were playing when we arrived. You remember: three word sentences, each word beginning with the same letter. Working through the alphabet.'

'Oh yes,' Dad said. 'Didn't we stop because I had to concentrate on driving into town?'

'That was your story,' laughed Vic.

'Yeah!' shouted Fish. 'I seem to remember that you were scheduled to have Z! Don't suppose that had anything to do with it!'

'I cant believe that,' Dad protested. He eased the car round the mini-roundabout at the end of the bay and up the long curved hillside stretch which led to the first of many dual carriageways they would use before reaching home.

'So, *Father*?'

'So what, *Fisher*?'

'Shall we play it?'

'Suits me. But I can't work out a "Z" sentence while I'm concentrating on these country roads. Let's start with A again.'

Fish glanced at Vic, who grinned. 'I'm afraid, therefore, that you forfeit that game. So we go back to… .'

Before Fish could say "A", Victoria cut in. 'I'll start,' she said, in a voice that brooked no objection. She paused for a moment. This will show them, she thought, then spoke:

'Apples appear abitrarily'

The silence in the car showed they were impressed. She was pleased to discover that, for once, she had shut them up, and sat back, looking out across the bay as they rose up the hillside.

'I still can't see the house,' she observed, and added, 'Come on Fish. Your turn!'

The alert reader will have noticed the reference to a poem on pages 35 and 36.

The poem in question does actually exist. It is "From Fishguard to Rosslare" by C Day Lewis and the author commends it to the reader as a reflection of the place, as it is and as my characters see it.